Alyssa turned around as the door opened and stared at the man who entered.

For one disorientating moment she thought she must have made a mistake—that this was surely not Adam. Even accounting for the ten years that had passed, there seemed nothing but a vague resemblance to connect this tall, hard-looking individual with the young man she remembered.

He was still handsome, but it was almost as if all those layers had been stripped away, exposing a hewn granite core. He was dressed for riding like any country gentleman, in pale buckskins and a dark blue coat, but there was a foreign air about him. Perhaps it was because he was tanned and his dark hair—which had once been carelessly long—was cut unfashionably short. But the greatest difference was in his eyes. She had remembered they were grey, but not that they were so dark and watchful. They expressed no emotion. No recognition. Not even curiosity.

'Miss Drake?' he said after a moment. 'You wished to see me?'

Author Note

I wanted to write a story about betrayal. Not just the cost of romantic betrayal, but the long-lasting emotional impact of the betrayal children experience at the hands of selfish, self-serving or abusive parents. How each subsequent betrayal in life just deepens the wound, driving us to thicken our armour, heighten our battlements, deepen our moats.

Our parents are our first models for learning about trust, self-esteem and unconditional love. If those models are faulty we can still learn from other sources—siblings, other family members, friends and, later in life, lovers—but there will always be scar tissue: a fundamental fault line of wariness and mistrust that any new relationship has to overcome. Trust will have to be earned, built, tested, and only then accepted. But couples who manage to overcome those barriers can often reach much richer emotional levels of intimacy than couples who come to love without question or challenge.

The Reluctant Viscount is just such a story about betrayal and redemption—how two scarred and wary individuals make a difficult and uneasy voyage to overcome the impact of early betrayals, risking their hard-earned emotional safety in order to experience trust and love.

THE RELUCTANT VISCOUNT

Lara Temple

First published in Great Britain 2016
By Mills & Boon, an imprint of HarperCollins*Publishers*
1 London Bridge Street, London, SE1 9GF

Large Print edition 2017

© 2016 Ilana Treston

ISBN: 978-0-263-06745-3

Printed and bound in Great Britain
by CPI Antony Rowe, Chippenham, Wiltshire

Lara Temple was three years old when she begged her mother to take the dictation of her first adventure story. Since then she has led a double life—by day she is a high-tech investment professional, who has lived and worked on three continents, but when darkness falls she loses herself in history and romance (at least on the page). Luckily her husband and two beautiful and very energetic children help her weave it all together.

Books by Lara Temple

Mills & Boon Historical Romance

Lord Crayle's Secret World
The Reluctant Viscount

Visit the Author Profile page at millsandboon.co.uk.

To Andy, husband, friend, lover and fellow
voyager through the rocky shoals of life.

Chapter One

Alyssa touched her gloved finger to the stone bust of Heraclites that stood precariously on the edge of the wide desk and gave it a push back to safety. The face of the ancient Greek looked worried, which suited someone who saw the world in a state of unrelenting flux and who was known as the 'weeping philosopher'. Or perhaps she was just reading into the rugged creases of sculpted skin a concern to mirror her own. And nerves. Right now nerves dominated even the concern that had motivated her visit.

She glanced quickly at her reflection in the large mirror on the other side of the study, but then turned away. Even in her best afternoon dress of palmetto green she looked small and insignificant in the imposing but dilapidated study which had once been the late Lord Delacort's.

It had all seemed easier in her mind once the

idea had surfaced. But facing the butler's obvious surprise and consternation at her request to see Lord Delacort had been enough to make plain it was extremely foolish to come here.

As Stebbins had led her through the large entrance hall which had been transformed into a maze of building materials and piles of threadbare furniture awaiting disposal, he had glanced worriedly back at her, as if debating whether to advise her to flee while she still could. Alyssa had kept her chin up and her demeanour calm, as if there was nothing in the least improper about calling, unchaperoned, on the scandalous new Viscount Delacort within a week of his arrival in Mowbray. She only hoped her reputation was robust enough to survive this very uncharacteristic act. Aunt Adele would be shocked if she knew what she was doing, but there was no way she could approach Adam in the staid presence of a chaperon. As risky as it was, if she meant to ask Adam for help, this was something she had to do alone.

Right now, concerns of propriety were overshadowed by the greater concern that this was a complete waste of time. However important the issue was to her, it was ludicrous to expect Adam to be willing to help her. And he wasn't Adam any more, but Lord Delacort, she reminded herself. Ten years and many dramatic events stood between this moment and the last time she had seen him.

She wondered if he would even remember her. She had been little more than a child at the time of the scandal. Not quite eighteen and both younger and older than her age. Perhaps he did—after all, he had been surprisingly kind to her and to her siblings in a town where everyone had regarded them as rather unfortunate and wild encumbrances on the brilliant and reclusive poet living in their midst, whom Mowbray society was proud of, though few in the town, if any, had actually read his poetry.

Adam had been young as well, just twenty-one, still up at Oxford, and a very serious student who had already secured a fellowship for the following year. Though he had clearly been the handsomest of Rowena's beaus, he had also been quite poor. That was why Alyssa had been immediately suspicious when her angelically beautiful cousin Rowena, the belle of Mowbray, had begun flirting with him.

Alyssa knew her cousin well enough to know that looks would count for little with Rowena, since the only beauty that interested her was her own. She'd had her eyes set on the wealthiest landowner in the area, Lord Moresby, who was almost thirty, and though he clearly admired Rowena, he was proving to be slow on the uptake. But Alyssa had never imagined Rowena would be quite as conniving, or daring, or brutal, as to manoeuvre Adam into believing she was about to elope with him while convincing everyone else he was trying to seduce and abduct her. Amazingly, such a melodramatic plan had achieved everything Rowena had desired, at the minor cost of Adam's reputation and future. His own family had repudiated him and he had been forced to leave Oxford, and the next Alyssa had heard Adam had left England altogether.

Alyssa had grown up in a flash. She had always known she could not trust her father or Mowbray society to support her, but she had not really understood their power to destroy. The day Mowbray expelled Adam in disgrace was the day she realised she could no longer afford to let her siblings, or herself, continue to be 'those wild Drake children'. Until that day she had focused on teaching them knowledge. From that day on she focused on transforming them and herself into proper members of society. She would not let them suffer Adam's fate. And she had succeeded beautifully.

But it was not just fear that had shaken her little universe that day. She had been too young and naïve to realise the significance of just how much she had looked forward to the occasions when Adam would stop by their little garden on his way to or from his family's home in the town to Delacort Hall, where he'd assisted Burford, the old estate agent.

She often taught her siblings outside in the garden so as not to bother her father, but no one had ever taken any interest in them until Adam had one day at the beginning of that fateful summer. They were so used to being ignored they had not even noticed he had stopped by the low garden wall that separated the garden from the lane and was listening to them with some amusement. When he had taken issue with Alyssa's interpretation of Homer she had been delighted at the opportunity to argue with someone who truly challenged her. And so, somehow it had become accepted that he could join their al fresco lessons whenever he liked. Then, by the time Rowena had carried out her coup, Alyssa had been unwittingly but very deeply in love.

His abrupt disappearance had left her stricken with a misery she could only force deep inside until it had eventually faded to an imprint, like the lacy skeletons of long-dried leaves she and her siblings had used to collect in the woods as children. And she had learned that unlike some poets' claims, one did not die of love or go into decline. In fact, she and her family had probably benefited a great deal from the whole affair. Her siblings were now all successfully employed or happily married and she herself had become as highly regarded in Mowbray society as any young woman. And if she had never tried to encourage any of the men who had shown an interest in her despite her lack of a dowry, it was just because none of those men had ever made her feel in the least tempted to go and live at the discretion of their whims and rules. She had enough of that with her father. Although at least he left her alone for six days out of seven as long as she helped him when he demanded and made sure no one interrupted his work.

She shook off her maudlin memories and focused on her task. She knew it would not be easy. Simply because Adam had been kind ten years ago was no reason to expect him to act on her behalf. If even a fraction of the tales about him that had surfaced over the past decade were correct, he was a very different person.

Still, she reminded herself firmly, she could not sit idly by without at least trying to stop Percy, and if there was even the slightest chance Adam might exert his influence, it was worth the embarrassment. For better or for worse, her reputation was sufficiently robust to withstand the possible gossip if it became known she had called on Adam. It might be considered eccentric, but then the Drakes would probably always be regarded as a little odd, despite all of Alyssa's attempts to smooth out her family's wrinkles.

The sound of steps in the hallway broke into her thoughts and she turned just as the door opened. For one disorienting moment she thought she must have made a mistake, that this was surely not Adam. Even accounting for the years that had passed, there seemed nothing but a vague resemblance to connect this tall, hard-looking individual with the young man she had known. She remembered most clearly his expression of devastated hurt when he had realised the extent of Rowena's betrayal that day at the White Hart. And his intent look when he had been explaining Homer in the small garden of their cottage. And the warmth of his quick, amused smile.

He was still handsome, but it was almost as if all those elements had been stripped away, exposing a hewn granite core. And he certainly did not look like he was capable of smiling. He was dressed for riding like any country gentleman in pale buckskins, top boots and a dark blue coat tailored perfectly for his broad shoulders, but he looked much larger than she had remembered and there was a foreign air about him. Perhaps it was because he was tanned and his dark hair, which had once been carelessly long, was cut short in an almost military style. But the greatest difference was in his eyes. She had remembered they were grey, but not that they were so dark and watchful. They expressed no emotion. No recognition. Not even curiosity.

'Miss Drake?' he said after a moment. 'You wished to see me?'

She drew a deep breath. She had no idea how or even whether to proceed. It had seemed natural to bring this problem to him when she heard he had arrived at Delacort Hall. She was honest enough with herself to admit that as much as she truly did need help, she had been happy for an excuse to see him again. But neither consideration seemed to apply to this stranger. She had an urge to protest—*you can't be Adam!*

'Yes,' she said hurriedly, before she lost what was left of her nerve. 'I need… I was hoping you could… This is about Percy.'

He frowned and moved further into the room, indicating one of the threadbare old chairs. She sat down and he took a chair opposite her.

'Percy Somerton? My cousin?'

'Yes. You see, he is courting my cousin Mary

Aldridge. She is an heiress and just turned seventeen. She is living with my aunt in Mowbray.'

'And why is it important that she be saved from Percy's clutches? He might be a dandy and a wastrel, but he is hardly a dissolute rake like yours truly.' He said it so blandly it took her a moment to register the self-mockery in his words. She debated telling him the truth and decided to take the plunge.

'Frankly I think being a dandy and a wastrel are sufficient reasons to discourage the match, but there is more than that at stake. The truth is that Charlie asked me to watch over her. He likes her, you see, and until he went away to Cambridge I had thought she liked him, too, very much. But he knows he can't offer for her until he can support himself. Especially since she is an heiress. He is too proud. And she *is* very young. And impressionable. She was miserable when he went away and Percy was very attentive. So...'

'So you have taken it on yourself to beat back the ravenous hordes until your brother can stake his claim?'

She ignored the mocking tone and continued.

'You make it sound like I am interfering. My father is her guardian, after all.'

'Good God, who in their right mind would appoint your father guardian over a gatepost, let alone a wealthy young woman?' he asked in genuine surprise and she pressed down hard on a smile. So he did remember something about them at least.

'Well, she is his niece. And my uncle, Mr Aldridge, was an avid admirer of my father's work. I often think that was why he married my aunt in the first place. You might not remember, but society considers my father to be a great poet.'

'Which might explain why society is in the state it is,' he replied laconically and she couldn't hold back a gurgle of laughter.

'So,' he continued. 'This is all very edifying, but what does it have to do with me?'

Alyssa's amusement faded at the coolness in his voice.

'He is your heir—' she began, but he cut her off.

'He is heir to Delacort when the world decides it has had enough of me. Just as I was Ivor's heir when the man was foolish enough to try to jump a hedge on a horse better suited to a farmer's cart before he managed to sire an heir of his own. Nothing more than that. Percy is neither my responsibility nor my concern and so I made clear to the tradesmen who seemed to share your opinion that I am responsible for him and should persist in Ivor's bad habit of bankrolling his extravagances.'

Something in the brutal dismissiveness of his words pushed hard at the knot of confused emotions that was roiling inside her and she felt a welcome surge of anger.

'He may not be your responsibility, but he *is* your concern. You may turn your back on it, but you are turning your back on something that exists whether it suits you or not!'

His eyes narrowed and to her surprise a slight smile lifted the corner of his mouth.

'So you haven't changed that much after all. I was wondering what all this diffident propriety had to do with the girl who spent most of her time in breeches and dispensing lectures from the branches of the Hungry Tree.'

She flushed. She had read somewhere that it was better to be remembered for something outrageous than not remembered at all, but she wasn't sure she would agree. She took a deep breath and changed tack.

'I do not presume to know what you have had to contend with all these years, but I do know that at one point you would not have calmly disregarded a blatant injustice. When Percy was bullying Charlie you—'

He interrupted her again. 'I had forgotten that! What a memory you have. It seems impossible that that little scamp is up at Cambridge. Is he doing well?'

His expression relaxed into a warm smile that was so at odds with what went before that she once again had a peculiar sense of disorientation. She felt herself smile in an almost involuntary response to this sudden glimpse of the Adam she remembered.

'Very well,' she answered. 'And at almost six feet he is definitely no longer a little scamp. Father wanted him to go to Balliol at Oxford like Terry and he did, but I can completely understand why Charlie preferred to get away from us all, for a while at least.'

The warmth in Adam's smile receded once again. It was as if he kept stepping in and out of the shadows.

'Very understandable. I seem to remember your household raised chaos to an art form.'

Alyssa felt the sting of insult. She had done all she could to instil some order into the muddle she had been raised in and she was well aware she had failed most of the time.

'You have no compunction about saying whatever you please, do you?' she blurted out.

He smiled lazily.

'I don't know why you are so sensitive about

some plain speaking. You used to speak your mind freely enough once. It is much easier that way. Principles are a damn nuisance, aren't they?'

'They may be, but not having any isn't much better!'

'How would you know?' He laughed.

'How would you know either?' she shot back. 'You may talk all you want about not having any, but it is obvious you do, or at least you did have. Otherwise you would not have helped Charlie.'

'That is different. I liked the boy. I didn't have to go against any inclinations to help him. And besides, that was a very, very long time ago.'

'Well, that's all principles are, in the end. Rules that make sure we don't hurt people we care about. Not having any principles means you don't care about anyone other than yourself.'

His smile twisted, turning cynical.

'You do go for the jugular, don't you? It won't do to try to box me in. I have no intention of getting involved in Percy's affairs. He is his own master. And frankly you would do better than to interfere in other people's affairs. I doubt you are doing your brother any favours by keeping Mary pristine for him. The best thing for him would be to fall in and out of love at least a dozen times before he is fool enough to think of marrying someone.'

She felt something close to a snarl of frustration bubble up in her and clamped down on it. She should not have expected anything from him. She stood up.

'Fine. I will do it myself.'

'That sounds ominous. Do what?' he enquired with mild interest as he stood up as well.

'What do you care?'

'I may not care, but I am curious. Percy is, as named, very persevering. It will take a great deal to detach him from his quarry if he feels he's closing in on the scent. And if your father is guardian, I sincerely doubt he will present Percy with much opposition. So you have quite an uphill task ahead. Can I watch you try to rout him?'

She knew he was being purposely aggravating and that by standing there glaring at him she was just feeding his amusement, but she was too upset to care. She had not expected him to be willing, but to realise she could elicit from him nothing but rather sardonic amusement on a matter that was so important to her made her want to do some damage.

'I don't remember you being so petty before Rowena got her hooks into you. She really took the man out of you, didn't she?' she shot at him contemptuously.

The lazy cynicism disappeared in a flash of fury that was no less alarming for being quickly reined in and for one moment Alyssa felt a spark of fear. Then his lids lowered and he shook his head.

'And I don't remember you being vicious. Time leaves its mark on us all. Heraclites had the right of that, didn't he?' He nodded at the morose statue on the desk, his mocking smile reasserting itself. Alyssa's own anger disappeared. She felt weary and depressed. She shook her head as well.

'I'm sorry, that *was* vicious. And foolish. And it was foolish to come. I should never have bothered you with this. Goodbye, Lord Delacort.'

She didn't wait for him to ring for someone to show her out, just walked out of the room almost absently, closing the door behind her.

Chapter Two

Adam remained standing for a few minutes after she left, staring at the door, his mouth flat and stern. He stared down absently at the estate accounts and papers that littered the desk, but turned when the door opened. The man who entered was tall and dark-haired like him, but his eyes were a rich warm brown and right now alert with interest and a hint of amused mischief.

'I thought we were going for a ride? Or are you too busy being besieged by young ladies? I just saw a very pretty specimen wander off through the garden. The English countryside must have changed quite a bit since my boyhood if young women feel free to call on bachelors unattended, especially bachelors of your dubious reputation. Or is she perhaps an old friend, here to renew your acquaintance?'

Adam shook his head ruefully at the innuendo.

'Miss Drake doesn't quite fall under any conventional category, Nick. But she most certainly did not come here on any romantic mission. At least not on her own account. She wanted to enlist my help in spiking Percy's guns. It seems he has got his mercenary sights on an heiress.'

Nicholas Beauvoir cast a critical eye at the worn and faded chairs, then sighed and sat down, propping his immaculately shining boots on a low table.

'Good for Percy. Why, does that pretty little thing want him for herself? She hasn't a chance unless she's wealthy.'

'Hardly. She likes Percy less than I do. Apparently her little brother is sweet on the heiress, so Miss Drake is guarding the sheep while her brother is off at Cambridge. And she wants me to help chase off this particular wolf.'

Nicholas opened his brown eyes wide.

'A very primped and pomaded wolf. But why on earth would she expect you of all people to do that?'

'No idea. She seems to think it is my duty now that I am the head of this misbegotten family.'

'I don't know why anyone would expect that,' Nicholas said reasonably. 'They never wanted anything to do with you until Ivor died without male issue. Who would have thought that old Lord Delacort would drop dead and lose two sons to mishaps in a mere five years? If you hadn't been halfway around the world at the time, I am sure they would have found a way of laying the blame at your door.'

'I wish one of them at least might have waited until they had sired a son before they died. It's bad enough being saddled with getting this ruin into some semblance of order, I certainly don't need furious little bluestockings stomping in demanding I do something about Percy's fortune hunting.'

Nicholas's brows rose. 'Is that what she is? She didn't look the part. How on earth do you even know her? She must have been little more than a child when you were booted out of the county.'

'I don't know, she must have been around sixteen or seventeen. And I know her because amongst other things she very kindly tried to warn me off Rowena. To be fair she was spot on—she told me she was sorry that I was about to be hurt, but Rowena was leading me on and had no real intention of marrying me because I was quite poor and that it was probably all for the best, since she would make me miserable if I were unlucky enough to marry her.'

'Good God! I would wager you didn't appreciate the lecture at the time.'

'I remember hoping she'd fall out of the tree.'

'What tree?' Nicholas asked, bemused.

'The lecture was delivered from a branch of the Hungry Tree, so named for its tendency to capture and demolish her siblings' balls and kites. Their cottage is on Rowena's family land and Miss Drake and her siblings were always underfoot somewhere.'

'Why the devil was she was up in the tree?'

'Rescuing a ball, I think. I offered to help and got that lecture for my pains. And she said I was too fat.'

Nicholas leaned back, clearly enjoying himself. 'Too fat? You?'

'Well, too big to help on any but the lowest branches. I was still in my chivalrous phase, but it was wasted on her. I forgot to mention she used to go around in breeches, of all things. It was the strangest household. Her father was always upstairs in his study, writing abysmal poetry, and I think I saw him less than half a dozen times the whole time we lived in Mowbray. Her siblings were always either up to some mischief or following Alyssa about like a tribe of Indians. They were a law unto themselves.'

Nicholas frowned.

'She didn't look wild.'

'Not wild, precisely. Despite the breeches and

the tree-climbing she was trying very hard to turn her ramshackle tribe into a proper little brigade. She used to tutor them *en masse* out in the garden so they wouldn't bother their father. She roped me into teaching them some Greek plays. It was very odd. The youngest one was seven, but they all sat there on the grass and drank in Antigone and Oedipus.'

'Oh, no, Adam, not Oedipus!'

'That's what I thought, but she insisted. She said it was important they know the classics. I toned it down as much as I could. They were a good audience—the only ones who showed any interest in what I was studying. My parents certainly never did. The only reason they consented to my going up to Oxford instead of starting work with old Delacort's estate agent right away was because I received a fellowship. That way I would be up there at Trinity earning old Delacort's goodwill by making sure Ivor did enough not to get himself sent down. Anything to insinuate us further into the Delacort social fold. My mother always made it clear that the chief redeeming feature of becoming plain Mrs Alistair was the Delacort connection. She was the reason we came to live in Mowbray on old Delacort's charity in the first place. She always hoped Timothy and Ivor would take at least one of my sisters off her hands, preferably both. Until I ruined everything, that is.'

'Yes, your mother is a piece of work, all right. Now that I think about it, you haven't said a word about your family since we returned to England. She should be delighted now that you've come into the title and estates, no?'

Adam picked up the bust of Heraclites from his desk and walked over to place him on the mantelpiece. He stood for a moment considering the morose face and his own reflection beyond it, then turned his back on both.

'"Delighted" is a word I wouldn't associate with my mother. Now that my sisters are eligibly married the benefit of my newly elevated status is minimal, certainly when balanced against my tarnished reputation. I think now that my father is dead she prefers to remain safely in Northumberland to bask in the borrowed glory of my sisters' husbands. And thank goodness for that. I am very comfortable with the current arrangement where any communication between us is through my sisters.'

Nicholas shook his head.

'I can see where you got your stubborn streak, man.'

Adam shrugged.

'I spent two-thirds of my life doing just about everything she wanted and for one act of folly she demands that the only way to make amends is to erase myself from our family's life and disappear. She didn't even have the decency to write to me when Father died. She left that task to Sybil and Cammie. But that knife cuts both ways. I promised myself that was the last time I would do what was proper. I didn't just erase myself from my family's life. I erased who I was. So now I can do whatever I want and be accountable to no one.'

'Well, you can certainly do almost anything you want. But I would argue against your being accountable to no one. You took pretty good care of me when I was sick in Punjab, for example.'

Adam smiled, relaxing.

'I would have done the same for my horse. Besides, I *was* responsible for you, in a way. I never understood why you decided to come along. You should have stayed at Oxford, then gone home to Berkshire and married one of those pretty little ladies you were always rhapsodising about.'

'There you have it in a nutshell. Unlike you, I always wanted to live an adventurous life and being a third son meant there wasn't much for me to do back in Berkshire, lovely ladies or not. I knew an opportunity when I saw it. That's not to say there weren't days I would have much rather stayed safe at home and I won't be going back to that particular village in Punjab in this lifetime, but all told, joining you was the best decision I've made. So, get this dilapidated old mausoleum into shape and let's return to London, where we can continue to reap the fruits of our labour. As long as you don't fall back in love with the mercenary Rowena now that we are in the neighbourhood. Is she very beautiful?'

Adam frowned in concentration.

'I think so.'

'You *think* so?'

'It was a long time ago. I thought so at the time, but I can't quite remember what she looked like.'

'For heaven's sake, Adam. This is the woman who broke your heart and you can't quite remember what she looks like?'

'I'm certain she had blue eyes. Everyone kept going on about cornflower orbs.'

'Blast you, Adam, you're about as romantic as a wet boot. How do you have such luck with women?'

Adam grinned.

'Luck has nothing to do with it. But I will certainly continue to leave the romance to you, you old fraud.'

'Well, I admit to being curious about the woman who was your Helen of Troy and catapulted you into battle, so to speak. She must be ten years married now, which is all for the best. Bored matrons are the easiest of prey. Imagine, Adam—if she had not been such a devious fortune hunter, you might even now be the proud owner of a brood of cornflower-eyed brats.'

'Thank the heavens she was, then.' Adam stretched lazily. 'As much as I resented it at the time, Miss Drake was right—marrying Rowena would have been one version of hell. And getting my pride handed to me so brutally has been very useful. Life has been much more enjoyable since. Sometimes it amazes me to remember just how serious I used to be. And stupid. I honestly thought Rowena was the embodiment of all that was good and right in the world. Unbelievable. As you said yourself, it was the best thing that happened to me.'

'Probably,' Nicholas conceded. He glanced sideways at Adam. 'Still, it is strange that you can't even remember what this beauty looks like. Seems to me you remember this Miss Drake quite well.'

'The Drake household was singularly unforgettable. It couldn't have been any more different from mine. She was a wild little thing with big eyes and her hair in a ribbon, and a mind which would have done an Oxford don proud. The last thing I thought she would become was a pattern card of propriety. Still, the fact that she dared come here, and unchaperoned, shows there is still something of that wilful girl she hasn't managed to tame.'

'I still don't quite understand why she came to you about her cousin and not to her father.'

'She has an overactive sense of duty and her father has none at all. He is one of the most self-centred people I've ever encountered, which is saying a great deal. Unfortunately for her I also don't have quite the same tribal loyalty. Percy is hardly my concern.'

'So Miss Drake and her little heiress "go to it"?'

Adam's eyes narrowed.

'If you are reduced to quoting Shakespeare, I gather you disapprove,' he stated, his tone flat. Nicholas shrugged.

'Not at all. I'm just thinking *you* might. Disapprove, I mean. Remember I've known you since we were eight years old.'

Adam stood up and walked over to the window, staring down at the gardens below.

'I don't know what she expects me to do. It's not as if I have any influence over Percy and I refuse to buy him off. I'll never be rid of him if I do.'

'That's true. The only thing that would convince Percy would be cold hard gold or a wealthier heiress.'

Adam turned back towards Nicholas, his eyes narrowing. 'You're probably right,' he said slowly.

'I mistrust that look, Adam. Last time I saw it we almost ended up in an Indian jail.'

Adam laughed, his intent expression lightening.

'Don't complain. That look, as you call it, earned you a nice fortune.'

'And I'm grateful. I just don't want to see you get into any trouble.'

'What possible trouble can I get into in Mowbray?'

Nicholas raised one brow quizzically. 'Wasn't the reason you had to leave England because of the trouble you got into in Mowbray? What if you fall back in love with the beautiful Rowena when you meet her again?'

'Back in lust, you mean.'

Nicholas shook his head.

'I don't know how you became so cynical, Adam. You're worse than I am.'

'That bad? Miss Drake attributes it to Rowena taking the man out of me.'

Nicholas's eyes opened wide. 'She didn't say that!'

'She did. Straight for the jugular, or rather, below the belt. To be fair, she apologised.'

'Well, that's all right, then. My goodness, I wouldn't mind meeting this peculiarity up close. So you're really going to stay here for a while?'

Adam shrugged and nudged a crate of crumpled documents with his boot. 'I have to spend a couple of weeks on the estate anyway. The place is a shambles. Apparently neither Timothy nor Ivor had any idea what they were doing, the poor fools. Someone needs to oversee the workmen getting this mausoleum into shape until Thorpe can take over and I can't leave all the negotiations with the tenants to him, at least not initially.

'Besides, I have an idea about Percy which just might provide us some entertainment while I am marooned here. Remember when we met with Derek and Ginnie in London? She said she missed her days on the stage now that she was a respectable wife and mother. Perhaps she might like to spend a few days visiting the famous Mowbray spa in the guise of a wealthy widow. She should have no trouble attracting Percy's attention.'

Nicholas shook his head ruefully. 'Ginnie would have no trouble attracting a blind man's attention. She will love the idea and will no doubt talk Derek into approving it. He never could say no to her. Still, take care what you're at, Adam,' he cautioned, but Adam merely smiled.

'For a rake, you're a timid old lady sometimes, Nick. If you're so worried, you can stay and keep an eye on me.'

'London society is a bit thin during the summer months, so I just might linger for a while. And I'll try not to cut you out with the beauty.'

Chapter Three

Adam pulled on the reins gently and halted the curricle just outside an old Tudor-style building on the High Street where a large sign announcing Milsom's Bookshop and Circulating Library hung above two large bay windows. This had been one of his favourite places in Mowbray ten years ago and it had not changed at all—the sign was even still very slightly crooked. In fact, it was amazing how little had changed, at least outwardly, in the ten years since he had left.

He handed the reins to Jem, his head groom and the only man amongst his staff whom he trusted with his horses, and jumped out of the curricle. A passing matron with a child hanging on to either hand shot him a look of alarm and hurried ahead, dragging her offspring with her, and Adam sighed. He was beginning to understand what it felt like to be a freak in a travelling fair. Mowbray might not be as large as nearby Oxford, but he would have thought it was large enough to ensure that not everyone had nothing better to do than either stare at him or look uncomfortably away. So far the only people who had treated him as a human being rather than an object of curiosity or a source of possible moral corruption were his servants and tenants, and that had taken a week of cautious interaction. It was as if the whole town had taken a leaf out of his mother's book and erased all memory of the serious young man who had lived there before the scandal. Now he was merely a caricature of a debauched rake.

He headed into Milsom's. None of the previous Lord Delacorts had been avid readers and this was one deficiency he wanted to right as soon as possible. He had no intention of spending too much time in Mowbray and he didn't particularly mind being a social pariah, but if there was no other entertainment to be had while immured in Oxfordshire, he might as well have some good books to read. A bell jangled faintly as he entered and two men on either side of a long counter turned towards him.

'Adam!' The younger man straightened abruptly from his lounging position and the ornate silver-rimmed quizzing glass he had been twirling slid from his fingers and hit the counter with a dull thud. He had a boyish face and very pale flaxen hair which demanded all of his valet's considerable skill to whip into the current *au coup de vent* fashion of artlessly disordered curls.

'Lord Delacort,' said the older man, much more pleasantly, and Adam nodded to him first.

'Good day, Mr Milsom. Hello, Percy. Mr Milsom, I was hoping you might assist me in purchasing some books. I brought a list…' He produced the folded list and handed it to the older man, who spread it out on the counter, his eyes brightening as he scanned its length.

'Yes, indeed…' he murmured absently, nodding to himself. 'We have some volumes here, but most I will have to request from London, My Lord.'

'I understand. There is no hurry, Mr Milsom. Whatever you can provide me with today, I would be grateful.'

'Of course, My Lord. Right way, My Lord.' Without a glance at Percy he turned and disappeared into a back room, leaving the cousins together.

Percy's gaze flickered towards the door and then back to Adam; he raised his quizzing glass and viewed Adam's riding clothes and caped greatcoat with a slightly derisive twist to his generous mouth.

'You know, Adam, you really should have Libbet give your valet some advice on tailoring now that you're settled. Stultz, my fellow. I can see you favour Weston and I can't fault his fabrics and his stitching, but really, that coat is quite commonplace.'

Adam surveyed Percy's nipped-waist coat, pale primrose-coloured pantaloons, the carefully arranged cravat secured with a ruby pin and the uncomfortably high shirt points. But the most impressive article of clothing was a waistcoat elaborately embroidered with what looked like tulips and long-tailed parrots, shot through with silver and gold thread.

'Stultz, you say? I don't think I could quite carry it off with the same panache as you, Percy. Did I pay for that pin or was it poor Ivor?'

Percy's hand rose towards the gleaming jewel, then dropped. He straightened, pushing away from the counter.

'It's not enough to cut off my allowance. You want to dun me now?' he asked bitterly.

'Not unless I have to, Percy. Just try not to annoy me too much while I'm here, will you? I'll be gone in a couple of weeks and you should have the field back to yourself. At your own expense, though, of course.'

'Blast it, man, you made your point—I told Libbet we need to scale back, but you can't cut me off completely, Adam. I'm your heir! I'm a Delacort!'

'Precisely, you're another in a long line of useless wastrels, myself included. And right now I happen to be in charge, which means you will have to make do with what you have.'

'Blast you, Adam, you have no right…'

'But I have every right, Percy. At least for the moment. Keep that in mind and keep your hand out of my pocket.'

Percy took a step forward.

'I wish you had—' He broke off, his face unappealingly crimson.

'What? Got myself killed and saved everyone the bother of dealing with me? Probably, but the fact is that I didn't. This is the reality. Deal with it. I am sure Libbet can keep you looking respectable even on your income. Though you might have to forgo these…entertaining waistcoats.'

The ugly look on Percy's face cleared with such rapidity Adam turned around even before the bells on Milsom's doors announced new customers. Three ladies entered. The first was a sweet-looking young woman in a bright jonquil pelisse over a white dress with several finely embroidered flounces, whose eyes lit up the moment they settled on Percy. She was followed by a plump woman of indeterminate age and unconvincing bright coppery hair tucked under an impressive high poke bonnet decorated with a spray of scarlet mock cherries. The last to enter was Miss Drake, dressed in a simple rose-coloured pelisse over a white muslin frock. Her gaze narrowed as it settled on the two men and Adam tried not to smile at the evident annoyance in her remarkable eyes.

'Mr Somerton…' Miss Aldridge breathed and Percy took a step forward.

'Miss Aldridge! Mrs Aldridge! Miss Drake! How fortuitous! Would it be too much to hope you might join me for a walk along the garden promenade? It would be such a pity to insult the sun by remaining indoors on such a beautiful day! I promise to escort you back to Milsom's at the first hint of a cloud.'

Adam watched the expressions on each of the women's faces appreciatively. Miss Drake's stony look did nothing to daunt Percy or the young Miss Aldridge, who continued to stare at him with a fatuously blissful look. And since Mrs Aldridge happily assented to the change in their plans, Miss Drake had nothing more to do than announce she would join them once she'd collected the book she had ordered. Percy bowed graciously, tucked Miss

Aldridge's hand about his arm and beckoned Mrs Aldridge to precede him.

Adam watched as the party stepped outside, Percy's fair hair gleaming halo-like in the summer shine before the doors closed behind them. He felt Alyssa hesitate beside him. He could already anticipate the repeat of her appeal and he cut her off before she could speak.

'It looks like the die is cast, Miss Drake. She could do worse, you know. He may be a selfish fortune hunter, but he is, as he reminded me, next in line for the Delacort spoils once I cash in my chips. She might even like being a dandy's wife. At least Percy has Libbet to keep him in good form. And the more I think about it, Charlie has no business thinking he is in love with anyone at his age, or frankly at any age. But certainly not until he has had a chance to enjoy life a little.'

She stiffened as he spoke and her eyes took on the hard glint of emeralds. Her eyes were not pure green, but encased a golden ring, like a sun settling into a lake. It was a strange contrast, both hot and cold, a physical manifestation of her contradictory character, he thought. It was a pity, then, that the cold should prevail.

'You made yourself quite clear when we last spoke, Lord Delacort. I can't force you to take your responsibilities seriously, but I can refuse to listen to your opinion as to what might constitute the future happiness of two people I care about.'

'That puts me in my place. You could always complete the effect by sweeping out.'

'I am sure that would gratify you, but I am waiting for my book. Why don't *you* sweep out, instead?'

Adam's grin deepened.

'Careful now. You've done a good job becoming a proper Mowbray Miss, but your tree-climbing ways tend to show under pressure.'

'I wonder if anything of what you once were would show under pressure,' she shot back. 'Or have you done too good a job at becoming what everyone thinks you are? I use to think most of the tales about you were the exaggerations of tattle-mongers, but quite frankly I think they weren't doing you justice. I am not surprised you are so sympathetic to Percy. Useless fribbles must stand by each other, no?'

Adam inspected her approvingly. The exotic slant of her green eyes elevated her face from merely pretty to fascinating. He had no idea why her attack amused rather than annoyed him. It was rather like being growled at by a kitten.

'That's better. It is so much more comfortable

with gloves off, isn't it? Unless you are going to try hitting me,' he added, indicating her clenched fists. 'In which case, keep your gloves on, it's less painful.'

She forced open her fisted hands and took a deep breath, stepping back. It was fascinating to see the almost physical transformation as she tucked herself back inside.

'Are you so bored here in Mowbray you have to resort to squabbling with me? Can you find no better sport?'

'I am perfectly willing if you are,' Adam offered. She remained suspended for a moment; then her slightly confused look gave way to a frown even as a flush swept up her cheeks.

'You cannot just go around saying things like that... Oh, for heaven's sake, I don't know why I am even arguing with you. It only seems to encourage you. You are determined to live up to everyone's expectations of the debauched rake, aren't you? If this is an example of how you mean to conduct yourself, your reception is unlikely to get any more inviting than what you have witnessed these last few days.'

She turned away resolutely, planting her hands on the counter, her gaze fixed on the closed door behind which Milsom had disappeared. Adam laughed slightly and leaned back against the surface, crossing his arms.

'Is that what all this anxious staring is all about? Is everyone waiting for me to commit my first act of iniquity? And here I thought it was my past, not my potential future that had everyone scurrying for cover. What on earth do they expect me to do? Set up a harem at the Hall? Hold orgies? Do you all gather to lay odds on the possibilities?'

'Believe it or not, but you are not the only topic of conversation in Mowbray, Lord Delacort. What on earth is keeping Mr Milsom?'

'He is busy gathering books for me. Are you in a hurry or are you concerned that too much time spent in my noxious presence will sway you from the true and narrow? Shall I leave? Or would that be presuming too much?'

Her lips pressed together firmly, but he saw a dimple waver. Then she laughed suddenly, her shoulders relaxing, and turned to him with a much friendlier smile, again reminding him of the young girl of ten years ago.

'I concede defeat. You are far better at provoking than I am at disapproving. Is all this to convince me not to bother you about Percy? I have learned my lesson—I assure you I expect nothing of you.'

Adam told himself his return to Mowbray had

made him unnecessarily sensitive to nuance. Her eyes were still warm with amusement and there was nothing to indicate that the bite he felt at her words was intentional. And even if it was, it should make no difference if her opinion of him was as low as everyone else's in Mowbray. He had long ago stopped caring about other people's opinions. If there was one thing he was used to, it was being weighed and found wanting. He was not about to pick up that bad habit again simply because he was in the one place he'd told himself he would never come back to.

'That is a relief,' he said drily.

She cocked her head to one side, her eyebrows lowering with concern.

'Have I offended you? I did not mean to, at least not this time.'

'I am not that easily offended. Being informed I arouse no expectations is hardly offensive. Expectations, like principles, are exceedingly tiresome. A great deal too much effort is spent either trying to live up to them or explaining why one has failed to do so.'

The disconcerting anxiety in her eyes faded, replaced once again by mischievous amusement.

'You have developed a whole philosophy on the

subject, it seems. I am glad your studies have not gone completely to waste.'

'Who's being provoking now? And I have made very good use of my studies. The classics set the ground for most challenges one encounters in life, and where they fall short, there are several very useful Sanskrit texts that fill the gaps.'

'From your tone I gather I should probably not ask which texts,' she said suspiciously.

'Not in public at least.'

Her eyes, intent and curious, searched his for a moment, but then her long lashes veiled her eyes and she sighed.

'And so, once again, we circle back to you trying to shock me. I'm afraid you can't outdo the moment ten years ago when I realised what Oedipus was *really* about and you didn't even mean to shock me then.'

'I was probably misled by your name. Anyone named after the founder of Carthage should be able to deal with Greek tragedy.'

She smiled, but there was a sharp edge to her expression.

'Queen Alissa? Nothing so grand. I believe my father suggested my name in one of his very few contributions to our upbringing—I am named after *alyssum*, the Greek word for sanity. Perhaps he feared having children might threaten his. Now I really should go and keep an eye on Mary and Percy. Aunt Adele is not a very effective chaperon. Could you please tell Mr Milsom I will return later for my book? Good day, Lord Delacort.'

She turned towards the door, not waiting for him to respond. He watched the door close behind her, turning as Mr Milsom stepped hurriedly out of the back room.

'I was quite certain I heard Miss Drake,' he said in a puzzled tone as he placed a wrapped stack of books on the counter and pulled a single book from beneath it, brandishing it at the closed door.

'You did, but she was in a bit of a hurry, I'm afraid,' Adam informed him.

'But her book!'

Adam glanced at the book Mr Milsom held and raised his brows as he recognised the title. He had once read part of *The Treasure of Orvieto* on a voyage between Cape Town and Zanzibar, but it had been lost along with some of his belongings when they had run aground on the African coast. Still, he had read enough to know it was hardly standard reading fare for young women. Perhaps she was collecting it for her father. He had not expected that the reclusive and very annoyingly moralistic poet William Drake would indulge in popular tales of adventure. Still, he had long since learned people were rarely what they appeared.

'I will deliver it to her, if you like,' he said and held out his hand imperatively.

Mr Milsom hesitated, looking rather worried, but in the end he handed it over. Authority had its advantages, Adam realised. He rather thought that however diffident people were around him, there was little he could not demand in Mowbray.

Adam added the book to the wrapped stack of books on the counter and stepped outside, heading towards his curricle. He knew he should probably go and deliver her book as promised, but he did not head towards the garden promenade. He wouldn't mind glancing at the novel again. The aggravating Miss Drake could wait until the next day for her book.

Chapter Four

Adam glanced up at the tree, now devoid of toys and looking somewhat smaller than he remembered. It stood just at the edge of the Drakes' cottage garden, its extensive roots creeping down the bank and into a small stream that ran alongside the lane towards Mowbray. The cottage was strategically situated at a fork in the lane that connected Mowbray with both Delacort Hall and Rowena's old home, Nesbit House. Adam had passed it more times than he could remember.

It was rather peculiarly proportioned, with the bottom half rather long and sprawling and the upper storey built on only half the cottage. That was, if he remembered correctly, where the poet was rumoured to live and work, often not appearing for days or even weeks on end. The children had all slept, cooked, eaten and played downstairs, in a world separate both from their parent and often from the outside world. Years ago the cottage had been surrounded by an unkempt wilderness which had been extremely useful for games of hide-and-seek. Now the lawn was trimmed and a profusion of vivid summer flowers crowded neat flower beds along the short gravel path to the house and under the front windows. Despite its small size, the garden looked lush and cheerful and the cottage itself had lost its ramshackle air. It seemed Miss Drake had tamed more than her own appearance and behaviour.

This was the first time since his arrival that he had ventured off Delacort land aside from his trip into Mowbray the previous day. He planned to go riding with Nicholas later, but for the moment he just wanted to walk down the familiar lanes. When his family had first moved to the town he had found every excuse to remain in his students' lodgings in Oxford, but from the moment he had laid eyes on Rowena, his dedication to the classics had melted under the heat of his infatuation for the local beauty. That last summer he had spent every available moment in Mowbray, vying with her many admirers for the privilege of a smile.

As a poor relation of the old Lord Delacort, effectively living in Mowbray on his charity, Adam had had few illusions about his ability to compete. He should have been suspicious when Rowena started encouraging his attentions, but at the time he had only been convinced that love was triumphing over lucre.

She had played him skilfully, ultimately convincing him that an elopement was their only chance for happiness. Yet he'd found their 'secret' rendezvous near the White Hart had been transformed into a scene from the worst music-hall farce with Rowena playing the kidnapped belle, himself as villain, Lord Moresby as Sir Galahad and most of Mowbray as either condemning chorus or avid audience.

He clearly remembered the scene, with his mother standing shoulder to shoulder with old Lord Delacort, demanding he leave that very day, while his father had stood mutely by, eyes downcast. And then there'd been the anticlimax of the farce as the young Miss Drake had elbowed her way past Lord Delacort and demanded that Rowena admit she had planned this all along. Rowena had cleverly fallen into a swoon, judiciously finding herself in Lord Moresby's arms, and Adam's fate had been sealed.

'Not Carthage! Dido is done to death!' a voice exclaimed and Adam turned around, dragged back from his memories. A man of about sixty was walking down the lane, slightly hunched and with his hands clasped behind his back. He caught sight of Adam and stopped, one hand on the cottage gate, the other extending an accusing finger in Adam's direction.

'Carthage will just not do! A different setting is called for!'

His eyes were a paler green than Miss Drake's, but this was unquestionably the acclaimed poet William Drake.

'What about Glasgow?' Adam offered.

'Glasgow?' the poet asked, aghast.

'It is certainly different,' Adam explained.

They both turned at the sound of a husky laugh.

'Why not, Father? You might start a new literary fashion,' Alyssa said as she stepped out of the cottage and headed up the short gravel path towards the gate.

'Are you acquainted with this philistine?' Mr Drake demanded.

'This is Lord Delacort, Father. Lord Delacort, this is my father, Mr William Drake.'

'Aha! You are the hedonist!'

'Father!' Alyssa exclaimed angrily, but Adam merely laughed.

'You honour me, Mr Drake, but I doubt the original Greek hedonists would consider me worthy of the title. And I don't think philistine is quite appropriate either. Perhaps you might care to try again? Third time lucky?'

Alyssa giggled and her father threw her a venomous look, swinging open the cottage gate, which gave a squeal of protest.

'Alyssa, did you find the name of Aeneas's brother-in-law?'

'Alcathous, Father.'

'Alcathous, of course. Well, I am not to be bothered further today. My Aeneas is at a most delicate stage. Good day, Lord Delacort.'

Alyssa remained standing by the gate as her father stalked into the cottage.

'I am so sorry he—' she began ruefully, but he cut her off.

'Don't apologise. You are not accountable for him.'

She frowned at the annoyance in his voice and pushed slightly at the gate, which squealed again.

'Fine. I won't. You are as bad as he is anyway.'

'Now, *that* is a worthy insult. Much more effective than your father's.'

She smiled reluctantly and as her eyes settled on the book in his hand she flushed.

'I was wondering if you planned to return my

book. Mr Milsom was mortified when he realised you hadn't delivered it as promised.'

'I almost didn't. I am only on the fifth chapter. But form prevailed. Do you mean to say this book is for you? Somehow I had thought it must be for your father.'

Her eyes lit up with laugher once more, but there was embarrassment there as well.

'Hardly. Father does not indulge in reading fiction. He considers all contemporary writing outside of his own to be a waste of ink and paper.'

'How very broad-minded of him. Still, tales of intrigue in the Sicilian court are hardly conventional reading material for a young woman.'

She shrugged and the light was extinguished from her eyes, as if a cloud had passed between her and the sun.

'You are an authority, then, on young women's reading habits? Why shouldn't a woman read, or even write, about adventures, and travel...or whatever she wishes?'

Adam raised his hands in surrender.

'I'm not saying they can't or shouldn't. Merely that they usually don't, that is all. I should have known no standard definition would apply to you. I apologise for even suggesting it might.'

'Your apologies are almost worse than your insults, Lord Delacort. Admitting that I might be right on the grounds that I am peculiar is hardly flattering. If that was even your objective, which I doubt!'

'Not peculiar. Special,' he offered. 'Exceptional?'

She shook her head, but one dimple threatened to appear.

'I can see you are well used to trying to talk yourself out of trouble. But if this is a sample of your usual efforts, I am surprised you have managed to survive so far.'

'I am usually more skilful. Fearing for one's life tends to sharpen one's focus. Here, take your book. I will ask Milsom for another copy so I can find out what happens after that very improbable hero tries to... Sorry, I shouldn't reveal the plot...'

Her brows drew together in a puzzled frown and again she looked much more like the resolute but overwhelmed young girl he remembered from years ago.

'It seems strange that you might enjoy a fictional adventure after you have lived through real ones,' she said wistfully.

'Real adventures are rarely as enjoyable as fictional ones, Miss Drake. My strongest memories of my so-called adventures are of fear, hunger, dirt and a very firm resolve never to find myself in a similar situation again if I were lucky enough to survive. Unfortunately I tended to forget these resolutions all too often when either curiosity or greed came into play. But for now I intend to only pursue adventures in printed form.'

He held out the book once more, but she shook her head.

'You may finish reading it, then. I am busy anyway. Perhaps it will keep you out of trouble. Were you heading into town?'

'Just wandering.'

Her eyes met his and they softened.

'Ten years is a long time,' she said sympathetically.

'True. I think the Hungry Tree has shrunk.'

Her laughter rolled out, husky and infectious. He moved towards the gate.

'Why on earth are you still here?'

Her brow contracted in confusion.

'What?'

'Why are you still living here, in Mowbray? You must be, what...twenty-six or twenty-seven? You should have been married and as far away from your parasite of a father as possible.'

To his surprise she didn't seem offended. Her eyes shone with amusement and he noticed now that she had only one dimple, conveying an impression of reined-in mischief. Or an internal battle between warring inclinations.

'And how is marriage any better? I believe I have a great deal more freedom than most wives.'

'But hardly the same benefits.'

Her eyes met his with a disconcerting directness. A slight flush spread across her cheekbones, but there was nothing coy or flirtatious in the look. Still, he was disconcerted by the tightening of his body. Without thinking he took another step towards the gate, but stopped as three figures on horseback appeared over the rise, heading in their direction.

Alyssa turned towards them, her face losing its animation, warning him what was coming before he even recognised the riders. He sighed in resignation as Rowena, Lord Moresby and Percy approached. He would have happily avoided this particular meeting, but he knew he would have to deal with this moment eventually. It was best to get it over with sooner rather than later. He stood by the gate inspecting the woman who had changed the course of his life and he felt a sudden stab of disappointment and a sensation of being quite old.

Rowena was undoubtedly beautiful, but he could hardly credit he had ever been young enough to have acted as he had. There had been so many women since her, some even more beautiful than her perfect English porcelain loveliness, but none had ever excited the kind of do-or-die fervour he vaguely remembered she'd inspired in him.

Though her betrayal had been very effective in wrenching him out of his infatuation, in some corner of his mind he had sometimes wondered what it would be like to see her again. The reality, as he watched her pull up her horse a few yards from him, was both a relief and a disappointment.

Even her demeanour now, with her lips slightly parted, her eyes cast down in patently false modesty, was as artificial as any actress on stage. He had fallen in love with a beautiful statue and endowed her with all manner of fine qualities which had absolutely nothing to do with the object of his desire. He felt a flicker of both contempt and pity for the boy he had been, that he hadn't been able to see what even the young Miss Drake had seen so clearly.

'Good morning, Alyssa.' Rowena nodded in Miss Drake's general direction, but her gaze was on Adam, her lashes dipping over her lovely eyes. 'Welcome back to Mowbray, Lord Delacort. Percy tells us you have already met since your return and I believe you know my husband, Lord Moresby?'

The power of form over inclination carried them

through the necessary polite exchange, but as soon as was decently possible Lord Moresby urged his horse onwards, his jaw set and his face flushed. Rowena, holding her playful mare easily, followed, her smile as serenely self-satisfied as a cat with the remains of a mouse between her paws. Surprisingly Percy lingered for a moment, bowing to Miss Drake with a boyish smile.

'I trust I will see you, Mrs Aldridge and Miss Aldridge at the Assembly on Thursday, Miss Drake?'

'I believe so, Mr Somerton.'

'Lovely, I am looking forward to it.' He smiled, not in the least abashed by her stiffness towards him. He turned to Adam and nodded abruptly in strong contrast to his sunny approach to Miss Drake, then rode off. Adam turned back to see her watching the riders disappear around a bend in the lane, her mouth tight. He felt quite tired suddenly.

'So this is what it is going to be like. The sooner I get out of Mowbray, the better.'

'At least it won't be boring,' she offered and he laughed.

'I think that is a Chinese curse—may you live in interesting times.'

'You have been to China?' Her eyes lit up. But just as quickly, the proper young woman reasserted control and she half-turned towards the cottage. 'I apologise. I dare say it is tedious to be asked questions about your travels all the time. Good day, Lord Delacort.'

'Was Percy referring to a dance at the Assembly Rooms?' he asked and she turned back, her brows rising.

'Yes. They have one every Thursday during summer. Why? You don't actually mean to attend, do you?'

'Why not? It might be amusing.'

'Amusing…'

'Yes, amusing. As in diverting. Entertaining. After all, this is now my home, at least for the next couple of weeks. It is time I became reacquainted with my neighbours.'

She stood, hands on hips, inspecting him suspiciously, the way she might look at her siblings when they were up to mischief.

'You do expect the worst of me, don't you?' he asked sardonically.

'Of course not. I was just wondering… You must do as you please.'

'I usually do.'

'That much is obvious if even half of what one hears is true,' she replied with disdain and he felt a surge of annoyance. Everywhere he went in this perfect little corner of England he found more proof that propriety equalled sanctimonious dis-honesty. For a moment he had actually thought this peculiar young woman might be cut of a different cloth, but it was all in the trimming—underneath she was the same as all the rest. She might have started out differently, but everything about her now was a statement of conformity. Even the well-tended garden that had replaced the wild jungle of ten years ago was testimony of her descent into grace. The familiar urge to undermine, to topple, prodded at him.

'Probably more than half, sweetheart. And you never answered my question.'

'What question?' she asked suspiciously. 'And don't call me sweetheart. You may delight in up-setting people, but I don't.'

'Did I call you that? A slip of the tongue. And you are still avoiding my question. Why did you never marry and get out of here? Are you too scared to leave the comfort of Papa's tyranny or did no one ever ask?'

She stared at him, her mouth slightly open in shock.

'Are you doing this on purpose? If you think the fact that I am unmarried gives you leave to insult me, you have forgotten who you are dealing with,

Adam!' She turned abruptly and headed towards the house.

Adam bit back a curse. Whatever he thought of her, he had gone too far. He surged after her, grabbing her arm, but immediately dropped it as she turned and directed the full force of her furious gaze up at him.

'Don't!' she bit out between clenched teeth and he took a step back.

'I apologise. I didn't mean… I'm a fool.'

'You don't have that grace! I never thought you of all people would become a bully! You may think I am weak to have stayed with Father while you were indulging in big, brave adventures around the world, but you know nothing of what it means to be brave for other people even at a cost to yourself. So don't you dare preach to me ever again!'

Adam remained standing as she swept up the path and into the house.

When Adam stalked into the breakfast room a quarter of an hour later, Nicholas was sprawled in a chair, still in his dressing gown, holding a cup of coffee.

'How was the tour of childhood pastures? The coffee's fresh—' Nicholas said, but broke off as he registered Adam's expression. 'Adam? What's to? Did something happen? Did you come across the beauty?'

Adam shrugged and poured himself some coffee.

'I came across the full cast of the Mowbray farce and managed to make a fool of myself.'

'In front of the beauty?'

'No. I insulted Miss Drake.'

Nicholas's brows rose.

'She of the Hungry Tree? How did you manage to insult her? Did she ask you for help with Percy again?'

'No. I didn't give her the chance.'

The silence stretched out for a moment and then Adam continued.

'I don't know why I did it. I'm just so tired of all the games people play here. The sooner I'm back in London, or frankly, out of England again, the better. But I shouldn't have taken it out on her. She is just doing what everyone else does. It's not her fault she is so desperate to conform.'

'Well, then, apologise. You've annoyed more than your fair share of women these past years, Adam, and you always seem able to get round them in the end.'

Adam met his friend's gaze.

'This isn't the same.'

'Fine. You'll probably be antagonising most of

the neighbourhood in short order anyway, so might as well start sooner rather than later. Anyway, I'm off to dress and then we'll go for a good gallop. It will clear your mind.'

Adam sighed and put down his glass.

'A gallop might be a good idea. There's an excellent run across the fields to Mare's Rise. Just be careful of the wooded area once we cross the first field, it gets very narrow between the trees for a hundred yards or so before opening up again.'

'Good. I'll let you win this time, since you're in a foul mood. No leniency the next.'

Adam shook his head, grinning reluctantly.

'Hubris unbound. Have you ever won yet?'

'It's not you, it's Thunder. He's an unfair advantage. He's like that Greek god horse in the *Odyssey*, you know, Poseidon's brat. What's its name? Marmion?'

'Arion, in the *Iliad*. And you've just given me an idea.'

'I have? Is it clever? I knew I'd be good for something.'

'Go and get dressed,' Adam suggested, unimpressed.

Chapter Five

'This came for you, miss.' Betsy laid a small paper-wrapped package on Alyssa's desk and stood back expectantly. Alyssa looked up from her writing, surprised.

'For me? From where?'

'I think it was one of the new footmen from Delacort Hall, miss, but I couldn't rightly say. I did ask whether it was meant for Mr Drake, but he said, no, it was for Miss Drake.'

Alyssa put down her pen and reached hesitantly for the package and then paused, glancing up.

'Thank you, Betsy. That is all.'

Betsy withdrew, clearly disappointed to be sent out before the unveiling, and Alyssa sighed. There was no way Betsy would keep this choice piece of gossip to herself and goodness knew what people would make of it. Alone, she untied the package to reveal a small silk pouch with something flat and firm inside. She emptied it on to the desk and an ancient silver coin rolled out and finally settled, showing a standing female figure holding a branch and sceptre. Two thousand years had rubbed away at the letters, but the word 'Clementia' was still visible encircling the figure.

She stared at this amazing treasure, a tribute to the Roman goddess of clemency and forgiveness, her heart thumping uncomfortably. After a moment she pressed the tips of her fingers to her eyes, wishing she wasn't such a fool. It was ridiculous to cry. It was ridiculous to feel anything because of him. She knew this gesture meant nothing. Selfish people were very good at manipulation. Her father was a master at interspersing his domineering commands with clever wheedling and Rowena usually managed to convince everyone around her to do precisely what she wanted in the end. Ten years ago Alyssa had believed Adam was very different, but that had been as much a fiction as any adventure tale she had ever read.

Well, she was through with selfish people who did what they pleased and then thought they could manipulate their victims into forgiving them. She was not a child any longer and she would give no one such power over her ever again. Adam was not a man worth risking her heart over a second time, even in the extremely unlikely event someone like him, who had enjoyed the favours of beautiful women all around the globe, might be interested in a thoroughly provincial oddity who was only mildly pretty. She shoved the coin back into its little pouch. She would return it to Lord Delacort as soon as possible. In a couple of weeks he would be gone from Mowbray once again and everything would return to normal.

The following morning, Alyssa dressed for walking and set out towards Mare's Rise. She had debated how to return the coin in the most discreet manner possible, which meant she couldn't have Betsy deliver it or send it by post. She tried to imagine what the gossipy postmaster, Mr Curtis, would make of it if she asked to send a package to Lord Delacort. Finally she decided her best chance was to waylay Lord Delacort near Mare's Rise. It was common knowledge he had taken to galloping his thoroughbred, Thunder, along the straight stretch past the rise every morning and this was likely to be her best chance to see him alone and be able to return the coin privately.

It did not take her long to reach Mare's Rise and before she had even made it to the top she heard the pulse of hooves approaching. She stood on the crest of the small hillock and watched as Thunder lived up to his name, moving across the field towards the lane that ran through the woods so fast he hardly seemed to need the ground beneath him to stay in motion. Rider and horse were beautiful together, she thought. Then they disappeared into the trees. She started walking down the rise, watching the point where they should come into sight again, then stopped abruptly.

The squeal of the horse was so unexpected she wondered if it was perhaps a bird's cry. Then she picked up her skirt and ran the rest of the way, forcing her way through the low, tight trees and brush that lined the path.

Thunder was standing over Adam and she could hardly see the man, only that he was stretched out on his side on the ground, unmoving. Thunder raised his head at her approach and nickered and Alyssa saw Adam was already raising himself on one elbow. But she didn't stop running until she had reached them.

'Are you all right?' she gasped, clutching her side. 'Don't get up yet.'

Adam was still holding Thunder's reins, but he let them go to brush at the dirt and leaves that clung to him and directed a puzzled look at his horse.

'What happened?' he asked.

Alyssa refrained from stating the obvious. 'I didn't see the fall. I just heard Thunder cry out and then nothing. He may have tripped in a rabbit hole. Were you off the path?'

Adam pulled himself to his feet with a groan and she resisted the urge to help him.

'Right in the middle,' he replied, brushing leaves and twigs from his coat. 'I always stay in the middle between the trees if we're coming in fast. There are definitely no rabbit holes or anything there.'

Alyssa frowned and moved towards Thunder. He stood calmly, his left foreleg resting on the tip of the hoof. She bent down to glance at his knee and cannon bone, but aside from scratches she could see no damage, so she turned in the direction they had come from and took a few steps down the lane. The ground was damp and she could clearly see where Thunder had stumbled. She went next towards the trees and knelt down again when she found what she was looking for. After a moment she pushed to her feet, ramming into Adam, who had come to stand behind her. He winced.

'Careful. I've had all the damage I can bear for one day. Let me see.'

She tried to stop him, but then realised the absurdity of the gesture and stood back. He didn't say a word as he took in the thin stretch of dun-coloured rope wrapped very low around the trunk of a poplar tree.

'That's one hell of a prank,' he said slowly. 'Did you see anyone around here?'

Alyssa shook her head and after a moment's hesitation she kneeled down again. She extracted a pair of small scissors from her reticule and sawed off the string.

Adam watched.

'A memento of my near demise?'

She glanced up at him.

'Don't be flippant. You might just as easily have broken your neck at that speed. You are lucky Thunder didn't break his knees.'

'Thunder!' Adam exclaimed, as if waking up, and went back to crouch down by his horse, running his hand gently down the stallion's legs. Thunder whinnied and nudged Adam with his muzzle.

'It seems we are both luckier than we deserve, old boy,' Adam said quietly. 'Just scrapes and bruises, but we will have Jem put something on that, just in case.'

'You should have someone put something on you, too,' Alyssa said, holding out a handkerchief. 'You're bleeding.'

Adam glanced down at the small white square of linen she extended.

'Does this white flag mean you've accepted my token of penance?'

She blinked. She had forgotten why she had come. She opened her reticule once again and extracted the silk pouch, holding it out as she had the handkerchief.

'I can't keep the coin. It's too valuable. And besides, I shouldn't have become so angry—'

'You had every right,' he interrupted her, but she raised her hand. She was very aware of the muddy rope she was still holding and she had the uncomfortable sensation of being watched.

'I may have had the right, but it was still foolish. And a waste of energy. But there is no point in discussing this. You should get Thunder back home. And put something on those scratches.'

'I'm not eight years old, you know.'

'So you say. Please take the coin.'

'It's a gift. I don't take back gifts.'

'Oh, for once, would you not argue! And we shouldn't be standing here like this. Not after what happened!'

His eyes narrowed.

'You really are worried, aren't you? It was just a stupid children's prank. If they had known what they were doing, they would have secured it higher off the ground. They probably didn't even realise anything serious might happen.'

She opened her mouth, then closed it.

'Fine. If you won't take it, I will send it by the post, which will be unnecessarily embarrassing and costly.'

He ignored her comment and glanced around the forest, frowning.

'Come, walk with me back to the Hall and I will send you home in the gig. I need to see Thunder back to the stables and I don't want you walking back alone.'

'It's not far…' she began.

'I know it isn't, but if there are mischief-makers out there now, I don't want you alone with them. Come, you can make sure I don't keel over on the way, weak from blood loss.'

She smiled reluctantly.

'So now it *is* serious.'

'Of course it is serious. How am I supposed to attend the dance with my face looking as if I've been tied in a sack with a wild cat?'

She smiled up at him, thinking he looked unfairly handsome, scratches included. She shook her head and started up the lane to the Hall.

'It will just lend colour to the stories already

making their way around the neighbourhood. I had no idea you were responsible for fomenting rebellions in South America.'

'I was?'

'Apparently. There is another one I particularly like. That you cleverly escaped the hangman's noose in Australia after abducting the governor's wife and daughter.'

'Both of them? How precocious of me. Especially since I have never been to Australia. By what stratagem did I effect this escape? It might be useful in case I need to do so in future.'

'They were sketchy on the details, unfortunately. And then there was the tale that you stole the Sultan of Oman's prize mare.'

'That has a grain of truth in it, I'm afraid. But it was the Sultan of Brunei and it isn't precisely stealing when he himself wagered I couldn't do it, is it?'

'Not precisely,' she admitted. 'One out of three is not bad. I am sure more tales will surface. It is quite wonderful how you have unleashed the creative forces latent in Mowbray.'

'I am always glad to be of service.' He bowed slightly and winced. Her hand went out involuntarily, as if to support him, and he grinned down at her.

'I repeat. I am not eight years old.'

'I forget,' she said tartly and kept walking.

'No, you're just used to managing everyone.'

His amused tone took the sting out of his words and she relaxed slightly. He might have changed a great deal in ten years, but his essence was still there. She had remembered him as serious and scholarly, but there'd always been this warm undercurrent of humour and even irreverence, which was probably why her siblings had liked him so much.

'I've offended you again,' he said suddenly, his voice more serious, and she came out of her reverie.

'Sorry? I wasn't listening...'

His frown faded.

'Well, that puts me in my place.'

They came out of the woods heading towards the stables which stood at the back of Delacort Hall. She barely registered where they were going; her mind kept replaying that moment she had come over the rise and seen him lying there, unmoving. And the image of the rope twined about the tree. They had almost reached the stable when she realised she was still clasping the rope and the pouch with the coin. She thrust them at him.

'Here, take these.'

He took them automatically, but before he could speak, head groom Jem came out of the stable and hurried towards them.

'My lord! What happened?'

'I am fine, Jem, and, more importantly, so is Thunder. We took a spill near Mare's Rise and Miss Drake was kind enough to come to our aid. Could you have a gig brought round to take her back to Drake Cottage? And have Thunder's foreleg seen to? I'll come by the stables in a moment. Oh, and send someone to ask Mr Beauvoir to join us in the stables as well.'

Jem cast Adam a searching look, but merely nodded and took Thunder's reins, leading him away. Adam pulled off his gloves, inspecting the damage to them ruefully.

'Thunder's foreleg and my favourite riding gloves. I'm beginning to be quite annoyed with whoever conceived of this prank. Come, we'll wait over here by the garden gate. I think it best we stay outdoors.'

She sat down next to him on a bench by the ornate gate leading to the gardens. He cast the gloves, muddy rope and silken pouch on the bench with a carelessness that amazed her.

'Concerned for my reputation, or yours?' she asked, ignoring the urge to remonstrate against his casual treatment both of what had just happened and of the precious coin.

'Mine, of course. There's a limit to how much abuse it can take.'

'You passed that limit eons ago, Lord Delacort.'

'Well, there's always hope I might come full circle. Who knows? I might even take to writing sermonising poetry like your esteemed sire. Put all my classical learning to good use.'

She shook her head, holding down hard on a smile, and stood up as a groom pulled out of the stable yard in a gig. Adam stopped her by moving between her and the stables, holding her arm lightly.

'About what happened today… I want to keep that between us.'

She looked up at him, realising she had been mistaken. There was something in his eyes that was anything but casual—he might have treated it lightly, but she could see past that to the implacable determination that probably accounted for his survival so far.

'What are you going to do?' she asked.

The hard look in his eyes lightened.

'Well, I won't be galloping Thunder for a while.'

She frowned, not in the least reassured by him reverting to humour. She didn't speak because she knew there was nothing she could say he would listen to. He watched her, his smile turning sardonic.

'You are a suspicious little thing, aren't you? But I am serious. I am asking you not to mention anything about this. All right?' he repeated, still holding her arm. She could feel the rough callouses on his palm and realised what strength it must take to ride a horse like Thunder. His grasp was impersonal, but his fingers were warm on her skin, and despite the fine weather she wished she had worn a long-sleeved dress. She didn't answer immediately and his grasp tightened slightly as he turned her to face him more fully.

'All right?' he asked once more, but his voice sounded distant. She nodded and he drew her towards the gig. She let him hand her up and settled herself beside the groom and didn't look back as they drove away.

Adam watched the gig pull away, absently rubbing his hand. When the gig had disappeared behind the trees he glanced down at the peculiar collection on the bench and went to gather the items up. He put the small silken pouch into the pocket of his muddied buckskins, picked up the rope and headed towards the stables.

Nicholas was already there, crouching down next to Thunder as Jem applied a sticky salve to the horse's scrapes. Nicholas pushed to his feet at Adam's entrance, but Jem kept at his work. Adam noted, thankfully, that the groom had cleared the stables of its many inhabitants.

'How is he, Jem?'

'Lucky, My Lord,' Jem replied. 'He'll mend quick. But I'm curious as to what did this.' He indicated a long scrape along the front and side of Thunder's leg and Adam held out the rope.

'This. Tied low between the trees on the narrow stretch near Mare's Rise,' he replied calmly and Nicholas's brows rose. Jem glanced up, but then went back to applying the salve.

'I know I am not very popular in these parts, Jem, but do you think there is someone here at the Hall or on the estate who has such a grudge against me? I am asking you to be honest. I won't hold it against you.'

Jem finished with the salve and rose stiffly to his feet, rubbing his hands thoughtfully on a rag.

'I know you wouldn't, My Lord. If you ask me, it is no one at the Hall or on your grounds. They live in hope you'll stay here permanent like. There's not a man or boy on the estate who wants to see Mr Somerton in your shoes.'

Adam smiled tightly.

'Somehow I don't consider that much of a compliment. But I take your point. Most likely not someone from Delacort. A child's prank, perhaps? Though somehow this does not quite strike me as a very childish act.'

'Any youth that malignant is likely to have done similar acts in the past,' Nicholas added.

'My thinking as well, Mr Beauvoir, and I haven't heard of any such mischief in Mowbray. May I see the rope, My Lord?' Jem asked.

Adam handed it to him. 'It looks like simple enough rope, I can't make much from it.'

Jem shook his head. 'Nor can I. Could find such rope anywhere. I don't like it, My Lord. Miss Drake isn't one for gossip, but the stable hands saw the state of your clothes and there's no hiding Thunder's leg. There's bound to be talk again.'

Adam frowned.

'Again?'

Jem sighed and handed back the rope.

'When Lord Ivor died so soon after Lord Timothy there was talk of a curse on the Delacorts.

Nonsense, but you know countryfolk. There's no avoiding it.'

Adam frowned.

'I thought Ivor was thrown by his horse. And Timothy died of inflammation of the lungs.'

'So did I, but there was some talk at the time. And now you were thrown from your horse as well. These things do happen. I am just saying you be careful. If I might be so bold, I've been in service at Delacort for more than forty years and this is the first time I'd be sorry to see a change of hands. We know what's said about you in Mowbray by those above us, but for all that work here at the Hall, what you've done since you came here has got people hopeful things will be different from here on out. So I'd as lief not see you carried back on a hurdle or worse, My Lord.'

Adam felt an uncharacteristic flush rise to his face. He almost told Jem not to count on him too much, but kept his peace.

'Not my favourite image either, Jem. Let's keep this between us for now. I need to think. And if you think of anything, let me know. Come on, Nick.'

Nicholas nodded and followed Adam out of the stables. Once out in the open and away from the building, Adam glanced at his friend.

'You have been unusually quiet, Nick. Impressed by the Delacort Curse?'

His friend's ready grin appeared.

'Hardly. I'm no more inclined to the supernatural than you, Adam. I'm just trying to reconcile this… prank, as you call it, with your very foppish cousin.'

'Not an easy thing to do. I was wondering the same. Somehow I find it hard to imagine Percy scrambling around the forest setting traps. And even though Ivor was unlucky enough to be killed when he was thrown, Percy was raised in the country and he should know the chance of that happening again is pretty slim. Most people don't break their necks being thrown from a horse. At best he might have hoped I would break a limb or be knocked unconscious. Just petty revenge for cutting him off?'

Nicholas shrugged.

'Stranger things have happened. You should keep your eyes open. What was that Jem said about Miss Drake?'

Adam grimaced. For some reason he did not want to discuss her part in what had happened.

'She came across me just after the fall. She found the rope.'

'What was she doing out near the Rise?'

Adam pulled the silk pouch out of his pocket.

'She came to acknowledge but return my apology.'

Nicholas took the pouch and emptied the coin into his palm. His brows rose.

'No wonder. It's just a tarnished old coin with some scribbles on it. You're slipping, Adam. That's what I call adding insult to injury.'

Adam took back the coin and pouch, shaking his head.

'What a waste of two years at Oxford, Nick. At least Miss Drake recognised its value. Which was precisely why she returned it.'

'A young lady of strict principles. Not your type. Pity.'

'Hardly. Since I have no intention of staying here for more than another week, a flirtation would have been impractical even if she was interested.'

Nicholas raised his brows again.

'Implying you are?'

Adam remembered the heat that had flowed through him when he had taken her arm. He wondered if it was in part because she insisted on not taking him seriously. He was not used to young women treating him with quite that combination of scolding amusement.

'Being treated like a schoolboy puts me on my mettle.'

Nicholas laughed. 'What a masterly tactic on her part. Are you sure she isn't just playing a deep game?'

'No such luck. She's no actress, just outspoken.' He changed the subject. 'Did you bring your dancing gear?'

'Of course. I have to have it on hand when I continue to the family pile in Berkshire. Why?'

'We are going to an Assembly on Thursday. Everyone who is anyone in Mowbray will be there. Percy certainly. And Ginnie.'

'She agreed? And Derek will let her come?'

'I received her letter this morning. She said Derek and the boys will have to survive without her for a week and she will be up by chaise tomorrow. She'll stay at the Fulton Hotel near the Pump Rooms. Apparently she spent the last two days buying clothes and I had my secretary in London supply her with some very expensive baubles so she can make a grand entrance at the Assembly.'

'Good old Ginnie. She will enjoy being back on the stage, so to speak. Do you think Percy will take the bait?'

'Hopefully it will keep him occupied and away from both Miss Drake's cousin and from me.'

Nicholas laughed and rubbed his hands together cheerfully. 'And I thought I was going to be bored to tears out here in the country. Next we will be attending Public Teas and playing whist with the dowagers. This is shaping up to be a fine holiday.'

Chapter Six

'What a reception,' Nicholas murmured appreciatively as they surveyed the Assembly Room and the Assembly Room surveyed them. 'Reminds me of the time we stumbled into a secret meeting of Thuggees, except that this is perhaps marginally more terrifying. Are you quite certain you didn't do anything other than try to elope with one of their fair virgins ten years ago? No buried bodies? Alchemy? Necromancy?'

Adam shot him a sardonic look. The ballroom was a slightly smaller copy of the room at the Ship in Brighton. It stood some seventy feet long and was lit by four massive glass chandeliers balancing hundreds of candles. Ten years ago Adam had thought it the epitome of splendour. After years of attending the most sophisticated ballrooms around the world he thought it still held a certain charm and certainly took itself very seriously. He knew Nicholas would milk this for all it was worth.

'Enjoying yourself, aren't you?'

'Of course. Who is that alarming dowager holding court in the corner? She either has a squint or she is giving you the evil eye.'

Adam turned in the direction of Nicholas's nod.

'Lady Nesbit. Alarming is right. She is Rowena's grandmother and the undisputed leader of Mowbray society and the Pump Rooms. I used to think she was the driving force behind the snaring of Lord Moresby, but then I realised it was a joint effort with Rowena.'

'Ah, I surmise that is the beauty next to her, then. My, she is a delectable piece, matron or not. And I see what you mean—she looks very used to leading the dance. Ah, she's spotted you, man,' Nicholas whispered. 'She's heading straight towards us!'

Adam frowned. He didn't really want to deal with Rowena now. He had other fish to fry.

'Lord Delacort. How nice you could come.'

There was such a wealth of innuendo in Rowena's proper greeting that Adam smiled grudgingly. He bowed.

'Lady Moresby. May I introduce Mr Nicholas Beauvoir? Nicholas, this is Lady Moresby.'

'An old friend of Adam's,' she clarified, extending her hand. Nicholas bent over her hand formally, his mouth clearly held firmly against a threatening grin.

'What a coincidence. So am I,' he replied. 'It is a pleasure to make your acquaintance.'

Her whole being seemed to convey her conviction that it was indeed a pleasure to make her acquaintance.

'Are you going to invite me to dance?' she asked Adam archly as the first notes of a cotillion strained to be heard above the murmur of voices that had increased in intensity as Rowena had intercepted Adam and Nicholas.

But Adam was watching a new couple entering the ballroom. Mr Figgs, the Master of the Pump Rooms, was short and round, with an amiable smile and an impressive head of springy white hair. He was walking proudly beside a woman whose entrance was causing quite as much of a sensation as Rowena's audacious waylaying of Adam. The new arrival glanced around the room insouciantly, and when her eyes skimmed past Adam and Nicholas, the hint of a smile played about her generous mouth, but her eyes did not linger.

'I don't think that is a good idea, Rowena,' Adam said casually. 'It was nice to see you again, though.'

He smiled down at her, bowed and moved on. The buzzing around them increased.

Adam found a good vantage point midway through the Assembly Room and he and Nicholas stopped to watch. Ginnie was easy to spot in her dramatic red gown and the diamonds he had provided shimmered as much as the extravagant chandeliers above them. Mr Figgs had introduced her to a serious-looking man Adam vaguely remembered as one of the landowners out by Cumnor. The man looked surprised but not displeased to find himself leading such a dazzling stranger on to the dance floor.

Nicholas glanced over at Adam.

'You've set the fox amongst the hens now, man,' he said, shaking his head ruefully, and Adam smiled but didn't answer.

'Here, isn't that your pretty tree-climber? What was her name again?' Nicholas indicated another dancing couple that had come into view and Adam turned.

'Miss Drake.'

'She *is* a pretty thing. And the best dancer here. Introduce me later, will you? I wouldn't mind seeing those eyes up close.'

'Don't be a fool, Nick. I told you she's not flirtation material. She's as proper as they come.'

'Devil a bit. That just ups the stakes. Where's Percy?'

'What? Oh. Over to the right, talking with Mr Figgs.'

'Well, he hasn't changed much. Still the dandy. Now *he's* giving you the evil eye.'

'He's furious with me for closing the Delacort purse. He seems to think that as my heir he is entitled to an allowance beyond his own income. I disabused him of that notion.'

'A kind of advance on your demise? How touching of him. I suppose it must have been a disappointment that you survived. There is a certain irony to that—the last two Lord Delacorts succumb to the most mundane of illnesses and accidents and you endure environments which should by all rights have shaken you free of your mortal coils.'

Adam grinned. 'That's the second time you've abused Shakespeare in the past few days. Have you been brushing up on your reading behind my back?'

'Not much else to do while you're out repairing your predecessors' damage to the estate. Now that we are making a foray into society I might find something or someone else to occupy me. Wait, look, Percy is on the move and has Mr Figgs in tow. This is almost too easy.'

They watched as the two men moved down the side of the hall, intercepting Ginnie and her dance partner as they stepped off the dance floor. Mr Figgs made the introductions, Percy bowed, smiled angelically and led Ginnie on to the floor to join the set forming for a country dance. Adam scanned the room. Miss Drake was standing by a rosewood sofa where Mrs Aldridge and Miss Aldridge were seated, the latter watching dismally as Percy took his place with the stunning stranger. Miss Drake herself was also watching the pair, her head slightly tilted to one side. Then she glanced down at Miss Aldridge and moved into her line of vision, blocking the dance floor from view.

Adam shook his head. He should have sent her a coin of Artemis, protectress of the vulnerable, rather than Clementia. Miss Drake persisted in trying to shield everyone around her. She took life far too seriously. Someone should teach her how to relax and enjoy herself. With Mr Figgs's Rules of Conduct at the Assembly Room in mind, he headed leisurely in her direction.

Alyssa wished she was anywhere but where she was. The whole neighbourhood had been awash with talk once Mr Figgs had disclosed that the new Lord Delacort would be attending Thursday's ball with his guest, Mr Beauvoir. Between that and talk of his accident, which everyone had bloodthirstily attributed to his notorious recklessness, Adam's name had come up so often at each of the neighbourhood teas or visits Alyssa had attended with her aunt and cousin that she'd begun to wonder what they'd all spoken of before his return.

The worst had been at Lady Nesbit's on Tuesday. Rowena had sat with a calculatedly pained look upon her beautiful face and hinted mournfully that Adam had clearly not recovered from his *tendre* for her, even after all these years. Alyssa had sat and fumed and wished again that he had never returned to Mowbray.

All this excitement reached fever pitch the moment he entered the Assembly Room. Alyssa waited with a sense of impending doom for something terrible to happen. When she saw Rowena approach him she held her breath along with the rest of those present. What followed was so anticlimactic Alyssa almost felt sorry for Rowena. It was worse than if he had snubbed her altogether. But to converse with her with apparent amicability and then move on to stand appreciatively viewing the dazzling widow who had arrived was possibly the worst combination he could have chosen as far as Rowena was concerned.

Alyssa tried to focus on her own concern, Mary, who was now gazing miserably at Percy as he talked animatedly with the lovely widow while leading her through the country dance. Alyssa sighed in frustration. She had still not come up with a plan to detach Mary from Percy. She knew her father would likely consent to any offer not overtly unsuitable. And as Adam had pointed out, Percy was suitable, at least on the surface.

Ever since Ivor had come into the Delacort title, Percy had acted as if he, and not Adam, was next in line. It had been clear that he had assumed, like many others, that Adam was unlikely to survive his exploits. It had not been an outlandish assumption. Even if one discounted many of the accounts of Adam's escapades as exaggerated, there were protracted periods of silence which gave as much or more food for speculation. Certainly Percy could not be completely blamed for his presumptions. But however disappointed Percy might be, it didn't mean he had any right to solve his problems by targeting Mary, not while Alyssa had a say in it, and furthermore...

'Do you waltz?'

She blinked and turned. She had been so intent

on the problem she hadn't even noticed Adam had come to stand beside her.

'Waltz?'

'Waltz. The dance. Do you?'

'I… Yes. But why?'

'Mr Figgs's Assembly Room rules state I have to try to make myself agreeable to the company present, by which I gathered he means squire wallflowers and converse with dowagers. So, I suppose if I am to be allowed to attend another dance I must do the pretty and invite some unfortunate maiden to dance. From the list he so helpfully provided I see the next dance is a waltz. Hence the invitation.'

She couldn't help smiling. She was beginning to realise this man enjoyed being deliberately provoking.

'How can I resist such a flattering invitation? Wait, I can. Go and find another wallflower. I am busy.'

'I know, glaring at Percy is hard work. Take a rest. Ah, they are just about to start.'

He grasped her elbow firmly and gave her a little push in the direction of the dance floor, attracting the attention of her aunt and the group of matrons to her right. She caught the alarmed look on her aunt's face and sighed inwardly. To break free now would attract more attention than to proceed.

'Fine,' she said grudgingly and saw the corners of his mouth quirk up in a smile. But he did not reply, just led her on to the dance floor and then, when they were in position, clasped her hand and placed his hand at her waist.

She loved dancing and over her many years at the Assemblies she had danced with most of the men of Mowbray who cared to indulge in the pastime. With some she flirted mildly and with most she stoically endured their total lack of skill while still enjoying the music. But even the most skilled or audacious of her dancing partners had never allowed their hand to sit quite so low on her waist and they certainly maintained a much more decorous distance.

Dancing with Adam was different. She could not point to anything conclusive other than that he employed the Continental rather than English style of the dance, holding her more closely than she was used to. Instead of a light, impersonal pressure his hand was insistent, slightly splayed along her waist, below the line of her stays, so she could feel each finger where it angled her towards him. And his other hand was contrarily so light against hers that his fingers kept shifting against the palm of her glove, only pressing in when he needed to guide her in the dance, so that her whole arm became sensitised. She was accustomed to talking while dancing, but somehow it was hard to focus on anything other than his hands.

She glanced up and met Adam's dark grey eyes. He wasn't smiling outright, but a shadow of amusement glinted in his eyes, the same look that she was becoming used to in her encounters with him. As if he knew what she was thinking and found her predicable but mildly entertaining. A wave of annoyance mixed with determination tingled through her.

'Your hand,' she said and his brows rose, the picture of innocence.

'My hand?'

'A bit lower, please.'

The heads of the dancers next to them turned as he burst out laughing. He slid his hand upwards slightly, very gently, and her body arched away momentarily from the contact before she could call herself to order.

'Too high?' he asked, his voice dropping suggestively and she fought a childish urge to step on his foot. She was not going to give him the satisfaction of knowing he had flustered her.

'No. That's perfect.' She gave him her sunniest smile and almost faltered again as his hands tightened on her and something shimmered in his eyes that wasn't quite amusement.

'Yes. It is,' he said softly and she had to struggle to remember this was a game and one he was all too used to.

'Just so I know,' she said calmly, 'who is our audience? Anyone in particular or Mowbray in general?'

'Why can't you believe I asked you to dance for the pleasure of your company? You dance beautifully, by the way.'

'That is why. You are clearly playing a role. It is all very well to turn that rakish charm on me, Adam, but please be careful with the likes of Mary and her friends. They are all ready to become enthralled with the "wicked Lord Delacort" and I don't think that is what you want.'

She had worried she might offend him, but his mouth merely quirked into a half-smile again.

'Quite right. I can think of nothing more tedious, frankly. Which is why, you note, I asked you to dance and not one of those empty-headed frothy bundles of flounce and tulle.'

She couldn't help laughing.

'I should have stayed with the compliments. So who is next? There aren't many indeterminately aged wallflowers present tonight. Will you proceed to matrons? Or perhaps the stunning widow? Please don't.'

He raised his brows again in genuine surprise.

'Why not? Dare I hope that you are jealous?'

'Not in the least. I am merely worried you might cut out Percy. Frankly given his behaviour so far tonight I hope he is realising there are better prospects to be had than Mary. Since you have declined helping, this lovely Mrs Eckley is my best hope of deliverance at the moment.'

'She is doing nicely, isn't she? And so quickly, too. I thought she might turn the trick,' he said innocently and her eyes widened with sudden suspicion.

'What? Adam! I mean, Lord Delacort!'

'Alyssa?' he enquired, still with the same spuriously innocent air. She flushed hotly at her slip in employing his given name, but forced herself to focus on the revelation that he'd had something to do with the widow's appearance in Mowbray.

'Do you mean to tell me you had something to do with…? No, that is ridiculous… Did you?'

He smiled cynically down at her. 'I am in a bind, aren't I? No matter what I say you are likely to disapprove.'

'Who is she?' she asked finally in a half-whisper.

'An actress and the wife of a very good friend

of mine from my disreputable days in India. She jumped at the opportunity to take a brief holiday for a good cause. If over the next few days she can manage to shake your silly cousin's belief in Percy's sainthood, good. If not, well, at least we tried.'

She shook her head, feeling slightly dazed.

'I don't know whether to be grateful or outraged,' she said finally and realised immediately she had said the wrong thing. He was still smiling, but there was no longer any warmth in his eyes.

'I don't need your gratitude or your approbation, Miss Drake,' he said and there was a hard bite to his voice that reminded her again that this was no longer the young man she had once known. 'Ten years ago you tried to do me a favour and, however many my faults, I take my debts seriously. Ginnie is how I see fit to repay that favour. If you don't like my methods, do your own dirty work. Or better yet, stop interfering in other people's lives and let your brother assume responsibility for his. If he is really so serious about your cousin, he should do something about her himself. But frankly, I think at nineteen the last thing he needs is to commit himself to a silly ninnyhammer like your cousin, no matter how wealthy. And as for you, you would probably do well to forgo your tendency to worry about all and sundry and put all that energy to use somewhere more enjoyable.'

Alyssa listened with a growing anger fuelled by the unwelcome recognition that there was truth in what he said.

'As you do,' she said contemptuously.

'Certainly as I do. I can show you how to enjoy yourself if you like.'

His tone shifted so abruptly, the anger in his eyes replaced by the taunting amusement again, that she was caught off guard and responded before she even registered the nature of the offer.

'Show me how to what?'

'How to...enjoy. Yourself. It's a very useful skill.'

She stared up at him, amazed that he had actually said what she thought he had said. She might not have much experience with men herself, but between her sister Minerva's revelations about the marvels of married life and the confidences of her brother Terry's charming wife, who had shared with her a few discreet and quite revealing books, she had learned a great deal about the relations between men and women. She had a fairly good idea what Adam was referring to, but no man had ever dared say anything as direct to her in the past.

Alyssa felt the need to step back, to mark a sharp line between them that there would be no mistaking. She could tell by the watchful, sardonic look in his grey eyes that Adam was enjoying her confusion. He was toying with her, but ultimately unconcerned whether she rose to the bait or swam away. She hated that part of her wanted to follow where he offered to lead.

'Having experience does not make you a good teacher,' she said dismissively.

His hands shifted slightly, his thumb moving to brush lightly over the inside of her wrist through the thin fabric of her long glove and a tingling surged up her arm before settling into an urgent thrum, like the quivering of a violin string after being plucked.

'True. Why don't you judge for yourself?' His voice had deepened again and she could not tell whether the urgency she heard there was anything but a clever tool, a well-honed instrument. With every encounter between them she felt something shift further and further from her memory of the Adam of ten years ago. Perhaps it was not really a memory, just a fabrication of her young, romantic and foolish mind.

This was Adam, she told herself. Charming, seductive, mocking, insincere. It was all a game for him. Even Percy was more sincere in his own way. She felt once again a surge of protest, almost of loss. She shrugged and twisted her hand so that he was forced to hold her more properly.

'I don't think I want to learn anything from you,' she said, looking away towards the other couples around them, wishing her voice had not sounded so morose.

His grasp tightened so sharply she gave a gasp of surprise and glanced up, but his face was expressionless, as he had looked in his study. The withdrawal lasted only a moment and then the mocking look returned, but his eyes had lost the warmth that had disturbed her.

'That is probably wise, Miss Drake. Unfortunate, though. I, at least, would have enjoyed myself.'

She shook her head, not able to hold back a smile at his determined destruction.

'Did you know you have only one dimple?' he asked curiously.

Heat flowed up and stained her cheeks, but before she could reply or even understand why of all the things he had said such an innocuous remark affected her most strongly, the band gave the final flourish and the dance ended. Adam guided her back towards where her aunt Adele was watching them with some trepidation. Alyssa shot a quick glance up at him, hoping he didn't succumb to the urge to say something outrageous in front of her very sober aunt.

By the look he shot her as he bowed very properly over her aunt's hand Alyssa could tell he was very tempted and she gritted her teeth as she made the necessary introductions. All the other matrons seated on the sofas in their direct vicinity were suspiciously silent, but Adam merely made some comment about the clement weather and strode off towards where his friend stood in conversation with Sir James Muncy, the local squire and Justice of the Peace. His departure was followed by another rush of whispering and Alyssa felt like picking up one of the very nice flower arrangements on the table next to the sofa, vase and all, and dropping it loudly on the floor.

She tensed even more as she saw Percy head in their direction. She knew that Mary's heart, though bruised, would probably forgive that he flirted with a dozen beautiful widows if he would only smile at her as well. She herself could not imagine how anyone would find that boyish dandy attractive. It was hard to imagine that Percy was merely a year younger than Adam.

Percy stopped by the sofa and grinned endearingly down at Mrs Aldridge.

'I know I shouldn't be greedy, Mrs Aldridge, but

may I beg for just one more dance with Miss Aldridge? I promise to content myself with that, at least for this evening.'

'Oh, please, Mother, may I?' Mary asked, pressing her hands together anxiously. Alyssa felt like kicking her.

Mrs Aldridge returned Percy's smile indolently.

'Well, I don't see why not. But that will be all for tonight, young man!'

Mary bounced to her feet and followed Percy to the dance floor while Mrs Aldridge watched them with a softened expression. Alyssa sighed and sat down.

'Aren't they so handsome together?' her aunt asked and Alyssa bit down on the range of answers she was considering. It wasn't her aunt's fault. She meant well. Another subtle groundswell of talk rumbled round the room and Alyssa wondered if Adam was doing something outrageous again.

'Have you heard about the new widow?' her aunt whispered, her eyes alight with interest. 'Almeria heard all about her from Mr Figgs. Apparently she is a Mrs Eckley, from Ireland. They say she is fabulously wealthy and has come here for the waters. But I think she has come here for a new husband. Apparently Mr Eckley was both extremely wealthy and extremely old. My goodness, just look at that dress!'

Despite herself, Alyssa looked. The dress *was* magnificent, as was the body it encased. This woman—Ginnie, Adam had called her—was absolutely stunning. She might have been anywhere between twenty-five and thirty-five, but her age was unimportant compared to the voluptuous body wrapped lovingly in deep red, almost burgundy-coloured silk and lace, and her neck and ears glittering with an almost indecent display of diamonds. Her auburn hair was dressed high, while one thick lock rested suggestively against her very white, very low *décolletage*.

Alyssa felt quite gauche and immature all of a sudden. She was probably not much younger than the widow, but she felt a vast gulf of experience lay between them. It seemed amazing to her that Adam had brought this woman to Mowbray because she had asked him for help. For a moment she felt a surge of something hopeful, a kind of yearning. But she pushed it down mercilessly. This was as much a game for him as his idle flirtation with her. It was just the kind of gesture he might make to please himself and his own sense of what was right. Trust him to come up with such an outrageous scheme.

'Quite shocking!' her aunt continued. 'Speaking of which, my dear, I know you think you are past the age of attracting gossip, but I assure you, my dear, that it is not so. It was really quite improvident to waltz with Lord Delacort. A country dance, perhaps, but a waltz…? What will Lady Nesbit say?'

Alyssa stood up impatiently.

'She will say a great deal of disapproving nonsense as usual. Pray forgive me, Aunt Adele, but I just remembered I am promised to someone for this dance.'

'Alyssa, my dear, I don't know what has come over you. You know you should wait for your partner to come to you…'

Alyssa did not stay to hear the rest. There was no point in staying anyway. Mary had already danced with Percy twice, which was hopefully all the damage he would do that night. And Alyssa had taken all she could bear at the moment. She felt raw and exposed and angry at herself.

The temptation to flirt with Adam, perhaps to prove she was not the callow, insignificant girl she had been ten years ago, was not worth the cost. She surely could not be enough of a fool to believe she could make any real impact upon him? In a few days he would be gone again. And she absolutely refused to find herself in the same dark place of loss and need she had wallowed in all those years ago. Before she was even ten years old she had removed her father from the position of being able to disappoint and hurt her. A decade ago Adam had breached her defences and left her in tatters without even realising what he had done. No one would ever, ever have that power over her again.

She manoeuvred through the crowd and out through the little colonnade of Ionic pillars leading to a courtyard that separated the Assembly Room from the Grand Pump Room. An ornamental fountain pumped out the curative waters in the centre of the courtyard and hooks held pewter cups for those patrons who wished to imbibe the foul-tasting liquid. There was no one there at this late hour and Alyssa sat down on one of the benches lining the wall and closed her eyes. The noise from the dance merged with the uneven sputtering of the fountain.

'Hallo, are you hiding?' an unfamiliar voice said very close to her and her eyes flew open in alarm. A tall man with dark hair and eyes was standing by one of the columns and watching her, brows raised. 'I didn't know young women were allowed to wander around here alone. Or perhaps you don't intend to be alone for long? Shall I leave?'

'If you are going to dispense any more opinions about what young women should or shouldn't do, then, yes, you *should* leave.'

After a surprised moment he gave a crack of laughter.

'Good lord, I see what he meant. No more opinions, I promise. You're escaping, then? So am I. This is my first social event outside of London in almost ten years. I had forgotten how terrifying they are.'

'Who is "he"? And meant what?' she asked suspiciously and somewhat incoherently, trying not to smile and failing.

Before he could answer a third figure entered the gloomy courtyard from the ballroom.

'What the devil are you doing out here, Nick?' Adam bit out and the other man turned to him, his face registering surprise at Adam's tones.

'We are escaping, Miss Drake and I. What are *you* doing here? If you came to play chaperon, I have to point out it is not only unnecessary, but probably counterproductive. Remember you're the *bête noire* around here, not I.'

Adam's face remained stony. He did not look at all like the man she had danced with just a few moments ago.

'We should all return to the Assembly Room,' he replied in the same flat voice.

Alyssa ignored him and addressed the other man. 'Are you Lord Delacort's guest?'

Nicholas gave a bow with a flourish.

'For my sins, I am. Until he ejects me, which by the look of it, might be sooner rather than later. And since he is apparently not going to introduce me, I must do so myself. Nicholas Beauvoir, at your service.'

Alyssa extended her hand promptly.

'It is a pleasure to meet you, Mr Beauvoir, I am Miss Drake.'

'So I gather. I heard you were a witness to Adam's unfortunate encounter with the forest floor. You will be pleased to hear Thunder is mending well.'

'I am very pleased to hear that. He is a beautiful horse. I hope there have been no further accidents,' she said, curious despite herself, and knowing it was much more likely this man would satisfy her curiosity than Adam. To her surprise Mr Beauvoir's gaze shifted to his friend and back to her before he answered.

'Was it an accident? I recollect a stretch of rope was involved, which rather defies the definition. In contrast, the collapse of the scaffolding on the east wing yesterday while we were inspecting the renovations might be deemed an accident, I suppose,' he said and Alyssa looked quickly at Adam, whose jaw tightened. His grey eyes narrowed ominously at his friend. But he did not respond, nor did he bother insisting they return to the ballroom again. He was clearly well acquainted with Mr Beauvoir and it was obvious even to Alyssa that this handsome and rather amusing man could be just as stubborn as Adam.

'Was anyone hurt?' she asked in concern.

'No one,' Adam interrupted. 'And it *was* an accident. My friend is just finding country life a bit boring and has decided to introduce some drama.'

Despite her worry and her annoyance at herself, she could not help smiling.

'Unlike you and the false widow?'

His stern expression faded, his grey eyes lightening with amusement.

'That is quite another matter. I told you, I consider that a repayment of a debt.'

She shook her head.

'And I told you, there is no debt. Which must mean I owe *you* now. Still, if it works and Mary sees Percy for what he is, it will be worth it.'

'It might work, but that still doesn't mean you should force your brother and her together. Do you mean to interfere every time that silly little girl fancies herself in love?'

She didn't answer right away. She had not thought beyond the moment. She knew she must appear hopelessly naïve and there was no way she could explain to him what drove her. With his jaded view of the world and probably no concept of love but the broken memory of his infatuation with Rowena or the multitude of relations he'd had with women over the years, she did not think he would understand her sense of commitment to her brother. She would never force Charlie to do anything he did not want to do, but she could at least try to prevent the girl he cared for making a mistake based on youth and inexperience.

The weight of these two men watching her from the height of their greater experience and their jaundiced view of the world made her feel futile and foolish.

'I appreciate what you are trying to do about Percy, but excuse me if I don't accept that you are an authority on the topic, Lord Delacort.'

Mr Beauvoir grinned.

'That's right. Put him in his place, Miss Drake. You're quite right not to take any advice from him on affairs of the heart, because quite frankly he doesn't have one, as many a damsel around the world could attest.'

Alyssa wondered if Mr Beauvoir was warning her or just taunting his friend. They did seem to have an unusual relationship, but though Adam's expression did not change, Alyssa could tell he was annoyed.

'Said the pot…' Adam replied caustically. 'You are hardly an authority on the topic either, Nick.'

'Never said I was, but you take the palm when it comes to antipathy to commitment of any kind. What was it you said once? That it was clear humanity was becoming steadily more stupid, since only idiots would willingly choose to marry and procreate.'

'I'm flattered. I had no idea you paid such attention to everything I said.'

Mr Beauvoir shrugged and winked at Alyssa. She could no longer doubt he was, in his light-hearted way, warning her to develop no expectations about Adam. He need not have bothered. She knew full well Adam's flirtation with her was no different from innumerable similar acts on his part. The fact that it stood out in the restricted landscape of her emotional life did not mean she should give it any particular weight. In fact, it meant she should be doubly careful to give it no weight at all. But though she knew all that, still his words left a bitter sting that mocked her. She looked up at Adam's strong face. Cut across with shadows in the dim courtyard he looked more unapproachable than ever.

You don't know him, she reminded herself. *Don't delude yourself into thinking you do.*

She extended her hand to Mr Beauvoir.

'Well, I should return before my poor aunt thinks I have abandoned her. I hope that if you are permitted to remain in Mowbray the rest of your stay is both pleasant and safe, Mr Beauvoir. Goodnight, Lord Delacort.'

Mr Beauvoir raised her hand audaciously and not quite properly to his lips. Adam crossed his arms.

'All right, Nick. You've had your fun…'

'Alyssa!' The three of them turned at her aunt's outraged exclamation. Alyssa snatched back her hand like a guilty child, then felt furious with herself for acting so gauchely. It was no business of her aunt, or of anyone else for that matter, if she wished to flirt with an attractive man. She was about to say something cutting, but she took in her aunt's kind, anxious face and relented. It was obviously not proper to be alone in the courtyard with two bachelors, one of whom was known to be a dangerous rake and the other who seemed to be little better.

She smiled, shaking her head at herself. If she had an ounce of sense, she should milk this opportunity for all it was worth. She took her aunt's arm and guided her back into the Assembly Room.

The two men watched them leave the courtyard. Nicholas turned to Adam, the mischief in his smile pronounced.

'Well, this is certainly more entertaining than I thought our country sojourn would be,' he said. 'I almost regret leaving tomorrow, even if it is only for a few days. Will I still be welcome once I've done my duty by my family?'

Adam shook his head ruefully. It was hard to stay mad at Nicholas, however aggravating he might be.

'You know you are. I need someone here who doesn't look at me like a two-headed wonder at the village fair.'

'Point taken. Try to stay out of trouble while I'm away, will you?'

'Yes, nanny.'

Nicholas laughed and shook his head. In the silence the fountain chattered merrily behind them. After a moment Nicholas indicated the colonnade.

'Should we go back in?'

'You go. I'll follow in a moment,' Adam replied.

Nicholas's brows rose, but he merely nodded and headed back towards the ballroom.

Adam walked over to the fountain. A faint sulphuric smell rose up from the water. It was fitting, since he felt this gathering was one version of hell, at least as far as he was concerned. He needed a moment of quiet before he went back into the Assembly Room.

He knew Nicholas well enough to realise his taunts had been primarily a warning to Alyssa, which he could have told his friend was unnecessary, since Alyssa took him no more seriously than he did himself. But Nicholas's words had struck home none the less. Adam wished he could live up to his own words and turn his back on this unwelcome inheritance and the way it tied him inexorably to the scene of his previous weakness and disgrace and to his memory of what a trusting fool he had been. He could hardly credit that he was the same man as the boy who had once stood in this ballroom, glaring after Rowena as she danced with other men, like a laughable impersonation of a Byronic hero.

He should just pack up and be gone tomorrow and forget about Delacort. The estate had limped along for decades and survived, who cared if it continued in the same vein? He already had more money than he would ever know what to do with. He didn't need the income from the estate and he didn't need the headache and he certainly didn't need the approbation of the people of Mowbray. It hadn't taken Alyssa's comments to make it clear the town was only waiting for the first signs of transgression.

His family, thankfully, now lived far away, but the whole place seemed to have subsumed that same narrow-minded, judgemental sourness that had ruled his mother's life. The only positive he could see in the whole situation was that everyone was so fixated on his notoriety that no one seemed to remember the serious and bathetic young man he had been other than himself.

He glanced over towards the haze of light spilling out from the ballroom and smiled. Alyssa appeared to remember enough not to be unduly impressed by his transformation. Surprisingly her insistence to call him to order didn't bother him. It only made him want to ruffle her feathers even more. He could never tell if she would scold or blush in response. He thought her own change was just as impressive as his, despite it being in quite the opposite direction. She might not give credit to his transformation, but she herself had put so much effort into turning her back on the wild young girl she had been and becoming proper that he wondered if she even knew who she was any longer. He knew only too well it was very easy to lose track.

What he could not understand was why she was still unmarried. He found it hard to believe it was simply because no one had asked her. She was attractive, intelligent, and she certainly seemed to have overdeveloped maternal instincts. It was probably as he suspected, that her tyrannical and selfish father had kept her well under his poetic thumb.

But he could see flashes of that girl—her mischievous bravado, usually accompanied by that single, distracting dimple. And then she would promptly disappear again like an errant child scolded back into the nursery. Except there was nothing childish about that side of her, quite the opposite. Strangely enough it was her proper demeanour that seemed young and rather endearingly severe, like a child playing at dress up, while the complicit, laughing, knowing sprite promised something much more mature.

It was a pity she hadn't taken him up on his offer

of a dalliance. Not that he had really expected she would. It had just been amusing to goad her and watch her emotions reflected in those amazing green eyes.

She was certainly adding flavour to his stay in Mowbray, but he knew he should not carry this rather unusual flirtation too far. However clever she had been at parrying his approaches, it was too uneven a battle to be quite fair. He might be a rake, but he had yet to pursue a serious flirtation with a woman who did not fully know the rules of the game. And he certainly should not confuse the degree of comfort he felt with her, which was based on some shared memory of another, simpler time, with any real intimacy.

Not that she showed any signs of being in danger of taking him too seriously or of fancying herself in love with him. But as proper as she was, there was that edge of heat in her eyes that told of a young woman who could enjoy physical passion very much if given half the chance. He had played unfairly on that conviction during the dance because it had been pleasant to forget for a moment that he hated being back here and wanted nothing more than to wrap up his business and be on his way. He had no right to toy with her of all people.

Adam turned and headed back into the Assembly Room in search of Nicholas. He had done what he had come to do and he wanted to get out of the oppressive morass of speculation. He'd had enough of Mowbray society for one night.

Chapter Seven

'She does not want to go.' Mrs Aldridge squeezed her plump hands together anxiously. She glanced at the mantelpiece clock in the neat little drawing room of the Queen Street house she had rented for the summer season in the fashionable quarter of Mowbray. 'And we just bought the most charmingly becoming bonnet with jonquil ribbons to match her gown. Whatever shall we do...?' She trailed off and looked hopefully across at Alyssa.

'Of course she doesn't want to go,' Alyssa replied, trying not to let her impatience show. 'She knows everyone will be talking about Percy and Mrs Eckley. For goodness' sake, Aunt Adele, this is just tea at Lady Nesbit's, hardly a court presentation. If she doesn't want to go for once, then we should not force her.'

'In Mowbray they are practically one and the

same as you well know, Alyssa. If she doesn't come now, the whispering will only get worse!'

Alyssa sighed. Her aunt was right. Every week during the summer months the best of Mowbray female *haut ton* joined the *grande dame* for a weekly dissection of events at the Assembly Room dances and other social gatherings. For years Alyssa had attended dutifully. As little as Lady Nesbit and Rowena seemed to appreciate her presence, she knew that to snub them might have serious consequences both for her and her family. The tedium of these afternoon gossips had been alleviated somewhat when her aunt and Mary had arrived in Mowbray. They'd just put off their mourning for Mr Aldridge and had clearly needed Alyssa's help navigating the often treacherous waters of Mowbray society.

But today Alyssa had a somewhat selfish reason for wishing to attend. She couldn't help wondering how Rowena was coping with the snub she had received from Adam. She also wanted to learn what she could about Mrs Eckley. If anyone had information about her, it would be Lady Nesbit with her faithful network of local gossips. Alyssa had heard from Betsy that Percy had been seen promenading with the widow in the town gardens that very morning. From her aunt's worried countenance when she had arrived at the house that afternoon it was clear the news had reached Queen Street as well.

Alyssa stood.

'I will talk to her, Aunt,' she said and headed up the narrow stairs to Mary's room. Her cousin was dressed very charmingly in a muslin dress trimmed with jonquil ribbons that matched the newly acquired bonnet lying on the bed by her side.

'I don't want to go,' Mary said petulantly when Alyssa entered. Alyssa sat down on the bed beside her and picked up one of Mary's delicate hands.

'I had a letter from Charles,' Alyssa began, hoping to distract her. 'He is doing well and is hopeful he will be able to visit for a few days in September.'

'That's nice. He hasn't written to me in weeks.' Her voice was flat, indifferent, and Alyssa could not make out if there was any pique there or just pure lack of interest. She was also surprised to hear Charlie had not written to Mary. When he had first gone up to Cambridge at the beginning of the school year he had written to her on a weekly basis. At least.

For the first time she wondered if Adam might have been right. After all, Charlie *was* young, and though he had seemed in love with Mary almost from the day she had arrived in Mowbray a year ago, he had never actively courted her. Alyssa had assumed it was because he believed, correctly, that Mary was still too young or because he felt her inheritance placed a barrier between them.

When he had gone up he had told Alyssa to take care of Mary for him and Alyssa had taken him at his word. She had therefore been surprised when he had written to say he would not come home for the summer vacation, but would be staying with friends in the area and would perhaps try to earn some money tutoring. She had rationalised this, deciding that he wanted to become as independent as swiftly as possible. But Adam's cynical observations as to the inconstancy of young men would not leave her.

She told herself she had done Mary no disservice by detaching her from someone like Percy. But if Adam were to ask Alyssa now if she intended to go to such lengths to separate Mary from any other potential suitor, she would have to answer that she wouldn't.

In fact, the more she thought about her blind insistence on preserving this pretty but not overly intelligent girl for Charlie simply because she thought he willed it, the more she felt foolish, even pathetic. It would have been better if she had acted out of purely mercenary aims rather than some romantic notion of constancy and love. Simply because she herself was foolishly still captive of the false image of someone she had loved years ago... She reined in her thoughts. There was no point in dwelling on ancient history. Right now she still had an obligation to her cousin.

'I know this isn't easy for you, Mary, and believe me I don't want to go either, but the brutal truth is that in cases like this the worst thing to do is hide and let people gloat and gossip behind your back. We shan't force you to go, but it really would be best for you if you came and tried to act as if you aren't in the least bit bothered.'

Mary raised her large blue eyes, now glistening with tears, and Alyssa felt she was being unfairly demanding. Mary was only a girl, after all. Why was it so necessary that she not show she was human and hurt? Surely it was healthier than holding everything inside.

The blue eyes dropped and Mary breathed in shakily, drying her eyes with the crumpled handkerchief in her hand. Finally she shrugged.

'Very well.'

Alyssa gave her a quick hug.

'Good girl. Let's get this over with.'

* * *

When they entered Lady Nesbit's elegant celestial-blue drawing room they were the last to arrive and it was clear they were entering a scene of unusual tension. Rowena was beautiful as usual in a lilac jaconet muslin morning dress with lace-trimmed sleeves, gathered below the bosom by a silver buckle. Her perfect complexion was enhanced by a slight flush. Alyssa, who knew her well, knew she was furious. Her heart sank. Rowena was never easy, but an antagonised Rowena was dangerous. She was not used to being the butt of either pity or derision and Alyssa could sense that there were those in the audience who felt either or both emotions towards the uncontested belle of the county.

It was not long after their arrival before Rowena made her move to deflect attention from her own ignominy towards Mary's. In a sweet but carrying voice she asked the young woman sitting next to her if she had chanced to see what a simply stunning gown Mrs Eckley had worn during her garden promenade with Percy. Surely it must be a French design! Only they could design something so dashing…

Mary's frail shoulders sagged and her fingers played nervously with the beading on her reticule and Alyssa wished she had not talked her into attending. She felt a flash of anger at Rowena for targeting someone who was so obviously unable to defend herself.

'I think you are probably correct, Rowena.' Alyssa spoke as calmly as she could. 'Probably the same *modiste* who designed that amazing creation she wore to the Assembly. But then she has a most perfect figure. Not every woman can wear such fashions and still appear elegant. It was clear *all* the men present remarked it.'

Rowena shot her a venomous look.

'Oh, quite, dear cousin. As they also remarked on the way you flirted so desperately with Lord Delacort. Really, my dear Alyssa, you cannot possibly imagine he might be interested in someone as *farouche* as you.'

It was such a blunt, inelegant attack, Alyssa felt more embarrassed for Rowena than for herself. There was a moment of disconcerted silence in the room; even Lady Nesbit took a moment longer than usual to re-establish her control over the conversation, turning it down avenues of gossip which for the first time that week touched upon neither Percy nor Lord Delacort.

Alyssa allowed the conversation to flow around her and waited for the afternoon to be over. There was no pleasure in kicking Rowena when she was down and Rowena's own taunt, though blunt, lingered. She knew she was right, that Adam's flirtation during the waltz had meant nothing more than a practised game. But at least it was an honest game. She needed to let go of the persistent fantasy that the Adam of her girlhood memory existed anywhere but in her imagination. And in a way the best way of doing that was to overlay that memory with reality.

Why not flirt with him? she told herself defiantly. It was about time she stopped being so careful about everything, and...

'...don't you think so, Alyssa?'

Alyssa blinked, startled as her aunt addressed her directly.

'I beg your pardon?'

Rowena gave a very unladylike snigger.

'Cousin Alyssa is daydreaming again. How many times has Grandmama reproved you on that tiresome habit of yours?'

Alyssa flushed. 'Not as many times as she has reproved you on your ill manners, Rowena,' she shot back.

Rowena raised her beautifully arched brows.

'My, my. Lessons on manners from someone

who wore breeches until she came of age? I find that rich,' she mocked.

Alyssa felt like replying that she would not have had to wear breeches if either Lady Nesbit or Rowena herself had taken enough interest in her family to ensure she and her sister had more than two dresses to their name.

'*"Who makes the fairest show, means most deceit,"*' she quoted sweetly instead. It was childish, since she knew that although Rowena had only contempt for her bookishness, it was the one area where Alyssa was clearly her superior and Rowena hated being second in any respect.

Before Rowena could find a response, Lady Nesbit gave the floor a sharp rap with her cane, leaning forward from where she sat enthroned on her favourite mahogany sofa.

'Now, now, girls. I would appreciate if you did not squabble in my drawing room. Really, at your age one would think you might have outgrown such nonsense. Alyssa, your aunt was enquiring whether you thought it would be a good idea for her to take Miss Aldridge to visit with the Aldridges in Windermere for a few weeks. You can see the unusually warm weather here in Mowbray does not at all agree with her delicate constitution.

A few weeks up near the Lakes may be just what is needed for her to recover her bloom.'

Alyssa turned to inspect the sad droop of Mary's pretty mouth and the confusion in her aunt's eyes.

'Would you like that, Mary?' she asked her cousin gently.

'I suppose. I think so,' Mary answered almost inaudibly, looking so much younger than her seventeen years that Alyssa wished once again she could strangle Percy with one of his own beautifully arranged cravats.

'Then I think that is an excellent idea, Aunt Adele,' she replied calmly and a look of relief spread over her aunt's plump face. Alyssa glanced over at Lady Nesbit and met the old woman's pale blue eyes. She had never quite understood her, but in that moment she could almost believe Lady Nesbit was motivated by compassion for the girl and she gave her a grateful smile. Lady Nesbit met the smile with one of her direct, expressionless gazes, before turning to address a comment to Miss Mott on the most recent fashion plates in *Bell's Court and Fashionable Magazine*, expressing her stringent disapproval on the distinct lowering of the waistline evident in the latest fashions.

Alyssa sighed inwardly and was extremely grateful when Lady Nesbit finally stood up, signalling the end of the gathering, and they all filed out to their awaiting barouches and landaus like obedient schoolgirls. On the ride back Alyssa went along with her aunt's determined prattle about the beauties of the Lake District and the pleasures in store there for Mary. For a moment Alyssa wanted to ask if she could go with them. But she knew that would merely be a cowardly evasion. It was time to stop hiding and make some serious decisions about her future, whether that be in Mowbray, or elsewhere.

Chapter Eight

Adam guided Thunder across the small stream and up on to the lane towards Mowbray. A thatch of leaves dislodged under Thunder's hoofs and Adam watched as they were snatched away, disappearing under a tangle of blackberry brambles that hung over the water. There was something soothing about these small lanes and streams, undramatic and undemanding. So different from the vivid but often unforgiving landscapes he had explored over the past years.

It wasn't just the easing of survival instincts; for a boy who had grown up outside a town smaller than Mowbray there was something relaxing in the familiarity of the countryside. In the steady pace and predictable rituals of country life.

His own memory of Mowbray had always been overlaid not just by his public shaming, but by the oppressive atmosphere of his parents' home, caught between his mother's ambitions and his father's weary surrender to her will. He and his sisters, who had also suffered under their mother's highly critical and often vindictive ambition, had been very fond of each other, but he had always preferred to avoid coming home from school when possible. Adam had spent many holidays with Nicholas's family in Berkshire, which his mother had agreed to with the very thinly veiled hope that he would ingratiate himself with his friend's highly respectable family. Now, with his mother in the far north and his sisters happily married, that aspect of Adam's memory of Mowbray no longer existed. That, at least, had rendered the town a much more pleasant place than he'd recalled.

In the three days since the Assembly, he had been surprised to receive a few judicious visits from the males amongst the local landowners. Although there had been no sudden embracing by local society, these visits indicated he was being assessed and his social fate considered. Against his better judgement he found there was something enjoyable about these tentative expeditions. Some were people he had known as a young man and once they spoke with him on an individual basis they were a great deal less judgemental than he had anticipated. If anything, they seemed rather envious of his travels and certainly appreciative of the contents of the restocked wine cellar.

His visitors had also been useful in reporting, also rather enviously, on Ginnie's progress. The consensus was that Percy was very close to clos-ing the deal with the widow Eckley. They joked that even Percy's debtors had relaxed their em-bargo sufficiently to allow him to acquire a few new items for his fashionable wardrobe. It seemed the tradesmen considered this generosity in the guise of an investment with a hope of return. Adam's own valet had reported that Percy's valet Libbet's star, which had begun to wane since Adam's return, was on the wax again. He almost felt bad about what was about to happen to Percy once Ginnie left Mowbray as she was scheduled to do the next day. Still, if Alyssa's heiress was fool enough to take Percy once Ginnie had wrapped up her role, she was welcome to him, as far as Adam was concerned.

Adam was only sorry Nicholas wasn't there to poke fun at his temporary descent into respect-ability. Still, it would be over soon enough. In a few days he would finally be on his way back to London. Or perhaps someplace completely new, like Australia. He smiled as he remembered Alyssa's comments about his supposed exploits in that country. Underneath her amusement she had sounded almost wistful. It seemed the carefully contained wild girl would not have minded some adventures of her own. It was almost a pity she was a gentleman's daughter. He had a feeling that under other circumstances she would have made an excellent adventurer.

Thunder nickered and raised his muzzle as if to breathe the air, and Adam tensed, focusing immediately on his surroundings.

'What is it, boy?' Adam asked. He told himself it was ridiculous, but he could not shake the occasional sensation of being watched, especially while riding or walking in the woods. He told himself it was absurd to feel he was missing something. It was just the tension of being back in Mowbray.

Thunder shook his sooty mane and huffed and Adam relaxed as he saw Alyssa's slim figure beyond the hedge that bordered the lane. She was carrying a small wicker basket, her brow contracted in an absent frown and her green eyes vivid in the sun that filtered through the trees. She was almost abreast of them when Adam nudged his top boots against Thunder's flanks and they moved through the trees on to the lane. She gave a gasp and stopped abruptly, clasping her wicker basket to her in a childlike gesture of alarm.

'I think one of Perrault's tales dealt with this situation,' Adam said mildly and the alarm on her face was replaced by laughter.

'Puss in Boots?' she enquired and he smiled appreciatively.

'I was thinking of the wolf and the fair maiden in the forest.'

'I see. Well, the gossips are definitely becoming frustrated by your good behaviour these past few days. Stalking village maids in the forest will stir things up nicely. Don't let me get in the way. Hello, Thunder, you are looking much better today,' she added as she moved around the large horse, just reaching up to rub his silky muzzle gently as she passed.

Thunder nickered and stepped forward, brushing his muzzle against her shoulder, and she laughed.

'You're like a big dog, aren't you?'

Adam swung out of the saddle, running his hand down the stallion's neck.

'Thunder doesn't appreciate being likened to a dog, do you, boy? He is much more discriminating than any canine I've met.'

'And yet he seems fond of you...'

'Very amusing. I have my good points. You just have to get to know me better.'

Her elusive dimple made a brief appearance and Adam resisted the impulse to reach out and touch it.

'You do know there is no one watching?' she asked amicably. 'This big-bad-wolf role is rather wasted without an audience, isn't it?'

'I consider it a dress rehearsal. Keeping my skills honed.'

She shook her head and stroked Thunder's flank gently and the horse lowered his head, delivering himself wholly to the pleasure of being petted. Adam watched as her fingers caressed the horse and his hand tightened on the reins. It was lucky she wasn't taking him seriously. Otherwise he just might be tempted to carry through on his big-bad-wolf threat and show her just what she was missing by insisting on being such a proper Mowbray Miss.

Standing so close to her reminded him how much he had enjoyed dancing with her. It wasn't just that she had danced well or that he had enjoyed her quizzical responses to his flirtation. It was ridiculous that something as innocuous as his hand on her waist should have been so potent, but even now he could remember how it had felt to slide his hand upwards, to feel the warmth of her skin underneath her dress. He shifted uncomfortably as his body heated. It was a shame she was unlikely to be willing to carry this banter into a more satisfying flirtation. He was increasingly convinced all her rigid propriety hid a very passionate nature.

'Well, I am glad to be of use,' she continued lightly. 'Is this dress rehearsal in aid of any particular grand production?'

'Since I will be leaving Mowbray in a couple of days I have neglected to schedule anything, but I am quite happy to arrange a private show if you are interested.'

She flushed, her bravado fading.

'You are very lucky Thunder doesn't understand what you are saying, Lord Delacort. He might be tempted to toss you on your back again. I certainly am.'

'Are you? If you wish to get me on my back, you only have to ask. There is no need to enlist Thunder's help.' He watched appreciatively as her flush deepened despite her attempt at sophistication. He knew he shouldn't push her like that, but each crack in her shell felt like an irresistible invitation to proceed.

'I must be going. I don't want to get in the way of your stalking. You might even find some willing prey, who knows?' she said scornfully. She moved to go around them, but Thunder ambled forward, blocking their path and boxing Alyssa and Adam against the hedge.

'How do you make him do that?' Alyssa asked, exasperated.

'I have nothing to do with it. Thunder has a mind of his own.'

'Don't be ridiculous… Here now, Thunder, move.' She gave the enormous black horse a gentle shove, but he merely shifted closer and Adam caught her around the waist before she stumbled backwards into the hedge.

'I told you.' He laughed, resisting the urge to tighten his hold and pull her to him fully.

'He must be very useful for you,' she said, fuming, but she did not try to move away.

'He is usually too fastidious to be of any use. You should be flattered.'

Her green eyes glinted up at him with the faintly mocking look he was becoming accustomed to, tempered only by her rebellious dimple. He gave in and reached up to touch it, just brushing his fingers over the elusive indentation and gently down the line of her jaw. The dimple vanished and as her lips parted he knew this was folly. They were standing in the middle of a public lane, for goodness' sake. And whether she was old enough to know better, she was still merely an unmarried gentlewoman and a virgin, two species he resolutely avoided dallying with. It was stupid to contemplate crossing the line simply because his body decided she would feel very right against him.

But his hand pulled her against him while his other slid against her cheek, into her hair, tilting her head. He forced himself to wait, pushing back at the tense hungry heat that swept through his body, magnifying the sensations radiating from every point of contact between them. It was mere seconds, counted out by the pulse under his palm where it rested on the side of her neck, but the time stretched out. The moment filled with images and sensations, of the contrast between the firm pressure of her hip bone and the soft flesh where his fingers rested, of the dip of her thick lashes as they lowered, obscuring the bright autumn colours of her eyes.

When she didn't react he gave in and lowered his head to hers, tension closing on his lungs as if he was preparing to cast himself off some height. His mouth had barely brushed over hers, feather-light, when he heard the clear sound of a vehicle coming down the lane. He breathed in and stepped away to pull Thunder aside just as a gig came into sight.

Alyssa nodded to the driver and his wife, who were regarding them with unveiled curiosity. She was slightly flushed but otherwise showed no sign of unease.

'Good morning, Mr Jeffries, Mrs Jeffries. How is Minnie?'

'Very well, Miss Drake,' Mrs Jeffries answered as the driver raised his cap in greeting. 'Just a touch of quinsy, but Dr Hedgeway says she's on the mend now.'

'I'm glad...'

She stopped and they all turned at the sound of another horse coming at a faster clip than was usual on such a narrow lane. Lord Moresby, astride one of his hunters, came into view, riding hard and recklessly. He pulled up at the sight of the gig and his large bay mare protested and tried to rear. His eyes swept over them and then settled on Adam with unmistakable enmity.

'You! Been meaning to tell you...stay away from my wife!' he slurred. He dismounted, stumbled slightly and had to lean against his horse, his face flushed above his high shirt points.

'Go home, Lord Moresby,' Alyssa said quietly. Mr Jeffries prodded his horse and the farmer's gig moved on with agonising slowness, but Lord Moresby didn't appear to even notice them.

'Stay out of this, Miss Drake!' he snapped at her and took a step towards Adam, his hand twisted around the reins of his mare. 'And you...you villain...you think you can come back to finish what you failed to do before? She is *my* wife! Stay away from her!'

Adam tensed, wondering how best to calm him down.

'Moresby, I am going to say this only once, so listen well. I have absolutely no interest in your wife. There has been nothing between us nor will there be. I don't even like her. Is that clear enough?'

'I don't believe you!'

'That is your problem, then. Don't blame me for whatever issues the two of you have. They are not of my making.'

'No? No?' Moresby took another step closer, his face hot and twisted with fury. 'She said if she had married you she would have sired a son by now. Do you think I don't know what she is planning? To have you foist a brat on me! Well, I'd sooner see her divorced! Is that what you are waiting for?'

He took another step forward and Adam braced himself. He did not want to brawl with a drunken man and give the town more food for gossip, but it looked like the only thing that would get through to Lord Moresby at the moment was the logic of a fist. But suddenly Alyssa moved between them and to Adam's shock she grasped the man's arms above the elbows and gave him a small shake.

'Lord Moresby. Arthur, look at me!'

Lord Moresby's hazy glance fixed on her, more in surprise at finding himself in the near embrace of a young woman than because of her words.

'Arthur. This is what Rowena does. She is trying to play you just as she has done countless times in the past. And she will continue to do so because this is how she gets what she wants. You know her. If you insist on fighting, or on giving any credence to what she says, you are merely going to look the fool and play into her hands. Do you want that?'

Adam watched as a range of emotions chased each other across the man's florid face and felt a surge of pity for him. Lord Moresby raised one hand, palm upwards in a kind of supplication, his eyes on Alyssa's.

'Nothing I ever do is enough,' he said, his voice husky. 'I try… It's never enough.'

'It's not you, Arthur,' Alyssa replied gently. 'She was always like this. From childhood. She is so beautiful, you see.'

He nodded morosely. 'She is, isn't she? Beautiful. Prettiest in the county.'

Alyssa nodded.

'And you have two beautiful little girls who love you very much. Don't forget that.'

His eyes softened.

'They do.'

His gaze shifted to Adam. His mouth opened and closed, then he turned and went back to his horse, mounting her with some difficulty. He nodded curtly in Adam's direction, then looked down at Alyssa.

'You're a good girl. Always were. Pity.'

They watched as he rode off. Alyssa stood with her arms on her hips.

'Good girl! As if I were a filly!' she said, annoyed. 'Not that I want to be like Rowena, but sometimes, just sometimes, I would like to make as much mischief and have none of it stick to me.'

Adam smiled despite himself. He was still tense because of the lingering heat of what had occurred before the appearance of the farmer's gig and from the near brush with violence. In contrast, Alyssa didn't seem at all embarrassed, which was disorienting in itself. He had not expected to be more affected than she and that thought made him drag himself back into the present moment. This was Alyssa Drake, he told himself. She was a good person who was trying desperately to become something he had no real patience for. He should stay away from her. He shrugged.

'I don't know. From what I have seen, you usually succeed in getting your own way. I wouldn't envy her if I were you.'

She frowned at him, as if trying to search his words for hidden meaning.

'You were very compassionate with him,' he added stiltedly.

She shrugged, looking down. 'He is not a bad person. I have never seen him drunk before. It cannot be easy for him to have you back here. I feel sorry for him.'

'So do I. There but for the grace of God—'

He broke off as her eyes flashed up at him, startling him with the intensity of the anger in them.

'Yes. You are lucky she was an expert manipulator even then. Otherwise her whole plan might have misfired and she would have been forced to marry you after all and you would have lost your excuse to do precisely as you please and be accountable to no one.'

Adam felt a surge of answering anger. 'You do like to lecture, don't you? Between your accusations and Moresby's I'm beginning to realise I am even more a degenerate specimen than I had previously considered. What a pity I can't live up to the exacting standards you all adhere to in this little corner of perfection.'

Alyssa half-raised her hand as if either to reach out to him or stop him, but he ignored her. He was vaguely conscious that his anger was out of proportion to her words, but this awareness was swamped by a wave of stinging bitterness.

'It must be very nice to have someone like me to put in a pillory so that you can all feel clean and righteous while you hide all your own petty deceits and duplicities. You're right I am accountable to no one. I spent most of my life being responsible and that counted for precisely nothing the moment I stepped off the straight and narrow. I'll be damned if I'm going to live my life on probation at the pleasure of hypocrites. Take a good look at yourself before you go throwing any more stones, Miss Drake.'

He swung himself on to Thunder's back and with a curt nod he cantered off.

Alyssa stood staring in shock at the horse and rider as they disappeared round the bend in the lane. Her heart was thudding uncomfortably and she felt ashamed and confused. Too much had happened in that short half hour. She could still feel the warmth of his hands on her, the heat of his body so close to hers and the knowledge that he was about to kiss her and that she desperately wanted him to, even knowing how little this meant to him. It was no good telling herself she didn't take him seriously. His casual statement that he would be leaving in a couple of days had struck her like a blow. She was a fool, but she had no right to vent her pain and her disappointment in herself by attacking him.

She would just have to stay away from him for those two days. She was not a foolish child any more. She might have allowed herself to enjoy his seductive flirtation, but she refused to fancy herself in love with him again. They spoke different languages and it was ridiculous to believe he might come to understand hers. Her father had taught her well that to live in expectation that people would change only led to pain and disillusionment.

Now *she* decided on her own universe, and if it was small, then at least it was safe and of her own making. And when she did decide to leave the safety of Drake Cottage as she knew she must do soon, it would be on her own terms and not at the mercy of people who were only concerned with their own needs and pleasures.

She turned and continued walking towards home, forcing her thoughts back to where they had been before Adam had startled her. With Mary's departure arranged for tomorrow morning she was now responsible for no one but herself. And her father, of course, but he didn't count. She wondered at the strength of her conviction. She had always taken care of her father in a way, even before her sweet but rather timid mother had died, but with neither affection nor a real sense of commitment. She had done so because he was her family's only source of income and out of sheer habit. But now that everyone else had left she could get up and leave and not look back. She did not even need to wait for the answer from London she was hoping for. If Burnley wasn't interested in her current project, she would find someone else.

In fact, if she had an ounce of sense, she would leave on the first stagecoach to London. At the very least she should just make up her mind to stay away from Adam for the next two days. Every time they met he made her lose either her footing or her temper and she didn't like the shaky feeling these encounters left her with. Nothing was ever normal around him. And most ridiculous of all was the fact that at the moment all she wanted to do was to go after him and apologise. She told herself he was hardly a child to be soothed, but the urge was powerful. There had been such bitterness in his voice behind the anger; she felt he had almost been talking to someone else, or to the world as a whole.

She pressed back on the thought. She was doing precisely what Adam had mocked her for doing, worrying about people she should not be. The brutal truth was that he was about to shake the dust of Mowbray from his boots and be off on his next escapade. She had no power to make an impact on someone like him. She had been broken once by his departure. She would not go down that path again.

She reached the gate to Drake Cottage and stopped, her hand on the gate, and looked up at the house she had lived in all her life. After years of gentle care it was as pretty as any cottage in the vale. It was peculiar that it was now almost empty with just herself and her father and Betsy. She raised her hand, just blocking off the view of the asymmetrical second storey, where her father was hard at work. That way the cottage looked better, less weighed down. She dropped her hand and opened the gate. It was hard to breathe and she didn't know if it was due to fear or anticipation. Something was changing and she was afraid she could not stop it.

Chapter Nine

Alyssa leaned on the counter at Milsom's Circulating Library and glanced absently towards the window. It was unlike Mr Milsom to leave the store unattended like this. She waited patiently for five minutes and then ventured to knock on the door to the back room. When that, too, remained unanswered she peeked inside, but other than his desk and stacks of books it was empty.

She glanced back at the interior of the store she had visited so many times she could not even begin to count them. But of all those times, the most vivid memory was of the last time she had been here and of Adam's tall, muscular figure leaning back against the counter, watching her with the mocking but not unsympathetic grey eyes that had always made her feel she was really seen.

With him she felt neither like the unusual, unpredictable Drake girl everyone had once thought her nor the proper Miss Drake she had become and whom everyone had come to esteem to such an extent she doubted if many remembered her wild childhood. When talking with him she felt just like herself, like the person who was with her even when there was no one else. Was this why she had never been tempted to open herself to any relationship? Like a fool, like that silly sleeping princess, waiting for someone to come along and make her feel present. Not even valued, or loved, but present. As real to them as she was to herself.

She closed her eyes against this image and against this seductive but false conviction. Whatever freedom she felt in Adam's presence, he did not really see her as she was, she told herself again, as she had told herself countless times ever since their encounter the previous day. To him she was just a temporarily amusing plaything and her main attraction appeared to be the tension he saw, and played upon, between those two extremes of her character. To delude herself into believing he saw what lay in the valley between those two defining peaks was folly. She was nothing more than a curiosity.

And if for a moment he were to suspect she felt anything more for him than amusement or annoyance or even attraction, he would be gone faster than her father disappeared when faced with a demand for his attention. Or perhaps not quite as fast and not quite so unkindly, but it would be just as bad. No, worse. Because her father no longer had the power to hurt her, and she was afraid that if she let him, Adam could have that power. Perhaps he was the only one who really could.

She pushed away from the counter. There was no point in waiting here. She should go and see if she could help Betsy with her errands and then return to Milsom's later. As she stepped out on to the High Street she almost collided with two men, who mumbled apologies and hurried past. She stepped back, realising with some surprise that there seemed to be a great deal of people heading hastily towards the town square. Before she could react, she saw Betsy herself running towards her, skirts grasped in one hand and her basket swinging precariously from the other.

'Miss! Miss! It's Lord Moresby! He's been stabbed dead! And it's Lord Delacort what done it!'

Betsy almost stumbled and Alyssa steadied her and gave her a little shake.

'What? Betsy! What nonsense is this?'

'It ain't nonsense, miss! I just come by the White Hart and Sir James has had Mr Will clear out the public room and there's Farmer Jeffries what saw

Lord Moresby and that Lord Delacort come to cuffs yesterday and now Lord Moresby is at death's door and Sir James's here to take Lord Delacort to gaol for murder! It's all true, miss!'

Alyssa left Betsy where she stood and almost ran the rest of the way to the White Hart. The yard was filled with townsfolk trying to hear what was going on inside, but she pushed through them ruthlessly and entered the public room of Mowbray's main posting inn. Out of the corner of her eye she saw Percy standing near the large bay windows, his handsome face intent. Beyond them, in the back, she glimpsed Lady Nesbit's butler alongside Percy's valet, Libbet, and members of all levels of Mowbray society. But though she registered all of this, her attention was focused on the other side of the room where Sir James and Adam stood in a clearing in the crowd, facing each other like pugilists assessing their opponent. Just at the edge of the crowd was Farmer Jeffries, his cloth hat crushed between his hands, his face pale and serious.

'I never meant... Mrs Jeffries and I didn't tell anyone we saw the argument between Lord Moresby and Lord Delacort yesterday on the lane. I surely don't know who left you that note saying I saw what I saw, Sir James, but it weren't me,' the farmer said with an apologetic nod to Adam, clearly uncomfortable.

'That's all right, Mr Jeffries,' Adam reassured him, turning to Sir James. 'We did argue...or rather Lord Moresby argued with me, but that does not mean I attacked him.'

Sir James stood stiffly, exuding both discomfort and resolution. 'I am sorry, but that will not do. There was a long-standing and well-known history of enmity between you, a report of a heated altercation on the day of the crime and the fact that you were not at the Hall but cannot account for your movements at the time Lord Moresby was stabbed in the back. I believe these are very incriminating circumstances, My Lord, and I advise you to take them seriously. I am afraid I cannot be seen to be swayed by your station. I have no choice but to ask you to accompany me to await His Majesty's pleasure until such time as his officers can take custody of you and a thorough investigation is conducted.'

'Frankly it seems to me you are being swayed by hearsay and not one bit of hard evidence, Sir James,' Adam replied scornfully.

'We got enough to hang yer!' a rough voice called out from the crowd and there was an answering round of sniggering.

Alyssa took in the expressions on the faces around her which were suffused by an avid hunger to the point where they looked almost animal. Though no one moved, they seemed to be closing in on Adam, circling him like wolves closing on a wounded stag, careful, biding their time as the stag bled out and weakened. And when they felt the moment was right they would surge forward, sink their teeth into its throat and choke out what was left of its life.

These people, who had lived for so many years on the tales of Adam's exploits, were already weaving the grand finale and could not care one whit for evidence. He might have cheated the hangman in their fictional accounts of his adventures, but he would not cheat the King's hangman if they had any say. He would go out in grand style and they would escort him festively to the gallows.

The fact that this was all occurring in the very place where ten years ago the fateful elopement had been brought to a dramatic halt was lost on no one in the room. Alyssa could hear the whispers around her, revelling in the poetic justice that had presented them with such a satisfying sequel to the decade-old scandal.

She felt such fury at the anticipation that rolled out in tangible waves from the whispering, excited crowd around her she wished she could physically expel all of them from the room, these people she had known all her life and at the moment hated more than she could remember hating anyone.

She didn't question her own conviction that Adam was innocent of the accusation. She just knew it was not true. Whatever he was capable of, she knew he could no more stab a man in the back than she could. But whether she was right or wrong, the most important consideration was that she was possibly the only person in Mowbray who had the will, and the ability, to save him. The fact that he was clearly being wrongly accused just strengthened her determination not to allow such a miscarriage of justice, even if it meant she must act against her own principles and interests.

Adam must have felt her gaze on him for he turned, his eyes dark and angry. She could tell he was well aware of the danger he was in, but he would not show weakness to this humming crowd. She had never forgotten the look of bitter hurt she had seen on his face a decade ago as everyone had turned on him. That look was not there now, just anger and determination. She knew he would not run this time, but then, he would not be given the chance. As far as those present were concerned, his fate was sealed. They did not truly know him nor did they want to. They smelled blood and would not be deflected from their prey.

But she would not let them succeed.

She held Adam's gaze and stepped forward, separating herself from the crowd.

'I think, Sir James, that you are being precipitate,' she said coolly, moving towards Adam. 'Lord Delacort, I appreciate your gallantry, but I think under the circumstances we can dispense with such gestures. Sir James, I hope you appreciate that Lord Delacort was merely trying to save me embarrassment by not disclosing his whereabouts yesterday evening. He was, in fact, with me.'

The effect of her statement was instant. A hiss of gasps shivered through the room, followed by a rush of murmurs, and the crowd seemed to shift towards them. Adam shook his head abruptly, his eyes darkening further.

'Alyssa, no.' His voice was low, but the crowd, focused avidly on the scene, caught his words and the significance of his use of her given name and tossed it around the room in a rush of nervous tittering. She ignored it, holding Adam's gaze resolutely.

'Miss Drake,' Sir James said, emphasising her name with a cautionary glance at Adam, 'are you quite certain of what you are saying? That you were with Lord Delacort yesterday at, or around, five minutes past nine in the evening, the time Lord Moresby was attacked and stabbed outside the stables of Moresby Manor? This is a most serious issue, both for your reputation and for this man's fate. So I ask you again, are you certain of what you are saying?'

Alyssa turned to him. She could not quite face Adam while taking her next step, so she kept her eyes on the Justice of the Peace.

'Quite certain, Sir James. I imagine I am not the only one who would remember quite accurately the time and place of one's betrothal.'

This master stroke had all the effect she could have wished for. Until now, the crowd had been somewhat subdued in its responses, but now the rumble became a roar. It was as if she had pulled the cork on a bottle of champagne, signalling the start of festivities. There was a roar of laughter and whistles. Someone even called out 'good for the gal!' appreciatively.

Alyssa let it all wash over her and despite the enormity of what she had done, the worst of her anxiety relaxed. She knew she had turned the pack from the scent of blood. She had provided them with an even richer feast and they would dine on this for many months to come. The fact that, for all the eccentricity of the Drakes, she was Mowbray born and bred would go far with these people.

Sir James desperately tried to regain control over the jubilant crowd and under the cover of the noise Adam grasped her arm and turned her to him, blocking out the rest of the room.

'What on earth are you doing?' he said urgently but quietly. 'Do you understand what you are saying?'

'I thought I was crystal clear,' she replied, keeping her voice low as well, amazed it was not as shaky as she felt. 'You needn't worry I will hold you to the engagement. Once you leave Mowbray, you may go back to your life and I to mine. But right now it is imperative that you are not held to blame for what happened to Lord Moresby. Because if it is true and he is dying, they will hang you. And cheer the hangman.'

Adam didn't answer, but his eyes were almost black with fury and frustration.

'Miss Drake! Lord Delacort!' Sir James had managed to reassert his authority over those present and now turned to address them. 'This is a most serious investigation into deeds most foul. Dr Hedgeway is even now battling to save Lord Moresby's life. I am afraid I must ask you to explain your actions insofar as they pertain to the matter at hand. We must all treat these proceedings with the seriousness they deserve!'

This speech quieted the last of the whispers and Adam turned back to face Sir James. Alyssa waited, so tense she could hear the rhythmic spasms of her heart. When Adam's hand closed gently on hers a wave of heat surged through her and she could feel herself begin to shake with relief. She breathed in deeply and forced herself to be calm.

'I am well aware of the seriousness of the situation,' Adam said with cool deliberation. 'Miss Drake and I did meet yesterday. And we are engaged. But this is not quite the way we wished to announce our engagement.'

In other circumstances Alyssa would have smiled in appreciation. He had managed to corroborate her statement and go along with her plan without actually lying.

The crowd now had itself well in hand, and aside from one hissing gasp, the silence held. Sir James breathed deeply, his generous side whiskers bristling alarmingly. Then he let his breath out in a rush.

'Well, if that is the case, you are, for the moment, cleared of suspicion, Lord Delacort. I have the greatest respect for Miss Drake's integrity and can only add that I congratulate you both on your impending nuptials. I share in your consternation at having to make the announcement in such circumstances, but quite frankly, had you chosen to enter into this engagement in a less clandestine fashion, we might all have been spared embarrassment and confusion. Well…that is neither here nor there. I suggest we all go about our business and mine is to uncover the perpetrator of this heinous crime. I appeal to all those present—if you have any information that might be of use, you are duty-bound to come forward.'

Adam did not wait for the room to clear, but, still holding Alyssa's hand, drew her out into the yard towards where Jem stood at the head of the two greys harnessed to his curricle. The groom, whose brow was clouded with anxiety, looked questioningly at Adam, but helped Alyssa up into the curricle before handing the reins to his master and hoisting himself up on to the perch at the back of the curricle. None of them spoke during the drive to Drake Cottage.

When they pulled up outside the gate Adam handed the reins to Jem and helped Alyssa descend.

She headed up the lane, unsure whether Adam

meant to follow and unsure whether or not she wanted him to. Her body still shivered occasionally with a spurt of fear and she needed time to calm herself before she had to face him, though she knew she was not likely to be granted this reprieve. She could hear him speaking softly to Jem and then the gravel crunched under his boots as he strode after her along with the rumble of the curricle's wheels as Jem headed back alone towards Delacort Hall.

Alyssa was grateful that no one appeared when they entered the cottage. Her father was no doubt upstairs in his study as usual and Betsy still in town, enjoying the excitement. She headed into the back parlour she had converted into a study for her own use, fully aware of Adam following closely behind. Once inside she turned to face him, bracing herself. He closed the door behind him and leaned back against it, his gaze hooded and inscrutable.

'I am still trying to understand what you did back there,' he said finally. His voice was calm and there was no discernible emotion on his face, but the tension about his mouth told a different story. He seemed very far away, as he had the time she'd gone to see him in his study. She raised her chin and went to lean her hand on her desk, reassured by its cool surface.

'Are you? I would have thought it was obvious. Or will it take another attempt on your life to wake you to what is happening?'

He didn't move away from the door.

'Are you saying they mistook Moresby for me outside his home?' he asked with just a hint of scorn. 'Since he is quite a bit more portly than I am, I hardly find that very complimentary.'

'Don't be facetious. Whoever stabbed Lord Moresby obviously knew what they were doing. They knew what had happened yesterday afternoon, they knew that Jeffries witnessed that scene between you and Moresby—Jeffries said someone left Sir James a note to that effect, didn't he? They also knew where you were yesterday evening, or rather that you would not be able to account for your whereabouts—perhaps they watched and waited until you had left on your evening walk before heading over to the Manor… And they knew what the likely outcome would be.

'They have tried to kill you at least once already, possibly twice if your friend Mr Beauvoir is right. And now they are trying to force Crown and Country to do their work for them. If I hadn't provided you with an alibi, you might even now be on your way to the local gaol in Faringdon to await His Majesty's mercy. You might have eventually succeeded in convincing the law of your innocence, but perhaps not, given your reputation and Jeffries's testimony. So now tell me if you wish to continue to act as if nothing unusual is happening or whether you are going to start taking this matter seriously! Because sham engagement or not, I give you leave to walk out of this room right now and I will not say another word.'

'That is very kind of you, no doubt,' Adam said mockingly, unimpressed by her speech. 'But since your actions this afternoon make such a course of action impossible, your generosity is a bit empty. You may have a low opinion of me, but if you think I could in conscience walk away after making that announcement at the White Hart, I underestimated your disdain. Let us be very clear about two things. The first is we are now betrothed and will have to figure out the implications of that action, and the second is that whatever fictional account you have concocted regarding recent events, even if you are correct, they have nothing whatsoever to do with you. They are in no way your concern. Is that clear?'

Alyssa raised her chin another notch. She had no intention of letting him treat her as if she was a child.

'Of course they are my concern! If you think *I* could in conscience ignore the fact that someone I know is in danger without doing a thing to prevent further tragedy, you have a very poor opinion of *me*! I wouldn't even turn my back on my worst enemy in such a situation. And whatever you may think of me, I consider you a friend.'

She was glad to note her voice was calmer than she felt. She was never sure where she stood with him, but now more than ever she felt raw and exposed. He was silent and still for so long she began to feel strangely shaky, as if she hadn't eaten in a long time. Finally she could stand the silence no longer.

'I know I am not much of an ally, Adam, but you should either leave Mowbray as soon as possible or make an effort to uncover what is really going on here. And for that you need allies. You need someone who can observe Percy and Rowena and everyone involved in this morass without being remarked. Fortunately, or unfortunately, depending on one's perspective, I am for the most part unremarkable here in Mowbray. No one is likely to be natural around you—Francis Bacon did say it was imperative in every scientific enquiry not to contaminate one's observations by unwonted influence and your presence in any situation here is one big contamination. You will never get a true, unbiased observation yourself.'

His severe expression lightened as her speech progressed. 'I have been called many things, but not yet, I believe, a contamination. And though you may be able to go about Mowbray society with ease, I don't think anyone would agree that you are unremarkable. But none of this is the point.'

'What is the point, then?'

'That on the off-chance that someone here is up to mischief, I don't want you or anyone put at risk on my account. I won't have that on my conscience.'

Alyssa shrugged.

'I am responsible for myself. Your conscience need not enter into it.'

'Don't be ridiculous. I have already caused enough damage.'

Alyssa waved her hand impatiently. 'This is all beside the point. I cannot undo what I said, even if I wished to. It would only make both our situations much worse, so I suggest we sit down and think sensibly how we are going to proceed. First, I guess we shall have to make at least some show of this engagement so that it is not too much a strain on credulity…'

Adam rubbed his hand over his jaw and to her stunned amazement she realised he was trying not to smile. Her pent-up fear and tension and confusion transformed in an instant into a surge of searing rage even greater than she had felt against the ravening crowd. All her anger was now directed towards this man who had, unknowingly, been the cause of her youthful misery. It was one thing to be disregarded at seventeen, but to be laughed at now, and after what she had just done for him, was intolerable. She felt a pang of hatred towards him, a clear, sharp need to inflict pain that both scared her and increased her rage.

'How *dare* you laugh at me?' she fumed, stamping her foot in unaccustomed fury. 'You are the stupidest, most infuriating… That is it. I am done here!' She stalked towards the door, but he moved to block her path. 'Get out of my way!' She tried to push past him, but he grasped her arms.

'Alyssa! Calm down… I'm not laughing, believe me!'

'I don't believe you and I don't want to be calm! Either you go or I do!' She tried to break free, but his grip tightened on her.

'Calm down, you little spitfire! We need to talk...'

'No, we do not!' She made another attempt to dislodge him, but to her shock he merely grabbed her by the waist, picked her up and deposited her with a thump on the desk, sending papers flying everywhere.

'Now listen to me!' he began angrily, but broke off as she grabbed at a stack of scrawled papers that were now teetering precariously at the edge of the desk. 'Forget the blasted papers... Give them to me!' he commanded as she clutched them to her.

'No! Don't tell me what to do!' She held the papers to her and tried to slide off the desk, but with an exasperated growl Adam stepped forward, blocking her descent so that she suddenly found herself pressed against him. She could feel the tense muscles of his legs against hers and the harsh thud of his heart under her hand which was splayed across his chest.

'Listen to me,' he said again. She was vaguely aware of the tension in his hands where they held her arms. Just as in the lane the day before, she felt turned inside out, so intensely aware of everything that it was impossible to think of anything else. Her body seemed larger, hotter and stinging and his body was almost an extension of her own.

He released one of her arms slowly, but instead of stepping back he touched her cheek gently, just tracing the line of her cheekbone.

'Believe me, I'm not laughing,' he said again, but his voice was muted. He breathed in and took a step back, breaking contact with her body. For a moment neither of them moved. Then he half-raised his hand, dropped it and took another, deliberate, step backwards.

'All right. Let's start again. Calmly. This whole day has been insane. I need to think.'

He turned away, pressing the heels of his hands to his eyes and she felt a surge of pain and pity drag her back to the moment. She pushed away from her desk, put the stack of papers carefully in the top drawer and went over to sit on the sofa and waited.

After a moment he drew up a chair and sat down opposite her. She raised her chin slightly, but did not speak.

'Do you want to get married?' he asked in such a matter-of-fact tone it took her a moment for the question to register. When it did she felt the heat of both shame and anger wash over her again.

'Do you think I did this to…to entrap you?' she demanded, outraged.

'No.' He laughed briefly. 'I think the idea never

crossed your mind. But the fact remains that saving my unworthy hide has put you in a very uncomfortable position. I may be a rake, as you so delight in reminding me, but I have never yet damaged a young woman's reputation and I don't plan to start now and certainly not with you. So, I will play by the rules. If the only way to get you through this unscathed is to go ahead with this engagement, I will do it.'

The silence stretched and after a moment he continued, still in the same even, practical voice.

'There are certain advantages you might want to consider. It would get you away from your dependency on your father. I never intended to stay here long anyway, which would mean you would mostly have the Hall to yourself, except when I would have to come back and see to whatever business couldn't be handled any other way. What do you think?'

She held herself rigidly, as if she could physically subdue the maelstrom of emotions his words inspired. No doubt he thought she should be grateful. She wished she was the kind of person who was capable of giving a man a resounding slap.

'I think,' she began, weighing each word, 'that we need not consider such drastic measures. In a month or so I will come up with a good reason to jilt you and frankly we probably won't have to look too far for something credible. It will be a little embarrassing for me, but everyone will likely be so occupied in feeling sorry for me and saying "I told you so" they won't even bother ostracising me. I dare say I will even be quite a popular dinner guest until they weary of the game. And since I, too, have no intention of staying in Mowbray for very long after we succeed in getting to the bottom of what is going on here, I won't worry too much about that. As for you, it will merely be another minor scandal on your list and they will probably even forgive you quite readily, because in the end you are very useful in alleviating the boredom of our little valley.'

She watched him as she spoke, but once again his face had become hard to read. When she finished he leaned back slightly.

'I see you have it all worked out. You are nothing if not thorough. What do you mean you have no intention of staying in Mowbray?'

She looked down. She felt tired and achy, as if she were becoming ill.

'I don't want to stay here any more. I suppose you have done me a favour, in a way. I don't think I can remain with Father much longer. There is a friend of Mama's in London who has always offered to have me visit. I might do that while I... explore other options.'

'I would have thought becoming Lady Delacort would solve that problem rather more simply,' he said abruptly.

'Perhaps more dramatically, but not more simply. Not for me. I am done living on sufferance in someone else's domain.'

'It would not be on sufferance—'

'Oh, would you please, please, just leave it!' she interrupted. 'Can't you just accept that I don't want to? I don't want to—' She broke off, aware of the childishness of her words, but she couldn't seem to help it. She was beginning to crack and any moment now she felt she would start crying. She breathed in and tried for a lighter tone. 'And one day you will thank me for not taking you up on your very obliging offer when you come across someone you actually wish to marry.'

He did not answer for a moment and his face remained expressionless.

'The whole point,' he said at last, 'is that I don't wish to marry. I am only willing to consider it with you because I do not wish to see you hurt by your actions on my behalf and because I don't think you expect anything from me. I have no intention of willingly walking into a relationship where I am to be held accountable to some absurd standards. I am done with that.'

'You might fall in *love*,' she threw out, as if it were something offensive.

He shook his head. 'Is that what this is about? Why you never married? Are you waiting for your prince? Well, there's nothing I can do about that, but I think it's a waste. There's a certain degree of blindness required to believe yourself in love, my dear, and I'm not convinced you have it. You would be better off giving up on that particular fantasy.'

He was smiling now, but there was also pity and contempt in his eyes and something harder, like the anger she had seen so clearly at the White Hart. As if she, too, was now ranked with the betrayers merely by believing in this emotion. She wondered what he would do if she told him she was not waiting for any prince—that *he* was the only man she had ever loved. He was hurting her so much she did not know what to do with the pain. She stood up slowly, stiffly. There was no point in talking. He stood up as well.

'If you change your mind at any point during this whole farce, you have only to let me know,' he said coolly. 'As far as I am concerned the offer is open. I would much rather you share in the Delacort spoils than all of them be preserved for the very man that is apparently trying to make away with me. My only hope of revenge is that hopefully I will live long enough so that when he does get his hands on everything he will be too old to enjoy it.'

He paused, mocking amusement obvious in his gaze. Something else was there as well, however—the glinting warmth she was sure served him so well with women. Despite the shaky cold that had filled her she felt its impact immediately. He reached out again, just touching the tips of his fingers to her cheek.

'And there are other, just as practical, benefits to being married. If you would relax that proper façade for a moment and let go of your fairy-tale fantasy, you might even enjoy life a little. I already told you I would be more than happy to oblige. This way you could have official sanction to do so.'

His fingers slid over her cheek to her temple, gently tucking a lock of hair behind her ear, and gliding lower down the side of her neck, softly easing up her chin with his knuckles so she was forced to look up at him. She knew this look of his already, half-smiling, inviting. And beyond it was the intent, banked fire that caught at her, touching something deeply hidden, threatening to drag it to the surface, shattering through defences she had spent her whole life constructing.

She had once seen Dr Hedgeway exhibit the effect of a magnetic lode on a pile of metal shavings, the way they had all turned and lined up, quivering. She felt as if her whole body was doing the same, shattered but aligned and drawn towards this man who was no more aware of what he was doing to her than the doctor's instrument.

But she knew there had been many women who had seen just that look, perhaps even been convinced of their unique ability to elicit it in him. She might be inexperienced in passion, but she was no fool when it came to the games people played with each other. She could not control her involuntary reaction, but she could control her actions.

This physical passion was almost trivial to him. A practical benefit, in his own words. She wished she could regard it the same way. That she could contemplate the thought of becoming Lady Delacort, of perhaps seeing him once or twice a year when he deigned to come and inspect the estate and supply his 'practical benefits'. And for the rest of the time she would be left to deal with the inevitable pity and whispering as the tales of his exploits and his mistresses continued to titillate the countryside.

Did he honestly think so little of her that he thought she would welcome such an offer? And the worst, the very worst, was that she desperately wanted to say yes and that was *his* fault. Because when he touched her like this, with that warmth and promise of pleasure in his beautiful stormy eyes, she was very close to being willing to pay that price.

His thumb brushed lightly just under her mouth and she breathed in involuntarily, her cheeks hot and tingling. She knew he was manipulating her, but she was losing the ability to judge his or her actions rationally. This was worse than the effects of wine. She *knew* there was a lie here, but she couldn't seem to care about it any more. Not enough to stop him when he bent to touch his mouth to hers, feather-light, gentle. She felt everything, the warmth of his breath on her sensitised lips, the coolness of his palm against her heated cheek, the way his other hand curved over her hip, to the small of her back, as he stepped closer, pulling her against the hard surface of his body.

'Alyssa…' he breathed against her mouth, before capturing her lips again and a scorching, urgent heat welled up through her, erasing parts of her as it went, destroying her control and her boundaries. With each caress of his hands as they moved over her body, with the coaxing slide of his mouth over hers, she was falling away, shedding herself like an unnecessary shell, and what was left was utterly with him. What was left was wrapping her arms around his neck, her fingers sliding into his hair, calling out his name on a whispered, agonised breath as he kissed the side of her neck and sent her nerves into a furious dance. It was almost so unbearable that if he had asked at that moment if she would do what he asked she would have said yes, wholeheartedly, without a thought to the consequences or whether it really reflected her will.

She was so far gone that even when she heard the vigorous striking of the knocker she tried, as in a dream, to include it in the moment, under the harsh beating of her heart. But the second time the knocking grew louder and longer and it woke her with a start and a rush of shame and anguish. She pushed away from him.

'I should go… I need to open the door. Betsy is probably still in town.'

He kept his arm around her, his eyes dark and intent.

'Leave it. Or let your father answer.'

She laughed at the absurdity of that suggestion. The knocker sounded again, more aggressively, and she pushed away resolutely. Adam cursed, shoving his hands through his hair.

'Get rid of them,' he said harshly.

She shook her head, not sure whether the interruption was a blessing or a curse. She walked out of the room and went to open the front door. She had no idea who to expect, but it had certainly not been Mr Beauvoir.

'Is Adam...Lord Delacort here?' he asked abruptly, taking off his hat, and Alyssa nodded, standing back to let him enter.

'Has something happened?' she asked quickly, her mind stumbling ahead towards possible disasters.

'That's what I want to find out. I just returned from Berkshire. Jem was going on about the Delacort Curse and told me the most outrageous...' He glanced up as Adam stepped out of the study. 'What the devil have you got yourself into now, man? Can't I leave for two days without you getting yourself accused of murder?'

Adam raised one eyebrow. He looked annoyed, but not at all like a man who had been interrupted mid-seduction, and Alyssa felt herself wake up a little further.

'Do you mind if we don't continue this conversation in the hallway, Nick?' he asked.

Mr Beauvoir barely waited for Adam to close the study door behind them before he began.

'Very well. Now, what's going on?'

Alyssa sat silently as Adam told his friend briefly about the attack on Lord Moresby and the accusations against him.

'Jem said you have an alibi for the time of the attack, is that correct?'

Adam glanced at Alyssa and some of the familiar cynicism shimmered in his grey eyes.

'In a way. Miss Drake kindly came to my rescue. Apparently I was busy becoming engaged at the time Lord Moresby was stabbed. A very effective bone thrown to the ravening crowds baying for my blood. At one moment they were ready to string me up, the next they were drinking to my good health. I think the good people of Mowbray appreciated the poetic justice in it.'

Mr Beauvoir looked quickly at Alyssa and then back at Adam.

'This is serious, Adam,' he said, more quietly than before.

'I'm well aware of that, Nick. But I suggest we take this conversation back to the Hall. For the moment, you should offer us your congratulations.'

Mr Beauvoir blinked.

'Of course. I mean, congratulations! This is marvellous news.'

'Thank you. Now, if you don't mind, Miss Drake, I will see Mr Beauvoir back to the Hall. You and I will continue our...discussion later,' Adam said, standing up.

Alyssa was wide awake now. And her earlier weakness only made her more determined. She would not be manipulated, or seduced, or intimidated, into doing what she felt was wrong or not doing what she felt was right. Adam would have to learn to know her better.

'But I do mind, Lord Delacort. We are not quite done here. Please sit down, and you, too, Mr Beauvoir.'

Adam remained standing, but Mr Beauvoir sat down promptly.

'With pleasure. And call me Nicholas. After all, you are engaged to my oldest friend.'

She couldn't help smiling. Somehow his light-hearted approach relieved some of the awful tension of the situation.

'I am sure you have understood this is a sham engagement, Mr Beau... Nicholas. But from your past comments I understand you are well aware that the events of the past two days are only part of something more serious that is unfolding. And escalating. At first I thought this had to do with some personal enmity towards Lord Delacort, perhaps someone from his rather chequered past, but I am afraid it may be more serious.'

Adam once again raised one eyebrow.

'More serious than someone trying to kill me or implicate me in a murder? I thank you. And if you are going to call Nick Nicholas, you might as well call me Adam. You were doing so freely enough earlier.'

She flushed, but ignored his taunt, knowing full well he was trying to distract her from the issue.

'The point is, *Nicholas*,' she continued resolutely, 'that the recent whispering about the Delacort Curse is not based on idle superstition. Or at least not only that. It began after Ivor died and frankly there were those at the time who had been more than willing to suggest that you had had a hand in both Timothy's and Ivor's deaths, *Adam*.'

Adam leaned back against the mantelpiece and crossed his arms.

'No wonder they want to get rid of me. I am not just omnipotent but also prolific. And what convinced them that I was not in fact involved?'

'The report that you were in Venice and having a very good and very public time with a certain Contessa,' she said drily.

Adam's mouth tightened and he flushed slightly, but Nicholas chuckled.

'You should send Seraphina a thank-you note, Adam. She was always convinced the universe revolved around her and she would love to hear of supporting evidence.'

'Quiet, Nick. So, what happened once I was removed from the list of suspects?'

'Nothing. Dr Hedgeway insisted on an inquest, but he had no hard evidence of foul play and so a verdict was turned in of accidental death. And that was that.'

'I don't understand. I had thought it was quite clear that Ivor broke his neck trying to jump his hunter over a fence. Why would Hedgeway ask for an inquest?'

'Because Ivor broke his leg as well. And he had a bump on his head.'

'So? Getting thrown from a horse, as I can attest, is painful. Why wouldn't there be more than one injury in a throw bad enough to lead to a broken neck?'

'That was precisely the view of the coroner and that's why he gave his verdict of accidental death. However, thanks to Mowbray's spa status it manages to attract quite a few wealthy patients and therefore a very capable doctor. Dr Hedgeway is a cut above the usual country doctors. He pointed out that a man who is thrown from his horse in a field and lands squarely enough on his leg to break it in that particular manner is unlikely to have also landed squarely enough on his head to have broken his neck. And the blow to Ivor's head was such that he thought it had been caused by an object of which there was no evidence at the scene. Unfortunately Dr Hedgeway then introduced his concerns regarding Timothy's death and the coroner accused him of paranoia and closed the meeting.'

'How on earth do you know all this detail?' Adam asked, his eyes narrowed in suspicion.

Alyssa flushed slightly.

'I was there.'

'At the inquest?' Nicholas asked in surprise and she shrugged.

'Yes. I wanted to see how an inquest was conducted. But what I—'

'Why…?'

'I had my reasons. The point is—'

'And they didn't mind having a woman there?'

She couldn't help it; she smiled.

'Of course they did. I didn't go as a woman,' she said simply and waited, quite content with the shocked looks they directed at her. Amidst all the chaos and confusion, she had derived significant pleasure from having so grandly shocked all of Mowbray earlier that day and she could not resist the temptation to shock again. There was something very rewarding about confounding expectations.

Adam rubbed his jaw, but the annoyance had faded from his eyes and there was only lightness there now.

'Do you often still don breeches?' he asked politely.

'Quite rarely nowadays. Only when absolutely necessary.'

Nicholas burst out laughing.

'I'm afraid to ask under what circumstances. And they really didn't recognise you? With your amazing eyes?'

She flushed, flattered despite herself.

'People see what they expect to see. Which is a country boy in a farmer's cap.'

'*I'd* like to see that,' Nicholas said appreciatively and Adam pushed away from the mantelpiece.

'Well, you aren't going to. And this is all beside the point. What did you say about Hedgeway's suspicions about Timothy's death? He died of inflammation of the lungs, didn't he? How on earth could that be misconstrued?'

'Well, he might not have suspected much if it

hadn't been for Ivor. It is true that Timothy fell ill that winter. He wasn't the only one. The influenza had spread through town and quite a few were ill at the Hall—Percy and Ivor and quite a few of the servants as well, and the few that remained had to take care of everyone else, since no one was willing to stay at the Hall unless they absolutely had to. You know how draughty and damp it is and that was a terrible winter, with the lanes impassable and everything frozen over. But Dr Hedgeway did say he had been certain Timothy was mending when suddenly one morning he was dead.'

Adam shrugged.

'So? It happens.'

'So it does. Which is why there was no inquest. But I know it always bothered Dr Hedgeway. He blamed himself for not bringing in proper nursing care. He also mentioned that he had noted, aside from redness of the eyes and a bluish tinge to the lips, that there was an unusual pallor about the mouth.'

'Meaning?'

Her shoulders slumped.

'I don't know. He merely said it was unusual and worth noting, since these were not symptoms he was familiar with in cases of inflammation of the lungs. But when the coroner asked him why he had not then raised these issues at the time of Timothy's death, he said they had not struck him sufficiently to make him enquire further and that it was only now in light of his concerns about Ivor's death that he was mentioning them.'

'I am sure the coroner was delighted at this point,' Adam said sardonically.

She smiled ruefully.

'He was a bit annoyed and poor Dr Hedgeway didn't insist when he wrapped up the inquest. And that was it.'

Nicholas leaned back and rubbed his face.

'Hell, Adam. What a mess.'

Adam didn't answer. His gaze was fixed on Alyssa, but seemed to be looking beyond her, and both she and Nicholas fell silent, as if on command. After a moment he breathed in, focusing back on her, and his eyes narrowed.

'This has nothing to do with you. You are not to get involved in this,' he stated and she straightened, incredulous.

'You cannot be serious! Have we been on separate continents today? Of course I am involved.'

'I am very grateful for what you did this afternoon, Alyssa, and we will sit down and discuss how to proceed with this engagement. But while I appreciate you sharing what you know about

Timothy and Ivor, you don't have to concern yourself any further with these suspicions. I will take care of it.'

'Will you, now? Do you know you have a very pompous streak? You sounded just like your mother,' she observed and watched with satisfaction as his proud stance was swamped by outrage. She had hit a sore point and had meant to. She had no intention of being managed.

Nick burst out laughing.

'You're a brave woman, Miss Drake. Remind me not to cross you.'

'All right, Nick. Go and wait for me outside. Miss Drake and I have some matters to discuss.'

Nick stood up promptly, winked at Alyssa and left the study. Alyssa raised her chin, waiting for Adam to resume either his commands or his persuasion, resolving this time at least to resist both, but he just turned to her and to her surprise she saw his anger had once again been replaced by amusement.

'Do you remember the time you lectured me about Rowena's intentions? You were halfway up the Hungry Tree at the time. In breeches then as well.'

She frowned, confused. She vaguely remembered something of the kind.

'I think so,' she assented suspiciously, wondering where this was going.

'I remember thinking that besides being presumptuous you were one of the most determined people I knew. Not like my mother, who was just selfishly bullheaded, or Rowena, who was the same—though I wasn't smart enough at the time to see that. You had a vision of the future, or at least of your siblings' future, and you had every intention of getting them there. I am not in the least surprised that they all turned out well. The point is, I understand how important it is to you to fit in here in Mowbray even if I don't share your outlook and I will do whatever possible to make sure what you did for me does not harm you. But you are going to have to curb that determination to manage this situation as you are used to managing everything that you believe concerns you. Because it doesn't. This is my problem and I will deal with it. Do you understand me?'

'I understand you very well, Adam.'

'You have no intention of doing as I asked, do you?' he asked suspiciously.

'Did you ask? I heard a command, not a request.'

'Would it make a difference if I asked?'

'It would be nicer and certainly less condescending. But, no, it would make no real difference.'

He threw up his hands. 'Unbelievable!'

She stood up.

'Why? And if our situations were reversed? Would you be content to do what you ask of me? I don't presume that simply because you're a rake you are also unconcerned with the welfare of others. If so, you would be a very different landlord to the one you have obviously become. So don't presume that simply because I am a woman and a wallflower, as you so quaintly phrased it, I will walk away when someone I know is in danger.'

'I did not call you a wallflower,' he protested.

'Yes, you did. And I suppose it is true in a way. But don't let that deceive you into thinking I am meek.'

He rubbed his forehead, half-laughing.

'Didn't I just say I thought you were one of the most determined people I know? The very last thing I think you are is meek. But I won't have you in danger because of me. It's as simple as that.'

'You're involving Nicholas.'

'Yes, well, Nick is used to putting up with my nonsense and I with his.'

She didn't respond. There was no point. He wasn't going to listen to her anyway. He might take the time to argue with her, but in the end he was as unbending as more overtly selfish people like her father or Rowena. He was merely smoother than both of them. But if he didn't get his way by charm and manipulation, he would become just like all the others.

She didn't know why she was even insisting. *Yes, you do know*, a voice inside answered her back and she looked away.

He moved towards her and turned her face back to him very gently. His hand was warm against her skin and the touch dragged up the sensations he had set loose before Nicholas's interruption. His thumb traced the line of her cheekbone and just brushed over the lobe of her ear, sending a tingling cascade through her body.

But she was too angry at her failure and foolishness to let him win her over so easily a second time. She forced herself to think of all the tales she had heard of his women. Of the Venetian Contessa. Seraphina! What a pretentious name! What on earth was she thinking, believing she could mean anything to someone like him?

She swatted his hand away and took a step back.

'You don't decide for me, Adam. The answer is no.'

She knew he was well aware that her refusal was referring to their earlier discussion about their engagement. His hand dropped and fisted. He took a step back as well and bowed ironically.

'Very well. For the moment we will call this a draw. I will return tomorrow so we can discuss how we are going to proceed with this engagement. Good day, Miss Drake.'

She didn't bother answering and he turned and left. She waited until she heard the squawk of the garden gate before she went and lay down on her comfortable old sofa. Everything was silent.

Overshadowing everything was the fact that someone was probably trying to kill Adam. She could not let that happen. And underneath that sharp realisation was a maelstrom of emotion she couldn't untangle.

She was engaged to Adam. Publicly. He had kissed her and it had been amazing and for a while she had allowed herself to sink deep into that part of her that wanted freedom and life and passion at any cost. But there was more to her than what he called 'the wild girl'. He certainly did not *really* wish to marry her. All he wanted was to banish this shadow hanging over him so he could get back to his freedom and his pleasure-seeking...

And what did she want? Now that he was gone there was finally enough room in her little study to face herself. And the truth.

In the public room his hand had closed over hers, warm and firm, and it had felt so very right. Somehow with him she felt so much more herself. Even at seventeen she had known it. He had entered their little garden without preconception or judgement. He had offered to help her teach Terry Greek and Latin out of real interest in her clever younger brother and not out of the patronising notions of charity they were so familiar with. And after he had seen Percy taunting Charlie, holding his favourite, ragged ball well over the little boy's head, the next day Percy had sported a black eye and had never bothered them again.

It would have been marvellous, she tried to tell herself, if she had not imagined herself a little in love with him. Except that she was now no longer seventeen, and she certainly didn't think him perfect, except, of course, for her. Because there was still that same unjudging acceptance about him. As much as he might disapprove of her actions she never felt he disapproved of her. Worse, she felt he actually liked the very qualities that she had learned early on to mask around other people. No wonder she felt more daring with him. It was like slipping loose the knots of an over-laced corset. She felt she could breathe freely and she had almost forgotten what that felt like.

And if she had even an ounce of Rowena's good sense, she told herself, she would take advantage of the situation and marry him and somehow force him to mind her.

But she was not Rowena and when the moment came when he departed on his next voyage, leaving her to keep an eye on the Hall, what would she do? Demand he stay? Demand he take her with him? He might even indulge her once or twice, because though he was a rake, he was not unkind. She supposed he would indulge her, a kind of gift of pleasure as part of his efforts to educate her in the art of enjoying herself. But there would be a vast gulf between that and what she really wanted from him.

And how long would it be before either her bitterness or her despair would show? Before those emotions would drive him and keep him away, each time longer and longer, until most of what she would have of him would be occasional reports of his amours with this countess or that actress whispered maliciously behind her back by the likes of the Mott sisters. And the worst, the very worst thing, was that at the moment she thought she might even be willing to sign such a Faustian contract and place her stake on part of his existence rather than lose him entirely.

She pulled the red blanket over her, pressed her fists to her eyes and cried for the first time in many years.

Chapter Ten

Adam stopped outside the cottage door. Nicholas was lounging against the garden wall, polishing an apple, and he glanced over as Adam approached, but didn't speak, just fell into step with him. Adam was grateful for the silence. At the moment he didn't want to talk with anyone. About anything. He felt that if he opened his mouth, he would say something he would very much regret about that impossible…

He forced down the confusion and frustration that threatened to take over as he thought of what had happened at the cottage. He was more furious with himself than at her. Someone was trying to kill him and he was more concerned with her rejection and unwillingness to back down.

He had to focus on what had happened earlier and what he was going to do about it. It seemed fantastical, unreal, but he could not afford to indulge in the futile hope that the accidents and the attack on Moresby were just an outrageous coincidence.

He knew it had been pure chance the whole scene had taken place at the White Hart again. But standing there, surrounded by some of the same people who had been present for his very public shaming ten years earlier, it had been hard not to feel the bite of betrayal once again. But this time whatever pain he felt at the ease with which these people were willing to condemn him had been swiftly trampled, first by fury, and then by the need to focus on action, just like all the other times he had found himself facing danger these past years. The last thing he had expected had been her intervention.

The moment she'd stepped forward everything had shifted. Like a drop of dye into water, her intrusion had spread through the scene and changed it irrevocably. He did not even understand how it had all happened. One minute he had been trying to figure out how to avoid a charge of murder and then suddenly it was as if they were all watching another show, like a seamless transition from tragedy to farce.

And the crowd had followed her. It amazed him that none of the people there, not even Sir James, who should know better, had really doubted her. She had stepped forward and spoken and they had backed down like children before a strict nanny. Even he had fallen into line and followed her lead.

He realised with some surprise that she had lied easily and without apparent compunction, something which did not seem to accord with her rigid sense of integrity. In doing so she had risked everything she had in this little community. And he hadn't even had the decency to thank her. Not really. What was wrong with him?

Worse, he had repaid her with mistrust and accusations. What was so wrong about having someone come to his aid, expecting nothing in return? He knew, fundamentally, that what she had said was true. She would have done the same for Percy, if the need had arisen, as much as she disliked the rat. Which was ironic, since it seemed it was probably Percy who was responsible for this whole mess.

Nicholas held out a whole five minutes before he spoke.

'So, what's the plan?'

'I find out who doesn't like me. And stop him.'

'Ah, simple. And the engagement?'

'That is my concern.'

'So it is indeed. You know, for a man who swore he would never fall into a parson's mousetrap, you don't seem to be too concerned she might be entrapping you,' Nicholas said curiously.

Adam smiled cynically.

'Hardly. She doesn't want to go through with this engagement any more than I do. She's a crusader on a mission, that's all. Now that her silly cousin has left the field, she needs another *cause célèbre*, but as soon as the danger is over she will be the first to cut the cord. She might well have done the same for Percy if he had been in my shoes. You saw what she is like.'

'So I did. The girl's a general *manqué*. I can't get that image out of my head—infiltrating the inquest in breeches. Good lord.'

Adam frowned.

'Don't dwell on it too much.'

Nicholas tossed the apple up in the air and caught it.

'I'll try not to. It's almost a pity she doesn't want to become Lady Delacort. She would lead you a very merry dance, old friend. But since she does not appear to have fallen victim to your fatal charm, I will have to forgo the pleasure of watching her bring you to heel.'

Adam shrugged. He did not particularly want to continue the conversation. He was still too raw from everything that had happened that morning.

Blast, it was almost afternoon already. In just a few hours everything had changed.

Right now the only thing that mattered was finding out if it was Percy or someone else who had tried to kill him, frame him, and was possibly responsible for the death of his cousins. He also needed to make sure Alyssa was not harmed by coming to his aid. He half-smiled at himself. It was a sign of the absurdity of the situation that right now that last point seemed to take precedence.

Whatever the case, he did not like being in anyone's debt, though it was somehow not quite so bad being in hers. Like Nicholas, he did not feel she was angling for any return on her action. It would almost be easier if she was. He could repay her and move on. But she was acting solely out of friendship and that almost aggravating sense of duty she had.

She had been very clear she wanted nothing to do with his offer. It was not as if he wanted to get married either. Actively inviting dependence and responsibilities which he was bound to only fail at, when he had been so opportunely freed from them, was to fly in the face of providence.

Still, if he could not in honour get out of this engagement without damaging her reputation, despite her rather sanguine belief in her ability to do so, he could think of worse fates than having to marry her. Because the fact was that beyond the desire she aroused with such aggravating ease, he respected her.

The problem was that she had a seriously obstinate streak, and if she decided not to do something, she probably wouldn't listen to reason. The same wild, tormenting girl that surfaced so tantalisingly at the promise of physical passion was inextricably tied to the proper girl waiting foolishly to love her prince. She would not marry for convenience, no matter how many problems such an alliance would solve for her.

For a moment he contemplated trying to make her fall in love with him. With women in the past the first signs of any real emotion towards him had always been his cue to move on. There was no pleasure in remaining in an emotionally unequal relationship, only a sense of oppression and sometimes guilt. But with her... But then again he was not at all certain he could achieve it. She knew him too well, in a way.

Once again Nicholas broke through his thoughts and Adam was almost grateful for the interruption.

'I wonder what she was really up to at the inquest,' Nicholas mused. 'That was over a year ago and she remembered it down to the tiny details. There's something strange there.'

'Nothing she does surprises me at this point. But I meant what I told her, Nick. I don't want her involved in this. Something is very wrong here. It will be hard enough to unwind this engagement without causing her too much damage. The last thing I want is to put her at any real risk.'

'And you think she'll sit back idly and wait for us to resolve this? I suspect she is much more likely to go off ferreting out information on her own account. It might be safer if we keep her inside the circle rather than exclude her.'

'I hate it when you make sense,' Adam said morosely after a moment of silence.

'You make it sound like such a rare occurrence. Well?'

'Fine. I'll talk to her tomorrow. You're right— on her own she's a loose cannon and the last thing I want is for her to get into any more trouble because of me.'

'Well, I don't see how you are going to avoid that once you terminate the engagement. Just out of curiosity—just how *will* you terminate the engagement?'

They had reached the drive leading to the stables and Adam stopped.

'She'll think of something. Or she might get lucky and whoever is after me will succeed in getting rid of me and she won't have to do a damn thing. Come, I want to talk to Jem. We need some eyes on the ground here and frankly he's the only one I trust.'

'Ah, good. Swell our ranks a little.'

'A motley crew. Two rakes, a groom and a crusader.'

'A very pretty and clever crusader. I put my money on her.'

Adam forced himself to keep walking. He knew Nicholas was toying with him on purpose. If he thought for a moment that his friend was really attracted to Alyssa or had any intention of exploring a flirtation with her...

'A very off-limits crusader, Nick,' he said curtly and his companion merely smiled and shrugged. Adam pushed down on an unfamiliar urge to make his point more vividly to his mischievous friend. He shoved open the door to the stables and the activity in the large building froze for a moment before everyone bent back to their various occupations, but this time there was almost absolute silence. Only Jem seemed unfazed by the intrusion.

'Good afternoon, My Lord. Mr Beauvoir.' He nodded.

'Jem, I need your advice on something.'

'Certainly, My Lord. Follow me. Jacob, fetch us some ale from the kitchen and some tankards, please.'

A young man with a striking resemblance to Jem nodded and headed off as Adam and Nicholas followed Jem through the back of the stable, out towards the small building attached to it.

'Was that your son?' Nicholas asked and Jem nodded.

'My eldest. A good steady lad. This way. I gather you would like to talk privately, My Lord, and not up at the Hall. I would think my kitchen would be nice and warm and we won't be disturbed. If you have no objection, of course.'

Adam assented and Jem led them to a kitchen where a great wooden table had pride of place at its centre. The groom motioned them to sit, not in the least perturbed by their presence in his home. Jacob appeared promptly with a jug and three tankards and after pouring out a measure of ale to each he nodded and left.

'Well, My Lord, it looks like you're fixed in Mowbray for a while yet at least,' Jem said laconically as they each took a tankard and Adam looked at him with amusement and understanding. He knew the servants were understandably worried about what would happen to the estate once he left and he knew the only way to allay their fears would be through the test of time.

'You make it sound like a good thing, Jem. This is a hell of a way to get me to stay.'

'We shall just have to make the most of it, My Lord. There's always more to be done around here. And there will be a great deal of to-do about the betrothal.'

Nicholas directed a look at Adam and then back to Jem.

'What's the word in the kitchens, Jem?' he asked comfortably and the groom raised his bushy brows at him.

'I am not one to indulge in kitchen gossip, Mr Beauvoir. However, the under-grooms are well provided with all the news. Naturally there is a great deal of excitement at the prospect of Miss Drake becoming Lady Delacort. She is a great favourite in these parts. For all she's of Lady Nesbit's stock, she is true Mowbray and always ready to show kindness or interest wherever there's a need. You couldn't have chosen better, My Lord.'

'Well, then,' Nicholas said comfortably and leaned forward to raise the jug in Adam's direction. 'More, Adam?'

'No, *thank you*, Nicholas,' Adam replied with

emphasis, without any real hope it would do any good. When Nicholas had the devil in him, he was unstoppable. He turned to Jem.

'Thank you, Jem, but for the moment the most important thing is that Miss Drake has offered to help try to unravel this mystery. If you are willing, I would like to ask for your help as well. Before you reply I want you to understand that if you feel this is not something you can become involved in, it will make no difference at all to your position here. I give you my word on that. Perhaps you should take some time to consider before you commit yourself.'

'Well, that's much appreciated, My Lord, but there isn't much to be considered. I've told you before it's in my interest to keep you alive and well. Now, what's to be done?'

'Can you discreetly make enquiries about Percy's activities yesterday evening?'

Jem did not bat an eyelid; he merely nodded.

'I'll look into it, My Lord. Most nights when there's no society do he's to be found at the Duck and Dragon over on the Oxford Road. You wouldn't think so to look at him, but he's one for the cockfights. It might be advisable to have someone keep an eye on him, discreet like, for the moment. If you like, I'll have Jacob do so. He's solid and won't ask questions.'

Adam breathed in. He didn't like the idea of widening the circle, but he had to admit he wanted Percy under steady observation and it would be better to have someone local do it than to bring in a stranger.

'I don't want your son put at risk.'

'Jacob can mind himself, don't you worry. Is there anything else?'

Adam hesitated.

'Yes. You were here when Timothy and Ivor died. I want to learn more about what happened to them.'

For the first time Jem's eyes lost their stoic focus and he frowned.

'Is that how it is, My Lord?'

'I don't know, Jem. Miss Drake told us of Dr Hedgeway's concerns at the time. Or perhaps they were just the imaginings of a medical man?'

Jem leaned his head slowly from side to side, rather like a curious rooster.

'I can't rightly say, sir. It was no surprise that Master Ivor got himself tossed. He always threw his heart over a hedge first, his mind following a bit more slowly, if you get my gist. And that horse was a brute. But I know bones and I know spills and it was in my mind at the time that the good doctor had a point about the leg and the neck and the crack on the skull. If he had been tossed down a gully, well then, but it was open field by that hedge. Still, I've seen all kind and can't tell.

'As for Master Timothy…well, I can't help much there. It was a bad winter and there were more sick than well. I was laid up myself or I might have been up serving in the hall. The ones what were well took care of the ill with no distinction of rank or position, let me tell you. Bodley—he was Ivor's man—and Libbet were the only upper men not afflicted and they had the care of Masters Timothy and Ivor and Percy, who were all ill, from bringing food to clearing chamber pots. There was no standing on dignity that winter. But who's to say that even being ill would have stopped a man's mission?'

Adam nodded. It was still hard to believe his dandyish cousin had managed to cleverly eliminate his two cousins without raising suspicion and was now hanging around the woods and the estate, stringing up ropes, weakening scaffolding and, most audacious of all, trying to implicate Adam in an attack on Lord Moresby. The lack of method and difference between the attacks indicated someone who waited and looked for opportunities. A quiet, patient determination and willingness to get one's hands dirty, qualities he would never have associated with Percy.

Still, it was possible. Percy was the only one who would reap any real benefit from his death. He could easily have made a move against Timothy in those circumstances, and since he was living at the hall at the time of Ivor's accident, he might have come across him after his fall and added to his injuries. Perhaps Adam had completely underestimated his fashionable cousin. There would be no way of finding out what had happened in the past. The only way to go forward was to try to find out what Percy was up to now.

'Thank you, Jem. Let me know what you and Jacob find out, but please be very careful. Gather what you can and we will decide tomorrow how to go forward.'

Chapter Eleven

'It's Lady Nesbit, miss,' Betsy announced, her voice an octave higher than usual and her eyes expressing a mix of terror and glee. Alyssa dropped her pen. She had heard the gate and had frozen in anticipation and nervousness. She knew Adam would come as promised, but it was still rather early for a morning call. But Lady Nesbit… The last time she had come to Drake Cottage was a very brief visit after Alyssa's mother had died. She frowned, wondering if she had perhaps misheard.

'Lady Nesbit?'

'In the parlour, miss.' Betsy nodded and giggled, clearly enjoying all the excitement.

Alyssa carefully stacked her handwritten sheets of paper. It was not as if she was getting anything done anyway. She didn't know why she was even bothering with the pretence of work, except that she was afraid of where her mind would go if she didn't keep it busy. She stood up and followed Betsy to the parlour, very much on edge. But when she entered the room, some of her wariness was replaced by concern. Lady Nesbit was seated in the best armchair, her hands resting on her cane, and she looked haggard.

'I hear congratulations are in order?' she barked out as Alyssa entered, her voice in sharp contrast to her looks, and Alyssa breathed deeply. She knew that Lady Nesbit's reaction to the engagement would set the tone for the entire neighbourhood. Everyone would be waiting for her verdict and Alyssa braced herself for what was to come. Her elderly cousin would undoubtedly demand her pound of flesh.

'Thank you, Cousin Harriet, you are very kind.' She sat down on a chair opposite Lady Nesbit and waited for the next stage of the attack.

'Rowena won't eat,' Lady Nesbit said flatly and Alyssa blinked.

'I beg your pardon?'

'She won't eat. Dr Hedgeway says she must. But she won't. She just sits next to Moresby's bed and stares at the wall. Even though the doctor says he is hopeful the man is going to recover. I told her it wasn't seemly.'

It took Alyssa a moment to reorient herself.

'I am so sorry,' she said hesitantly after a moment. 'Is there anything I can do?'

'I want you to speak with her!' Lady Nesbit banged her cane hard on the floor and the sound echoed off the walls of the parlour.

'Me? I hardly think Rowena wishes to speak with me, Cousin Harriet.'

Lady Nesbit's eyes fixed on Alyssa shrewdly.

'You do not know her as well as you think, Alyssa. She might make game of you, but that is because she has never succeeded in managing you. And that is why she trusts you. She may listen to you. I am asking you. Please. She is making herself ill.'

The old woman's voice wavered on these last words and her eyes fell. Without thinking, Alyssa dragged her chair next to the armchair and picked up one of the papery hands clenched about the head of the cane. They sat in silence for a moment.

'I will go with you now, if you like?'

Lady Nesbit nodded briefly and pushed herself to her feet, leaning heavily on her cane.

They did not speak on the short drive to Moresby Manor and, aside from ascertaining that Rowena was still in Lord Moresby's room, Lady Nesbit did not say a word as Alyssa left her at the foot of the stairs and headed up towards the bedchambers in the east wing.

Lord Moresby's valet was seated in a chair outside the room and stood up as Alyssa ascended the stairs.

'I am here to see Lady Moresby,' she explained and the valet nodded with something like relief.

'Of course, Miss Drake, she is inside. If you please?'

He opened the door and she entered. It was like walking into a painting. The room was quite bright; the curtains had been drawn back and sunlight was pouring in, creating stark contrasts of light and shadows. Lord Moresby was lying on his back, his tall frame diminished and pale. He looked more like an effigy than a live person, nothing like the stocky, ruddy-faced man she was used to. Rowena was seated upright on the other side of the bed, as white as her dress aside from her vivid blue eyes, which stared vacantly ahead of her. She did not acknowledge Alyssa's entrance.

Alyssa drew up a chair beside her and picked up one unresisting hand. It was very cold and dry and Alyssa rubbed it absently, trying to think of what to say. Rowena continued to stare ahead, but after a moment her hand twitched in Alyssa's and an almost furtive look entered her eyes.

'I think he is dead,' she whispered.

'No, Rowena. Dr Hedgeway says he has a good chance of recovering.'

'No. They are saying that to make me leave the room. But I won't. I won't let them take him.'

Alyssa continued rubbing the delicate, frozen hand between hers. She felt rough and unworthy suddenly. She had never credited Rowena with any real feelings. Lady Nesbit was right. Alyssa did not really know her older cousin. She had allowed her own jealousy and insecurity to colour her view of this woman. She might be selfish and pampered and often cruel, but there were other sides to her as well.

'He loves you very much, Rowena,' she said softly and for the first time Rowena looked at her, with an almost childlike entreaty.

'Does he? Does he really? I think he hates me now. He used to love me. More than anyone ever did. But I made him hate me. Even if he lives, he might leave me, and I could not bear it. I could not bear it.'

Alyssa stared in shock as Rowena suddenly cast herself on to the floor by the bed, grabbing one of Lord Moresby's immobile hands and covering her face with it as she sobbed. After a moment Alyssa drew her chair over and sat gently stroking her cousin's hair as she cried. Both women started violently when a frail voice spoke.

'Ro?'

Rowena's hands closed convulsively around Lord Moresby's hand.

'Arthur? Arthur!' She dragged herself shakily to her feet, leaning over to touch his face almost fearfully. 'Oh, please...'

His eyes opened and closed a few times before fixing on her.

'My lovely Ro,' he said hoarsely, trying to smile, and Rowena crumpled. She curled up on the bed beside him, sobbing and stroking his hand.

Alyssa left the room quietly and closed the door. The valet stood in the hallway, clearly unsure what to do.

'His Lordship is awake, but I think you should give them a few minutes before you enter. Perhaps you could send for the doctor meanwhile? He might want to know Lord Moresby has recovered consciousness.'

The valet nodded and hurried off and Alyssa went downstairs to the morning room, where Lady Nesbit sat, still ramrod stiff, staring out at the wide, well-tended lawn. She was once again in possession of herself and she sent Alyssa an arctic glare.

'You weren't up there very long. Given up already?'

In the past Alyssa might have been hurt by Lady Nesbit's derisive tones, but today she merely walked over and sat by her.

'I think she will be all right. Lord Moresby is awake and she is crying.'

'Crying!'

'Yes, sobbing, actually. I think she really cares for him. I never realised she could. You are right that I don't understand her very well. I never knew this side of her.'

Lady Nesbit raised one shaky hand to her eyes and nodded.

'I tried to do right by her when Verena died. She was very young and I think… I made mistakes. But I do want her to be happy.'

The pale milky-blue eyes met Alyssa's with the same kind of childish entreaty as had been in Rowena's. Alyssa smiled and gave the bony hand a comforting squeeze.

'She might have a chance now. I hope she does.'

Lady Nesbit nodded and cleared her throat.

'Well. Good. I will have someone see you home in the gig.'

Alyssa subdued a smile at this brusque dismissal. Probably both Lady Nesbit and Rowena would make her pay for having seen them in their weakness, but she didn't mind. If Lord Moresby was recovering, then one immediate threat to Adam was removed. Still, even without the possibility of being charged with murder, he was still in danger. She needed to think and she thought best while she walked.

'Don't worry, Cousin Harriet, I prefer to walk.'

'As you wish. And bring your young man to Nesbit House with you. I will be busy today, but tomorrow afternoon will do. For tea. I want to speak with you. Both of you.'

It took Alyssa a moment to realise Lady Nesbit was referring to Adam. A gurgle of laughter bubbled up in her, but she kept her lips prim and nodded.

'Of course, Cousin Harriet. Tomorrow afternoon.'

Lady Nesbit nodded once more and returned her attention to the window. Alyssa showed herself out and headed back towards Drake Cottage. Her mind kept going back again and again to the scene in Lord Moresby's bedroom and Rowena's haunted, almost unfamiliar face. For the first time she had not looked merely beautiful but human, tragic, alive. The more she thought about the fear and the need in her cousin's pale face, the more confused she felt. It was like a magic trick and she felt dense and rather stupid that she was unable to grasp where this revelation had come from. How had she never seen any signs of this humanity and love in either Rowena or Lady Nesbit? Was she so blind and prejudiced against them?

She stopped for a moment on the bridge over the stream leading towards her home. The sun twinkled on the water as it rushed beneath her and the heat warmed her back after the coolness between the trees and she closed her eyes for a moment.

The thought, as cool and clear as the water beneath her, appeared in her mind: if Rowena was capable of loving like that, why not Adam? Whatever he himself thought of his capacity for caring, she knew he was not fundamentally selfish. The very degree to which he had been hurt by Rowena's and his mother's rejections were signs of someone who felt deeply. He might not believe it, but he was capable of love.

She opened her eyes to the swirl of light and colour beneath her. There was no point in deluding herself. He might be capable of love, in time, but not for her. He knew her too well, and even if he esteemed her, he obviously didn't love her. There was no reason why he should suddenly fall in love with her simply because she was fool enough to still cling to her fantasies.

Even if she had been beautiful and accomplished and charming and all the things his previous women had so effortlessly been, she would still be connected with everything in his life that he resented and abhorred—with Mowbray and Rowena, the memories of his parents' betrayal and his own humiliation. He obviously wanted nothing more than to do what he considered to be his duty by the estate and then to leave it and her. It was not as if he had offered to take Alyssa on his journeys. Just to wed her and leave her here with everything else he sought to escape. And then one day he *would* fall in love and she would have to live with that.

The water winked and gurgled merrily, like a delighted animal, and she thought of that bust of Heraclites sitting so precariously on his desk and the words of that Greek philosopher: 'You can never step into the same river twice.'

She had been a mute and wounded witness to his love for Rowena. She would not stick around to go through that again, never knowing when it would happen and always hanging on to the hope that she might succeed in making him care for her.

What kind of existence would that be? No better than the barren emotional life her own mother had led with her father.

The fact that part of her was willing to consider it a worthy existence merely for the price of being able to be with him once or twice a year made her feel a burst of self-contempt. How many years had she spent suspended in this tiny corner of the world, content to be safe, never making any serious effort to encourage any other man because somewhere she was still holding up that ridiculous image she had of Adam? No one could ever have met that standard. And now, well, neither could Adam. He was just as flawed as any of the men she had ever met. Worse, even. His only redeeming feature was that he knew her and didn't seem to be very outraged by her oddity. And that he could be amusing when he wasn't reverting to acting like a schoolmaster. And other things which were best not dwelt on...

As painful as his return to Mowbray was, it was a good thing, she told herself. It was about time she gathered enough courage to strike out on her own. She had already taken one significant step towards that independence, which she would keep close to her chest. If that didn't work, she would just keep on trying until something did work. But first, they had to remove the danger to Adam. Besides that, everything else paled.

Chapter Twelve

Adam guided Thunder into the little orchard behind Drake Cottage and hitched his reins on to the branch of an apple tree. He stroked his horse's sooty mane as Thunder bent to feast on the lush grass and fallen fruit between the trees. From here he could see the back door of the cottage and once again the memories of what had happened there yesterday came back to him as they had too frequently for his peace of mind. Again he reminded himself he had more important matters to worry about than the insistent conviction that the most pressing order of business was to explore just how far he could coax out the sensual, wild girl Alyssa was at such pains to keep under control.

But if he was still standing once this threat on his life was defused, he knew he would have to come to terms with the fact that the events of the past couple of days had irrevocably curtailed his choices. Rowena and his mother and the whole of Mowbray had once taught him a very valuable lesson about ever having or creating expectations, but there was no honourable way he could see of getting out of the current situation that did not involve going ahead with this marriage. Alyssa was nothing like either his mother or Rowena—those self-centred, manipulative women—but she was a romantic and a crusader, and by definition was bound to be disappointed in him, even if their union was based on convenience.

He would just have to be very clear about the terms of that union.

It would have some definite advantages. It would mean he would definitively be taken off the list of matrimonial targets, a result which none of his scandals seemed to achieve. And as Jem had pointed out, she was well liked and trusted and would probably keep the estate in order as well as any estate agent. Between her and Thorpe they could easily keep the place running smoothly and it would give her financial security and freedom.

And of course there was the benefit of being able to bed her, as long as he took precautions not to get her with child. It was one thing to try to negotiate terms with an intelligent young woman, but he was not about to actively and inevitably set himself up to disappoint the absolute trust of a child.

This determination was followed immediately by a long-lost memory of stopping by Drake Cottage on fine days in the summer when Miss Drake and her siblings would sit on a blanket spread out on the high grass, like a boat riding green waves. Alyssa was a slim and intense captain, with her sailors looking up to her with trust and conviction. She was a natural mother, as far from his own as imaginable. It would be unforgivably selfish to force her into a union when he had no intention of being a real husband or even of giving her the possibility of having children. She deserved much better than anything he had or wanted to offer. She was no fool. It was clear she would want nothing to do with such a sterile arrangement.

He turned and headed towards the cottage. The sooner this whole story was over and he was out of Mowbray again, the better.

Betsy answered his knock on the cottage door and curtsied.

'Could you take me to Miss Drake?'

'Oh, no, sir, I mean, My Lord, I can't. I mean I could, if she were here, but she isn't.' She giggled nervously and Adam frowned.

'Where is she?'

'Lady Nesbit took her to Moresby Manor. This morning. She came by in her barouche and I showed her to the parlour, sir, I mean, My Lord.'

This seemed to be a very dramatic event for Betsy, but Adam focused on the one thing that interested him.

'To Moresby Manor? When did they leave?'

'An hour ago, My Lord. Shall I tell Miss that you called?' she asked, drawing herself up importantly.

Adam nodded absently and headed back towards Thunder. This did not sound good. Probably Moresby had passed away, the poor devil. It was terrible that he might be in some way responsible for this man's death. The worst of it was that Alyssa was now squarely in the middle of this, with that lie hanging over her. He swung on to Thunder and headed towards Moresby Manor. He knew he would not be welcome, but he did not want her facing that situation alone.

He almost did not see her. He was turning off the main lane on to the smaller path over the bridge at such a sharp pace it took him a moment to focus on her still figure standing by the bridge railing, looking down at the water. Relief mixed with exasperation as he realised she was alone and he drew Thunder up just as she turned. He swung off the horse, dragging Thunder's reins over his head and leading him forward on to the bridge, his eyes on her face, trying to gauge how she was as she watched him approach, but her expression was neutral.

'Betsy said you went to Moresby Manor. Is he dead?'

Her eyes widened slightly at his blunt question, but she shook her head.

'No, he recovered consciousness just half an hour ago. Cousin Harriet brought me over to talk with Rowena.'

He relaxed slightly, the knot of guilt easing.

'Talk with Rowena? Why? And why are you alone here in the middle of the woods?'

She laid one hand on the railing.

'Because Rowena has been very much affected by her concern for Lord Moresby and Lady Nesbit wanted me to try to convince her to take care of herself. And I am hardly alone in the middle of the woods, but on the lane on my way back home.' Her voice was patient, as if she was speaking to a dunce, which only aggravated Adam further.

'All Rowena does is take care of herself. I fail to see why she had to drag you out there or allow you to walk all the way home without an escort through the very woods where a knife-wielding maniac attacked Lord Moresby less than two days ago. Or why you agreed, which is much more to the point!'

'I hardly think...'

'That's just the problem! You hardly think! You are very clever when it comes to other people, but you are blind as a day-old newt when it comes to yourself! You were the one lecturing me about taking this seriously and here you are—' He broke off, raising his hands in front of him as if warding something off. He breathed deeply and took her arm in a firm grip, propelling her down the path. 'I will see you home.'

Alyssa allowed herself to be led and didn't speak until they were within sight of the cottage.

'Are day-old newts blind?' she asked curiously and Adam tightened his hold on her arm.

'Don't be flippant.' He bit down on the anger that was threatening to be let loose. It was bad enough that she was acting so irresponsibly. Compounding reckless folly with deliberate nonchalance was a clear provocation.

When they reached Drake Cottage he tethered Thunder once more to one of the apple trees behind the cottage and followed her through the door which led to her private parlour. She moved resolutely towards the window seat and sat down, fold-ing her hands demurely in her lap, but her chin was raised in a gesture he was now very familiar with.

'Well?' she asked as he remained silent.

'Well what?' he snapped.

'You might as well get the lecture off your chest,' she replied. 'You know, for someone who doesn't appreciate lectures, you give an awful lot of them yourself.'

'I wouldn't have to…' he began with a resolute effort to calm down '…if you would act with a modicum of sense.'

'By your definition.'

'By anyone's definition! What is more reasonable than to expect you not to go walking alone unprotected when you yourself are convinced several violent attacks have taken place in the vicinity unless you have an excellent reason?'

She regarded him with sudden suspicion.

'I am just curious. Were you out in the woods again last night?'

'That is different. I was armed,' he said impatiently and she stared at him.

'Do you mean…? Well! That is beyond anything! You have the audacity to tell me I am not to walk out on my own in the middle of the day in what is practically my back garden, while you purposely go and try to put yourself in harm's way? Let me tell you, Lord Delacort, that your definition of sense leaves a lot to be desired!'

'Let me remind you that whoever this villain is is probably after me, not you…'

'Precisely, which is why *you* should be doubly careful, not I.'

Adam clenched his fists and started pacing the room with restless fury. It was so like her to resort to logic to confuse the issue when she knew what he said made sense. Before he could think of a response that she was not likely to rip to shreds, she spoke.

'I know this situation is abhorrent to you, Adam, but if it is any consolation, your situation has just improved. With Lord Moresby recovering, even if blame swings back in your direction, at least a charge of murder is no longer on the table. I have been thinking and I believe the best course of action is for you to leave Mowbray.'

Adam stopped pacing as the meaning of her words sank in. The silence stretched for so long Alyssa shifted in her chair and a wariness entered her eyes that had not been present before.

'Do you?' he said carefully. 'Would you care to share your rationale, or am I deemed too dense to understand?'

She waved his sarcasm aside.

'Not at all. Even though I can't quite get my mind around the thought of Percy as a perpetrator of violent crime, I can't think of anyone else who might be behind all this. But if you were to leave the area, he would either have to follow you, which would be telling in itself, or he would have to give up. In either case we would be in a better position than we are now.'

Adam stood by her desk, his fist pressing against its cool surface as if he could somehow push it through the floor and into the ground below.

'We...' he repeated slowly. 'And wouldn't my precipitous departure look a little odd in light of our recent engagement? Or are we going to go the full length of making me appear a cad and a coward while we are at it? It would hardly surprise anyone and it just might excite quite a bit of sympathy for you, no?'

Alyssa's composed expression dissolved into shock as he spoke.

'Do you honestly think that is what I want?'

He did not answer for a moment. The anger was still there, sharp and present, but he knew he was wrong. It did not make sense to be angry at her, of all people. He walked over to the window overlooking the garden. He could just make out Thunder, peaceably munching on the rich grass between the low branches of the trees. It was such a calm, sane view.

'Lady Nesbit said I must bring you to tea tomorrow,' she said, her voice calmer.

Adam turned around, grateful for the olive branch she offered.

'Did she? Should I come in full armour?'

Her smile peeped through, lighting up her eyes.

'Well, she did call you "that young man", but tea is a good sign. Teas at Nesbit House are rather a sacred event. I think she is trying to gauge whether to rescue me or redeem you.'

'Are those our only two choices?'

She laughed.

'Today is the most human I have ever seen her. Her and Rowena.' Her smile dimmed slightly as she watched him. 'I've never seen Rowena like this. I know what you think of her, but I think she really cares for Moresby. She was shattered, almost like a little child.'

'I don't doubt the strength of her dependency. Just her ability to give anything in return.'

Alyssa shrugged.

'Sometimes just showing need is enough of a gift. I am glad Arthur saw her like that.'

'And thus Rowena earns a place on your list

of wounded animals,' he mused and she raised her chin.

'What bothers you so—that I might have added her to this fictitious list, or that you might be on it as well?'

Adam wandered over to her desk, holding down forcibly on the need to react to that. He should not be surprised if she pushed back when he prodded. She stood up suddenly and strode over to the desk and began stacking papers and placing them in one of the drawers. He frowned. There was something distracted about her suddenly and he wondered if there had been something in those papers she had not wished him to see. He ignored the jab of curiosity. It was none of his business. Before he could answer her question, she continued.

'Believe me, I have no more wish to remove Rowena from my "Most Aggravating" list than you do. But I'm willing to concede that she is capable of more human emotion than I gave her credit for.'

'And so, inevitably, we circle back to love,' he said cynically. 'I'm well aware that people prefer to cloak self-interest under loftier façades, but I would have thought you were too intelligent to fall for such ploys.'

'Simply because you've never experienced something yourself, it doesn't mean it doesn't exist!'

'True. Like angels and fairies and guaranteed returns on investments.'

'Oh, for... Never mind. I should know better than to let you provoke me when you are in one of your moods.'

She sounded so exasperated that his anger faded on an instant.

'I do not have moods. You make me sound just like one of those crotchety, dyspeptic old biddies coming to Mowbray to take the waters.'

Her dimple appeared and she shot him the mischievous look he knew she had no idea was so seductive. It once again amazed him she had not secured a husband. What on earth was wrong with the men of Mowbray, or rather what was wrong with her? It could not only be the lack of a dowry. Men needed encouragement, of course, and as far as he could tell she gave none. It was amazing she had learned so little from her very adept cousin. Could she really be waiting for some fairy-tale prince to come charging into Mowbray and sweep her off her feet? It was hard to credit that someone so practical could also be so naïve.

She sat down, her eyes still glinting with amusement.

'No, you are just very used to having your own way and tend to get colicky when crossed.'

'Don't push your luck.'

She laughed.

'Fine. We should get down to business anyway. Did you talk with Jem? What did you find out? What are you going to do about Percy? You should probably have someone keep an eye on him. Perhaps…'

'Perhaps you might let me speak?' he asked politely and she sighed.

'Sorry. There is just so much… However, please go ahead.'

'Thank you. As for Percy, Jem's eldest son Jacob is keeping an eye on him, as much as possible. We know he was at the Duck and Dragon last night. They hold cockfights there several nights a week and Percy is a regular, but you can imagine it is not exactly a place people keep tabs on each other. Jacob did report that he spent yesterday evening there until well past midnight when Libbet came to drag him home to his apartments on Turl Street, which is also apparently a common occurrence. There is always the possibility of course that Percy has hired someone rather than doing the dirty deed himself.'

She nodded. 'That would make more sense. Try as I might, I can't seem to picture Percy actually doing any of this himself. But wouldn't it be expensive to hire someone?'

'Not as much as you might think and he could easily meet some very unpleasant characters at the Duck and Dragon willing to cause mischief for a few coins. And certainly for some of the jewels and fobs he has purchased at the estate's expense before I cut him off. There would be something poetic about Percy using funds borrowed from the estate to do away with me.'

'But what about Timothy? And Ivor? Do you mean that Percy has managed to find reliable tools to do his dirty work on two previous occasions in very different circumstances? It all seems so fantastic.'

'I agree, which means there may in fact have been nothing suspicious about those deaths after all, or simply that we are underestimating him and that he, like Rowena, has hidden depths yet to be plumbed.'

She frowned at him.

'Which, by your tone, you don't believe in the least.'

'Let's just say I will have to be convinced. For the moment I am willing to explore all possibilities.'

'Who is next in line? After Percy?' she asked abruptly and he smiled.

'I'm afraid I can't give you the pleasure of adding them to the party. The next in line to the estate after Percy is our cousin George Ingram, who is a very staid and proper middle-aged Methodist minister living outside Newcastle. He is already quite well to do, but lives extremely simply, basking in the glory of his flock and dispensing a great deal of charity. His son is currently somewhere in Africa, establishing orphanages. And while George does deeply disapprove of my way of life and occasionally sends me long letters calling on me to renounce my wasteful and licentious ways and find comfort in sincere prayer, I challenge even you to draw him into this plot. I am afraid we will have to make do with Percy, the possibility of someone from my disreputable past who has followed me here or that this is merely an unfortunate string of coincidences.'

She sat back with an annoyed huff.

'I don't like any of those options.'

'I am not very fond of them myself, but that is the current situation. I promised to keep you informed and I will continue to do so on the condition you don't go off on your own like some misguided Bow Street Runner. Now, unless you have any practical suggestions, we should move on to our other business.'

The wariness returned to her eyes.

'The engagement,' he clarified and that dimple appeared.

'Of course, I had forgotten.'

'Which is why I thought I would remind you. Given Lord Moresby's condition no one will be expecting festivities, but they will be expecting something. You know the rules here, so this is your province. Just tell me my role.'

'Very well. Our first move must be to convince Cousin Harriet—Lady Nesbit, that is—to give us her support. If she is seen to favour the match, the whole neighbourhood will follow without question. We could even appeal to her for advice. That would gratify her and give her motivation to promote the match. And then perhaps we could attend an Assembly or a concert in the Pump Rooms together. Something undramatic and yet public... Are you laughing at me?' she asked suspiciously as she caught the amusement in his eyes.

'No. Just an appreciative audience of your machinations.'

'You're impossible! Not everything exists for your amusement, Adam. How can you be so flippant when there may be someone out there plotting his next move against you? Would you please take this seriously?'

There was such concern in her eyes his amusement faded. It was a strange feeling, having someone so focused on his welfare. It made him uncomfortable and he wasn't sure he liked it.

'You seem to be taking it seriously enough for both of us. Are you really so worried?'

'Of course I am,' she answered, surprised, but it struck him that the very sincerity of her answer cheapened her concern. It placed him squarely in line with her other objects of worry, like her siblings and her cousins. He told himself, again, he should be very happy that he occupied no loftier position, but some vanity, or pique, resisted this sensible conclusion. It wasn't that he really wanted to make her believe herself in love with him, but just to have her admit that there was a natural attraction between them that placed him in a rather different category than her usual list of needy causes. There was no way he was going to be classified alongside that silly Mary and now Rowena.

'You don't have much faith in me,' he mocked, moving forward and raising her chin gently. It was as much a warning as a statement and to give her credit she recognised it as such immediately, her eyes darkening from a soft, almost golden green to the shade of shadows in the woods outside.

'Up to a point,' she answered, her voice subdued and wary.

'Smart. I'm tempted to ask what point. And then cross it.'

'Why?'

'Because I think I might enjoy myself there. I have a feeling you would, too, if you would just give yourself some freedom to do so. What did Herrick write? *"Gather ye rosebuds while ye may"*? Starting with these.'

He brushed his thumb along the tense line of her lower lip, caressing it, pulling at it gently as if he could physically tease out her inner struggle. Her lashes dipped, fanning over the faint colour that spread across her cheekbones, and he felt the undeniable surge of triumph mix with the desire he was getting tired of keeping at bay. Good intentions were thoroughly inconvenient, especially when there was someone out there determined to get rid of him permanently. Why not take and give some pleasure while he yet could? He wouldn't go further than a kiss or two.

"'The grave's a fine and private place, but none, I think, do there embrace,"' he quoted lightly as he tucked a honey-brown lock of hair behind her ear.

'That is Marvell, not Herrick,' she said faintly, but she did not move away.

'So it is. Another cynic and a much better poem for my purposes. Not the title, though. I am well aware you are neither coy nor my mistress, unfortunately.'

'Are you trying to shock me, again?'

'No, I am trying to prepare you for the fact that I am going to kiss you, again.'

'Why?'

'Now, that is a foolish question, even for you,' he said and raised her chin as he bent to brush his lips over hers. 'We were doing quite nicely before Nicholas interrupted us on that rather eventful day and we might as well derive some degree of pleasure from this engagement, don't you think? If you want me to stop, just say so.'

She didn't speak and he slid his palm over her cheek, into her hair, registering every texture and fighting back the drive to let slip the manacles on his control. The last thing he wanted to do was scare her. She didn't move and he bent to skim his lips over hers very gently, waiting for some sign that she was with him. Some release in the tension that held her rigid.

He touched his mouth to her cheek, her throat, to the pulse that rushed beneath her soft skin, then up to the hollow beneath her ear, and a slight shudder ran through her, echoing through him with sharp immediacy. An unfamiliar vice tightened on his body, bordering on pain, and he had to forcibly restrain the urge to pull her against his body. Until she was fully with him he had to keep this light.

'See, wild girl?' he whispered against her mouth, just teasing her lips with his. 'That's not so terrible, is it?'

She shook her head and her lips finally relaxed against his on a small sigh. Once again the unfamiliar vice closed on him and for a second he wondered if he could control this. He knew he would have to stop soon, but it seemed absurd not to explore just a little further the obvious passion she kept so firmly under lock and key.

He slid his hand down, spreading his fingers over the small of her back. He could feel her skin, hot and pliant beneath the loosely woven muslin dress she wore. He wanted to feel just that curve under his hand, feel her skin directly, its soft heat, and slide down over her backside, pulling her to him… He curved his hand over her nape, holding her as he gave in and kissed her slowly and thoroughly, revelling in the way her body softened and sank against his just as it had before.

His mind moved ahead of him, telling him to lock the door, that it was time to stop playing games and take her up on the promise of pleasure she was expressing in everything but words. He would probably have to marry her anyway; so he would only be anticipating…

'The gate…' she gasped suddenly.

Adam shook his head, neither comprehending nor caring, but then he, too, heard the squeal of the garden gate and the snap as it closed behind someone. Alyssa pressed her hands to his chest, pushing him back.

'Maybe it was just someone leaving,' he said hopefully, but then they both heard the knock on the front door and before he could stop her Alyssa turned and hurried out of the room. He moved towards the mirror over the mantelpiece, fixing the folds of his cravat and cursing long and silently. It was probably Nicholas. He didn't know whether to berate his friend or thank him for the interruption.

The door to the study opened and Alyssa re-entered, followed by Sir James Muncy. Alyssa did not meet Adam's eyes, but other than the flush on her cheeks he could see she had herself in hand and that the wild girl had been resolutely banished for the moment. Sir James paused for a moment on the threshold as he noticed Adam and bowed apologetically.

'Good day, Lord Delacort. I mean no offence, sir, but I had hoped to speak to Miss Drake alone.'

Before Adam could voice any objection Alyssa raised her hand.

'There is no need, Sir James. I assure you Lord Delacort's presence here will have absolutely no impact on my answers.'

She sat down on the sofa and indicated the chair opposite her. Sir James hesitated, his pale blue eyes searching hers for a moment, then he nodded and sat down.

'Very well. I have just come from Moresby Manor, where Dr Hedgeway informed me that Lord Moresby has recovered consciousness. I have not yet had the opportunity to question him, but Dr Hedgeway did agree to enquire on my behalf whether His Lordship had any memory of the attack and apparently he is still in such a confused state that he has no clear recollection. Indeed, as the knife wound was inflicted from behind, there is every possibility he might not have seen his assailant at all. This means we still have no clear direction in our enquiry. We are of course looking into tenant grievances and the like, but the fact remains that the most glaring motive for an act of enmity against Lord Moresby, as you yourself must be aware, My Lord, is still yours. Am I clear thus far, Miss Drake?'

'Perfectly clear, Sir James.'

'Very well. As you might surmise, with Lord Moresby's recovery, the criminal proceedings have by their very nature taken a less dire turn. However! I still intend to pursue this investigation with no less rigour. I cannot permit such acts of wanton violence to be perpetrated under my jurisdiction with impunity!'

'That is both understandable and commendable, Sir James,' Alyssa replied. 'I assure you that I understand the gravity of the situation and I am absolutely sincere in stating that I know of a certainty that Lord Delacort did not attack Lord Moresby.'

Adam forced himself not to react. However convinced Alyssa might be that he was indeed innocent of the attack on Moresby, he hated the fact that she had to continue lying. But once that first lie had been spoken, there was no way of retrieving it without exposing her to even greater censure.

Sir James wavered and it was obvious to Adam he wished to probe further. Perhaps the fact that this meant enquiring about their 'clandestine' meeting as he had termed it was too embarrassing for someone as diffident as he. At least Adam hoped so.

'Very well,' Sir James said at last. 'That will do

for now. I might have further enquiries as the enquiry progresses—' He broke off as they heard a heavy step in the hall, then the door opened and Mr Drake entered.

'Betsy told me Sir James… Ah, Sir James! Well, what's to? And *you*, what are you doing here?'

The latter was addressed to Adam, who straightened, readying himself to deal with this complication. Sir James, who had known the poet all his life, was unfazed either by the interruption or by Drake's ill manners.

'Good afternoon, William. I have come to confirm with your daughter certain points regarding the attack on Lord Moresby. And to congratulate her again on her engagement,' Sir James added somewhat self-consciously. Alyssa clenched her fists and groaned inwardly. It was sheer bad luck that her father had chosen today of all days to descend from his lair. She prayed he at least would keep true to form and remain oblivious to anything that was of no direct concern for his poetry.

'What the devil?' William Drake demanded and Alyssa stood up, taking a step towards Sir James, who stood up as well, somewhat confused.

'I have not yet told my father of the attack on Lord Moresby, Sir James. You know he does not like to be interrupted with outside concerns when he is at a sensitive point of his writing. Thank you so much for coming and, as I said, I would like to be of whatever assistance necessary in your enquiries. Good day, Sir James.'

'Yes, of course, thank you, I mean…good day, Lord Delacort, William.'

Alyssa herded him mercilessly out of the room, leaving Adam alone to face the poet across the room.

'What the devil was Sir James about?' William Drake demanded. 'Engaged? To whom? And what in the blazes does it have to do with Moresby?'

'Engaged to me, Mr Drake.' Adam replied. 'And it has nothing to do with Moresby. I hope you will give us your blessing.'

'I most certainly will not! Alyssa! Where are you? Ah, there you are! This person tells me you are engaged. What nonsense is this? Why was I not consulted?'

Alyssa sighed.

'It is not nonsense, Father. You were not consulted because I am of age and do not require your approval, though I obviously hope you do give your blessing to whatever choice I make.'

'But this is utterly unnecessary. I thought it was

understood that you would stay at the cottage and assist in my work. It was all well and good for Minerva and Terrence, but I don't see any purpose in your getting married as well...'

Alyssa stared at her father for a moment, then shook her head slightly, as if denying something.

'It is over, Father.' Her voice was calm, but Adam could clearly see how stiffly she held herself. 'You will just have to manage on your own.'

'On my own?' Mr Drake stated in stark incredulity. She might as well have been telling him the sun would be rising in the west the following day.

'Yes, or hire someone to act as your secretary.'

'This is arrant nonsense. You have none of the skills required to be Lady Delacort and you know I won't be able to find someone who can understand metre properly and whom I can trust with historic detail. I won't have it and that is final.'

Alyssa didn't respond; she merely turned on her heel and walked out the door and into the garden.

Once the door closed behind her, Adam turned to inspect William Drake. He had kept purposely silent during the interchange. For her own good this was a battle Alyssa needed to fight alone. But now that she was gone there was nothing wrong with Adam telling her parasitical parent what he thought of him.

'Do you have any idea how wrong that was?' he asked.

'What on earth are you talking about?' Mr Drake asked testily.

'Unbelievable,' Adam said wonderingly. 'You really have no idea. You know, I thought my own father was a pretty poor specimen of the breed, but you are actually making me remember him with fondness. Has it really never occurred to you that you have been abusing your daughter's love and sense of responsibility ever since she has been a child?'

Mr Drake faced him, livid with outrage.

'How dare you speak to me like that, sir?'

'Don't worry, I'm done speaking to you. It's a waste of air. Just take care—one day you will demand too much and she will break with you. I just hope she does it sooner rather than later, for her own sake.'

He walked out into the garden before he succumbed to the need to do Drake some physical damage, leaving the older man standing in the middle of the room, his face as furiously red as the dog roses surrounding the house.

Adam scanned the small garden, but there was no sign of Alyssa. He walked over to unhitch Thunder from the tree, trying to think where she might go, then led Thunder towards the Hungry Tree. She was standing there, looking up at the topmost branches.

'Oh, it's you,' she said absently as he came to stand beside her. 'Do you know I just remembered I spent the night up in the tree when I was six?'

'You did?' Adam asked carefully. There was something distant in her voice that made him wary.

'Yes, my mother went to visit her family with Terry. He was just three and I think she was hopeful they would do something for us, because they had not approved of her marrying a poet. They are very strait-laced and live near Aberdeen and I never heard them mentioned again after that trip. Anyway, I was to stay with Father because they weren't interested in girls. And we didn't have a maid then, just a girl who came in some days to help.

'I climbed up, I don't remember why, and for some reason I was too scared to come down. I'm not afraid of heights and I had been up a hundred times before that and again after, but somehow that evening it seemed impossibly high. I finally fell asleep just up there where the branches cross.

One of Lady Nesbit's tenants found me the next morning and helped me down and took me inside. Father told him he hadn't noticed I wasn't at home that night, but that I was usually a good girl. The farmer was upset with Father, but I just wished he would go away so I could sleep. I wasn't angry, just numb, but I knew I would never ask my father for anything ever again. And I haven't. It makes no sense that I stayed here except that it has been comfortable, in a way. Other than the work I do for him on his manuscripts we hardly ever talk— he rarely comes out of his corner of the house, he even eats there. Sometimes I might not see him for a week or more. It is just that when Mama died I knew that I could never leave my brothers or sister with him. He just didn't see us. So it was up to me. And I didn't mind. We were good together. But now even Charlie is gone and Mary, too. So once this is all over I shall also leave.'

Adam didn't move.

'Leave?'

She brushed a hand over her eyes.

'Yes. I told you about Mama's friend. I wrote to her to see if I could stay with her for a while.'

'Aren't you overlooking the fact that we are engaged?' Adam said tightly.

She looked surprised and the distant look faded slightly.

'Of course not. I did say once this is all over—when we unwind this tangle and you go back to your life.'

Adam turned to look at the stream, willing himself calm.

'I need to get back to the Hall and see if Nick and Jem are back,' he said after a moment.

'You won't go outside again at night any more, will you?' she asked abruptly, her eyes wide and insistent.

He wished he could lie outright, but somehow it seemed a physical impossibility under the pressure of her green-and-gold gaze.

'I told you this is not your concern.'

'Adam! You cannot possibly...'

'As you have just pointed out, we are not actually engaged, which means you do not have scolding rights.'

'I am not scolding, I am just...'

'Yes, you are.'

'...trying to be sensible,' she finished resolutely.

'Reserve your sense for our dealings with Lady Nesbit. I will come and report to you tomorrow as ordered and then we will go and beard the lioness in her den.'

Before she could reply he reached out, his hand sliding over the warm silky hair at her nape. She stumbled slightly and he pulled her against him as he lowered his head to hers.

He had meant it to be a quick embrace, a way to distract her, but her lips were soft and warm and opened under his and just as in the study it seemed mad not to sink into her, to touch her, to take what she was offering. Her taste and smell seemed to be part of everything around them—blackberries, honeysuckle, apples. He pressed her back until she was half-seated on a long branch of the tree behind her and her eyes drifted open.

'Adam,' she murmured. 'Someone will see—' She broke off on a moan as his mouth teased the spot on the side of her neck that had made her shudder back in the house.

'There's something about you and trees, wild girl. Besides, we are engaged,' he replied hoarsely and she answered with a small broken laugh. He pulled her more tightly against him, but even as her body pressed against his, soft and pliant, he knew she was right. It was madness to be doing this at all, and certainly just a few yards off a country lane where anyone could see them.

He forced himself to step back. He wanted to say something, anything, to make light of the urgent blaze she kindled in him so effortlessly, but he could think of nothing and after a moment he nodded to her, swung up on to Thunder's back and left.

Chapter Thirteen

Alyssa sat down by her dresser and pulled open the bottom drawer. At the very back of the drawer she found them. A pair of long dark breeches that had once belonged to Terry which she had appropriated ever since he had outgrown them. She had never quite been willing to let them go. She'd not had any expectation of using them again, but they reminded her how far she had come from those days.

She stood up and after a moment's hesitation she undressed except for her short chemise and slid her legs into the trousers. They were a bit more snug than she remembered, but still comfortable, and they felt both familiar and quite strange. She next pulled on a simple cotton shirt that had once been Charlie's and glanced at her small clock—eight thirty. She should be going.

She knew this was nothing short of madness and

should anyone ever discover what she was doing she would be mortified, but against these fears stood her conviction that whatever he had said, Adam meant to go out into the woods that night. Most likely in the expectation that whoever had perpetrated the attacks would try again. She had no clear idea what earthly good she might be if something horrible happened, but she also knew it was impossible just to stay safe in the cottage and do nothing. She would head to the path by the bridge and then decide what to do. Hopefully nothing would happen and she could slink back home unnoticed.

She tied on her long dark winter cloak over her unconventional clothes and hurried downstairs to her study. Betsy was a firm believer in *early to bed, early to rise* and would probably be already sound asleep in her room at the other side of the cottage, but it was still best to leave by the study door so she could go directly through the garden to the woods. Just in case her father took it into his head to break with habit as he'd done that afternoon and go anywhere in the house other than his study and adjacent room.

She unlatched the door and stood for a moment inspecting the dark garden and the even darker shadows of the trees beyond. The only colour was the pale grey shimmer of a very slight mist which hovered just above the ground. She knew what country nights were like, but only from the safety of her study or a carriage. The last time she had gone out on her own into the woods like this at night had been many years ago when Terry had run away after a tantrum and got lost. She had found him near the bridge, cold and terrified.

But back then all her terror had been focused on finding Terry; she had barely noticed the oppressive blackness. Now she became fully aware of it. Of the sense that everything was larger and closer even though she could not see more than a couple of yards in front of her. Trees that she knew were straight seemed to lean over her and she kept stumbling, like a babe learning to walk. Yet everything was familiar enough that she knew instinctively which way to go, heading through the woods alongside the paler slash of the lane towards Mare's Rise. After a few moments she realised she could see quite differently from before. Black became shaded with greys and blues and deep greens and she could make out the shapes of trees.

The closer she came to Delacort the more cautious she became, keeping near the trees and stopping often to listen. She had just reached the small rise which overlooked the stone bridge when she heard someone moving ahead of her. She froze, listening. It was just a faint slithering sound. It stopped for a moment, then it resumed before stopping again. It might be an animal, she thought, as she tried to pinpoint the direction of the sound. Whatever or whoever it was, it wasn't Adam. She had no idea how she knew, but she did. She closed her eyes, focusing only on that occasional, faint sound, until she was certain she knew which direction it came from and how far away it was. Then she began moving cautiously in that direction.

She saw and heard Adam before she had moved more than a few yards. Coming out of the woods on the other side of the bridge, he was momentarily a dark blot on the pale gravel path leading up to the bridge and the sound of his feet on the gravel carried sharply. She froze in shock as the darkness shifted between the trees ahead of her. A hunched shape with a glinting protrusion was moving away from her, in Adam's direction, and she realised what was happening and lurched forward towards the shape. She must have cried out, because she heard Adam's name in her own voice, high and shrill. The shadow ahead twisted in her direction as she surged towards him and the barrel of a rifle slammed into her arm. She stumbled and fell, her hands barely stopping her fall as she slid part way down the rise. She heard shouting and running and someone grabbed her by the arm, half-dragging her to her feet.

'Alyssa? Alyssa!' Adam's urgent voice was close to her ear. 'Are you all right? What happened? Are you hurt?'

She shook her head dazedly.

'No. I didn't see... Did you?'

He didn't answer. His arms had closed around her, his body was stiff with tension and the outline of the pistol he held pressed against her back. Through the pounding of blood in her ears she heard someone running and then Nicholas Beauvoir's voice.

'Adam! Where are you, blast it? What... Oh, Jem, is that you?'

'Aye, sir. He got away. I'm sorry.'

She felt Adam draw a deep breath and he moved back slightly without letting her go. Nicholas and the groom came towards them up the path. Even in the gloom Alyssa saw they were both holding flintlock pistols as well as unlit lanterns.

'Miss Drake!' Nicholas exclaimed as he saw her. Jem placed his lantern on the ground and bent down to strike a French match with a practised hand and the single candle caught, flickering and dancing until he closed the glass cover. He did the same for Nicholas's lantern and the dark transformed into a dance of shadows and soft gold light.

'He disappeared, My Lord,' Jem said calmly. 'I heard him running and then nothing. He might even still be out there, but the chances of us finding him in the dark are slim. I don't think we should linger.'

Adam scanned the woods and nodded.

'You two head back to the Hall and I will see Miss Drake back to the cottage.'

'Perhaps you should take the gig, My Lord?' Jem asked with a dubious look around them.

'I think we should get her back as unobtrusively as possible, Jem. Don't worry, I doubt he will try anything again tonight. You and Nicholas go on and we will talk later.'

The groom hesitated, but Nicholas nodded and handed Adam the glowing lantern.

Without a word Adam grasped Alyssa's hand and led her down the path. As he turned she saw the glint of the long-barrelled silver-tipped pistol tucked through a belt under his dark coat and she shivered. He glanced down at her but didn't speak. Still, she knew him well enough to know he was furious. The light of the lantern accentuated the sharply carved lines of his face and stripped it of colour. He looked like a marble statue of a particularly unfriendly deity. Alyssa watched the dark forest around them warily and told herself again and again she didn't care that he was furious. At least he was alive. When they were almost at the cottage he slackened his pace.

'Front door?' he asked curtly.

'No. I left the back door open. This way,' she said quietly and, pulling free from his grasp, she led the way through the garden. She hated the thought that he would be walking back to the Hall alone now, but she did not have the nerve to protest. She hoped he was right and that whoever had been there in the forest that night was long gone.

He led the way through the back corridor into the hallway, sweeping the lantern about as if expecting someone to leap at them from the shadows. She waited tensely for him to turn and leave, holding back against the urge to demand he not go out alone into the night again. But he just placed the lantern on the small side table in the hallway. He opened his mouth to speak, then closed it, and she saw the muscles about his jaw tighten and flex. She held herself very still.

'I need a drink,' he said finally. 'Is there anything here?'

She nodded and hurried towards the front parlour, where they kept a decanter of brandy for rare guests. She needed a drink, too. She was shaking, from cold and fear and shock, and her arm ached dully where the rifle had hit her. The gloom in the parlour lightened as he followed her, placing the lantern on the modest dining table and striding over to pull the curtains closed. She didn't look around as she poured him a large measure of brandy. Glass chattered against glass as her hands shook at their task. Finally she handed him his glass and went to sit down, untying her cloak and draping it over the arm of the sofa. She didn't feel steady enough to take what was coming standing.

He placed the glass down on the table with a snap.

'Of course. Breeches. Why am I not surprised?'

She glanced down at her legs.

'I needed something comfortable...'

He covered his face with his hands and drew a deep breath.

'Hell, where do I start?' he mumbled through his hands and she felt a welcome spurt of annoyance focus her and her shaking eased slightly.

'You can be as condescending as you wish, but I am not the idiot who went about playing bullseye for a murderer! He was about to shoot you when I scared him!'

'No. He was about to reveal himself when you

warned him. Pay me the compliment of believing I might know what I am doing, Alyssa. There are not that many places along the path I am known to walk in the evening which provide cover for someone wishing to attack me. We found traces of earlier tracks in two of them when we searched the woods earlier. Nick and Jem were each positioned to watch one location without being seen while Jacob was set to track Percy from the Duck and Dragon, where he had shown up earlier this evening. I had to be seen, but I would not have come within ten yards of either spot. At that distance Percy would have been no more accurate with a rifle than a dog. He is too vain to admit it, but that quizzing glass isn't just ornamental. In the dark and at that distance he would have the devil's own luck to do any damage. And we needed to catch him in the act so he couldn't claim he was just wandering around old haunts!'

Alyssa's assurance faded with each additional, coldly furious word.

'You should have told me,' she said miserably.

He didn't answer immediately.

'Perhaps, very foolishly, I thought it would hardly be considerate to have you concerned about what was going on. How was I to know you would decide to go into the woods in the middle of the night when there is a murderer about…? Damn it, Alyssa!'

Alyssa felt utterly humiliated, but even worse was the realisation that she had ruined perhaps their best chance of capturing the villain. There was only one thing she could offer as palliative.

'It wasn't Percy,' she said numbly as once again an icy cold coursed through her, as it had the moment she had seen the figure gliding between the trees, black on black…

Her statement distracted Adam momentarily from his anger.

'Of course it was Percy.'

She shook her head.

'No. Percy is almost as tall as you are. This man was smaller. And right-handed. Percy is left-handed. I remember Ivor once saying that they tried to break him of the habit in the nursery when he was growing up at Delacort but finally they gave up. That man, the man in the forest, held the rifle in his right hand.'

She closed her eyes as that moment, sharper now even than when she had been there, flashed before her. The cloaked figure, the long dull glint of the rifle barrel and beyond it Adam's blurry silhouette against the path. Then the moment when the figure had turned towards her, swinging the rifle. The moment before the barrel had knocked her sidewise she had seen him fully—all in black and hooded like a hangman.

'You could have been mistaken,' he said, his voice cold, and she opened her eyes to dispel the vision.

'It is possible. He was hooded. But I don't think so. It was not Percy.'

He took a restless turn around the room and then stopped, levelling an accusing finger at her.

'Whether it was or not does not change the enormity of what you did! What were you doing out alone, in the forest…?' He stopped as his voice turned into something like a snarl.

What had she been doing? she wondered wearily. She could not explain to him that it had been impossible not to go, knowing that he was going to be out there tying himself like a sheep to a stake to draw the wolf. The implications of that admission were more than she was willing to acknowledge even to herself. She stood up and shrugged, and he seemed to bound forward.

'Don't you dare shrug at me! Answer me!' He seized her arms and she gasped in surprised pain as his hand closed on the spot where the rifle had struck her. She tugged her left arm from his grasp and he let go immediately.

'Are you hurt?'

'It's nothing.' She pulled away instinctively as he reached for her again, but he took her arm, gently this time, and pushed up her sleeve. She glanced down at the large, already livid bruise.

'It isn't serious,' she mumbled, but he ignored her and just stood there for a moment, looking at the bruise before very tenderly lowering her sleeve again, his fingers brushing along the soft skin under her arm, and she wavered as a tingling rushed up to her chest, mixing with the pain and spreading scalding heat through her whole body. It was sudden and urgent and she moaned slightly in protest and need.

Adam pulled her to him, his arms enfolding her as he had in the forest. She felt bared and scorched and she pressed closer, as if she could merge into him. His voice, hard and urgent, pulsed through her.

'Alyssa…you are never, ever to do something like that again. Do you understand? Ever.'

She shook her head against him, breathing him in, wishing this was her rightful place. How could she stand it if something were to happen to him? Even if she was not willing to be with him on his crippling terms, she needed him alive and well. She felt beaten and tired and hopeless. She wished he would just hold her until it was all over and he was safe.

'Your luck will run out one day, Adam,' she said wearily, forcing herself to push away from him, and his arms fell to his sides.

'That is my concern,' he said after a moment and she didn't answer. There was no point. She went and sat on the sofa and pulled a blanket towards her. She felt so cold recently. The silence stretched, but she didn't look up, not even when Adam spoke at last.

'I want you to stay here at the cottage until I come to drive you over to Lady Nesbit's tomorrow afternoon, understood? And lock the back door behind me when I leave.'

Alyssa debated taking issue with these commands but just nodded and pulled the blanket more closely about her. Adam stood there for a moment, but then he picked up the lantern and left the room, closing the door quietly behind him.

Chapter Fourteen

Adam walked swiftly across the lawn. It was rather cold, but he was hardly aware of the chill. When a figure pushed away from the long wall marking the line between the cottage lawn and the orchard behind it both body and mind went into shocked alert. He had already pulled out his pistol when he recognised Nicholas.

'Nick! What the devil? Has something happened?'

'No. Just making sure it doesn't,' Nicholas replied phlegmatically.

Adam noted the pistol Nicholas tucked back into the pocket of his greatcoat and realisation sank in.

'You were on guard? You must be frozen through!'

'Not quite, but I'll be glad for some brandy when we get back. I can't believe I forgot to bring a flask to a night vigil. I'm getting rusty. Jem will be waiting for us and hopefully Jacob as well. Is she all right?'

Adam debated how to answer that question.

'She is. She caught quite a blow to her arm, but I think her pride took the worst bruising. But she's luckier than she deserves. He might have killed her.' He kept his voice as level as possible, but he could not help the anger and fear that seeped through. The memory of that moment when he'd heard her call out his name kept coming back. Until that moment, fear had been present, but it had been subdued as he'd honed his senses in the darkness. But her voice, high and urgent, had shattered his focus and he'd headed towards her as blindly as any fool stepping into a trap. If the murderer had had more sense, or experience, he could have made the most of that moment.

The image of her bruised arm refused to leave him. He had fought back the urge to cover the already purple-brown contusion, gently, with his hand, as if he could erase it. He could still feel the smooth warmth of her skin as he slid his fingers down her arm. And her soft cry, which he could not tell whether it was one of pain or pleasure. It had seemed natural to pull her against him. All he had wanted was to continue what he had twice begun in her study and carry it to its natural conclusion. Even knowing it would be unforgivable to take advantage of her in that state, he had no idea what he would have done if she had not moved away. The transition from danger to fear to the physical desire she evoked in him had held him at the edge of his control.

'She said the man she saw there wasn't Percy,' Adam said, forcing himself back to the present.

'She saw who it was, then?' Nicholas asked urgently and Adam shook his head.

'She said the man was hooded and dressed in black, but she is convinced he was smaller than Percy. And that he raised the rifle to his right shoulder, while Percy is left-handed. I think she's right about that, but I'll ask Jem.'

When they reached Jem's house they found the fire lit and a bottle of brandy and mugs on the rough wooden table.

Jem nodded in confirmation to Adam's question.

'Ay, Master Percy is left-handed without a doubt. Masters Ivor and Timothy were wont to taunt him as a boy for that, but he could never break himself of it, poor lad.'

Adam refrained from commenting on Jem's somewhat misplaced sympathy.

'I'm still curious as to what your Jacob reports.'

'He's here already, My Lord. I sent him to the kitchen for some bread and cheese. Ah, that'll be him. Come in, boy.'

Jacob nodded a greeting and silently set about cutting slices from a large loaf of bread. Nicholas sighed contentedly and reached over, happily tucking a chunk of cheese between two slices of the doughy bread.

'Why is the simplest food always the best? Now, fill us in, Jacob.'

Jem's son nodded serenely, looking very much like his father.

'It's as I told Pa just now. Mr Somerton was at the Duck and Dragon from just coming on eight o'clock this evening. There was a cockfight and the betting was heavy. Mr Somerton won on a Bloomsbury Red what come all the way from Faringdon. There was talk that Percy was drowning his sorrows after trying his luck with the wealthy widow and getting shot down. Aside from once when he went outside to relieve himself, he was there until Mr Libbet came to take him home half an hour ago. I followed and they went directly to his lodgings in Turl Street. Then I came back here. So whoever it was out there tonight, it wasn't Mr Somerton.'

'Thank you for that, Jacob,' Adam said. 'You've done very well. Why don't you go get some rest?'

Jem nodded and handed his son a mug with a small brandy.

'That's right. You go on now, lad.'

The young man grinned and headed out, mug in hand.

'So. Miss Drake was right. It weren't Master Percy. At least not last night,' Jem said after a moment.

'So what now?' Nicholas asked practically.

'We go back to the possibility that he has hired someone,' Adam said wearily. 'All the more reason to spend the night at the Duck and Dragon establishing an alibi. We need to find the man from the woods. If Percy is involved, he will have to make contact with him at some point. Also, this man must be staying somewhere in the area to be able to spend so much time around the Hall. We need to find out if there are any strangers staying in or near Mowbray or if Percy has been in contact with anyone from the area who might fit the bill. We'll need you and Jacob for that, Jem.'

Jem nodded.

'Jacob and I can do the asking. Carefully.'

Adam nodded and Nicholas stood up resolutely.

'All right. First things first—we need to get some

sleep. You both look like something I scraped off my boot and I feel like it. Everything will seem clearer once we all get some decent sleep.'

Adam stood up and nodded.

'Point taken. We will talk again tomorrow.'

Once in his room Adam dismissed his valet and sat down on the side of the bed. He was drained, but his mind was tumbling over itself with ideas of what they needed to do. And underneath was the rumble of the images and sensations that would not be subdued and compartmentalised. What on earth was he going to do with Alyssa? He had about as much control over her as he had over the weather. Everything else he could deal with, even the danger, but her...

This was partly his fault. Either he should have lied more convincingly about not planning anything that night, or he should have, as Nick had warned him, taken her into his confidence and established the ground rules absolutely clearly. But how could he have guessed she would do something so mad? Maybe he should have. He remembered she had once demanded what he would have done if their situations had been reversed and he knew for certain he would not have let her go into the forest on her own without intervening. He could tell himself a million times, and believe it, that it was different—that he was a man, and that he had had to deal with danger in the past—but none of that would mean anything to the little crusader.

Well, he had learned his lesson. Next time he would sit her down and make it clear that if she set one foot outside the cottage in such a situation he would have her kidnapped and sent to the Antipodes if that was what he had to do to keep her safe. And if she dared call him domineering one more time or tell him he had no authority over her, he would…

He lay down, rubbing his hands over his face. The only ideas that surfaced were ones he shouldn't be entertaining. It had taken every ounce of his willpower not to seduce her tonight. He shifted on the bed, trying to get comfortable, pressing down on the physical heat that surged every time he let his mind slide back to the memory of her body against his, softening, and the faint moan that had caught in her throat, the promise of the wild girl waiting to be set loose. He pulled the covers over him and turned resolutely on to his side. He needed to sleep and then he could try to consider what he had to do about her. Sleep now, think later.

Chapter Fifteen

Alyssa looked at her reflection in the mirror. It was sunny outside and the light streamed in strong and warm, raising golden lights in her gathered hair. It reflected in the hazel flecks of her eyes and the pale orange ribbons that adorned the bodice of her best afternoon dress, which Betsy's nimble fingers had copied from a fashion plate in *La Belle Assemblée*. A matching pale orange pelisse hid the bruise on her arm, which throbbed intermittently, though she did not need it to remind her of what had happened the previous night.

It was another uncharacteristically beautiful summer day. Which was strange, since she felt a little cold. She placed her palms lightly on her pale cheeks. Cold, and tired, and scared, and now she had to go and act in front of Lady Nesbit that all was well.

She heard the unmistakable sound of a curricle

pulling up outside and she picked up her reticule and bonnet, breathed in and stepped out of the cottage, tying her bonnet.

'How is your arm?' Adam asked once he had helped her into the curricle.

'Well, thank you,' she replied properly. 'Have you discovered anything? About Percy or last night?'

Adam flicked the reins and the team pulled forward.

'You were right, it wasn't Percy. Jem's son watched him the whole evening at the Duck and Dragon. Which means it was probably a hireling. We've been out all day making discreet enquiries about strangers in the area or about the people Percy has been seen with, but no luck so far. And that is the end of our report. Believe me, if we discover anything I will inform you promptly. But right now we need to concentrate on convincing Lady Nesbit not to show me the door.'

She flexed her shoulders, trying to relax them.

'You make it sound like a difficult task. You really don't believe you can charm her?'

He glanced down at her with a slightly wry smile.

'My faith in my powers of persuasion has taken a slight beating recently. I depend on you to smooth my path.'

She turned away slightly to hide the flush she

could not control. She had never considered herself a blusher, in fact she could hardly remember
blushing before Adam's return. Just another sign
part of her was stuck firmly in the schoolroom
when it came to him.

'I have a great deal of faith in your ability to be
suave, Lord Delacort. And we don't need a Drury
Lane performance just to be moderately convincing.' She could not completely subdue the bitterness in her voice and he smiled without mirth as
he pulled his team skilfully to a halt at the foot of
the stairs to Nesbit House.

'Very well, then, let us go "strut and fret our
hour" on Lady Nesbit's stage...'

He jumped down, handing the reins to the footman, who had run down the steps at their approach, and walked around to help her descend.
She accepted his arm, trying not to let him see the
impact of his words. She knew the continuation
of the quote he had employed. And so their story
was, in a way, 'a tale told by an idiot, full of sound
and fury, signifying nothing'.

They walked into the blue drawing room and
Alyssa noted with dismay but without surprise that
they were not the only visitors. Lady Nesbit sat
enthroned on her favourite sofa with Rowena at
her side. And opposite them sat the Mott sisters,

two of Lady Nesbit's cronies and Mowbray's chief gossips, who watched with avid, almost gleeful concentration as the matriarch greeted Alyssa and Adam with every appearance of approbation. Rowena, too, though pale and slightly defiant, came forward uncharacteristically to kiss Alyssa's cheek.

'Arthur is very much better,' she said without preamble, but low enough so the others did not hear. 'Dr Hedgeway thinks he may be allowed downstairs in a few days if he continues to mend like this. Grandmama asked me particularly to come to tea today and Arthur said I should, too. So I came.'

Despite the slightly sulky delivery of this message, Alyssa smiled, touched. She didn't know whether to trust this side of Rowena, but she could not help being affected by it.

'I'm glad, Rowena. And I am glad you came. Good afternoon, Cousin Harriet.' Alyssa bent to kiss Lady Nesbit's wrinkled cheek and then obediently went to sit on the sofa the older lady indicated with her fan. Adam followed, bowing over Lady Nesbit's hands and then bowing politely towards the Misses Mott before joining Alyssa on the sofa.

Once the introductions had been made, there was a moment of awkward silence and Alyssa felt a spurt of panic that none of them would be able to think of anything to say. Then Adam took her hand casually in his and turned to address Rowena.

'We were very glad to hear that Lord Moresby is better, Lady Moresby.'

The gaze of the two Mowbray gossips drank in the clasped hands and Rowena's gracious inclination of her head. Alyssa knew their presence here was no accident and was even reassured by it. It was clear Lady Nesbit would not have invited them if she disapproved of the engagement. No doubt everything that transpired here this afternoon would be common knowledge in Mowbray by nightfall. She hoped Adam knew what he was doing. His hand was warm on hers and the insistent cold that had held her since the attack last night was dissipating slightly.

'It was kind of you to invite us, Lady Nesbit,' Adam said smoothly after a few moments of commonplace enquiries led by Lady Nesbit, his hand tightening on Alyssa's warningly. 'I hope you don't mind, but we would like to seek your advice on a slightly sensitive issue.'

Lady Nesbit directed a shrewd gaze at him and the Mott sisters appeared to lean forward without even having moved.

'Advice?'

'Yes. We are having…a little trouble convincing

Alyssa's father to give his support to our engagement. While we do not formally need his approval, clearly we would prefer to receive it. I recognise that I may not be anyone's ideal choice for a son-in-law, but whatever my past, now that I have come into the title I intend to take my responsibilities seriously. We were hoping that you might help us in convincing Mr Drake that I am worthy of his daughter.'

Alyssa looked down at their clasped hands and pressed her lips firmly together against the need to laugh. She had no idea how he had the audacity to talk such nonsense. It was so ridiculous she wondered that Lady Nesbit did not lean over and give him a good rap on the knuckles with the fan she was plying rhythmically. Alyssa decided to contribute her bit to the farce.

'Do please speak with Father, Cousin Harriet. Adam...I mean Lord Delacort, would not have been in trouble in the first place if Papa would have allowed him to call on me at the cottage. I know it was wrong of us to meet unchaperoned, but I am of age after all, and what are we to do if Papa remains so stubborn?'

For a moment the verdict hung in the balance as Lady Nesbit inspected them. Finally she closed her fan with a snap.

'Your father is a fool, Alyssa,' she said categorically, and though Alyssa was not watching the Mott sisters, she could feel the quiver of excitement that went through them as even the swish of their fans seemed to pick up speed. The sentence had fallen and it would now be reported that Lady Nesbit had given her seal of approval not only to the engagement, but to Lord Delacort as well.

'I will speak to him myself,' Lady Nesbit stated grandly and nodded briskly to herself. 'Meanwhile, you are more than welcome to meet under my aegis here at Nesbit House and under my chaperonage where necessary now that Mrs Aldridge has travelled north. As your poor mother is not here to guide you, Alyssa, I will also willingly act in her stead. As such we should also discuss the marriage arrangements. Lord Delacort, my agent informs me you have already made significant progress in restoring the estate and that there is general approbation amongst the tenants, who quite frankly were less than content under Timothy's and Ivor's mismanagement, and even under old Delacort, who was a crotchety old fool. I am of the opinion that a marriage at the Hall chapel would be very well received in the valley and go a long way to put to rest all these grossly exaggerated tales of your exploits, young man.'

'You are very kind, Lady Nesbit,' Adam replied so meekly Alyssa had to struggle against the urge to giggle. It didn't help that she was so aware of the warm hand resting on hers and the way his fingers were almost imperceptibly caressing her palm through her glove. She had no idea if he was aware he was doing it as he listened so intently to Lady Nesbit, or whether it was pure absence of mind, but those tiny movements seemed as loud as a scream echoing inside her body. Part of her wanted to pull her hand away and remove this proof of her susceptibility, and the other part wished she could strip off her glove so she could feel his fingers directly.

She tried to concentrate on Lady Nesbit's lecture, which had somehow moved on to a discussion of the best dates for the wedding. She listened, fascinated, as Adam and her elderly cousin debated August or September. Lady Nesbit suggested August, since some families might remove to London for the Small Season in September and therefore might miss the ceremony. Adam countered that September had more clement weather and when he added offhandedly that he had been hoping to take advantage of the good weather in Europe in September for their honeymoon, before the cold set in, the two Mott sisters all but tittered excitedly. Lady Nesbit smiled serenely and conceded he had a point and the deal was closed on September.

It was to be a small family ceremony at the chapel followed by a ball for the neighbourhood and there were to be separate festivities organised for the Delacort tenants and their families. Adam accepted this graciously and even managed to remain quite calm when Rowena suggested that Adam's mother be invited to oversee the bridals. Thankfully Lady Nesbit smoothly countered this, stating that she herself would be only too happy to assume the roles required by the mother of the bride.

Once the negotiations were complete, Lady Nesbit wrapped up the meeting with resolution and suggested that Adam take Alyssa back home, while she herself would immediately write a note commanding Mr Drake's presence so she could, in her own words, 'set him straight'. Her final edict was that they attend the Assembly the following day in her company and held out her hand imperiously to Adam. He stood up and smiled as he bowed over her hand and for a moment Lady Nesbit's bony fingers closed tightly on his.

'You're a clever one, Delacort, and providential. But luck only gets you in the door. It don't keep you in the room,' she said, too low for the Mott sisters to hear, and he inclined his head.

'I am well aware of that, Lady Nesbit. Thank you for this.'

She nodded and let his hand go.

'You might do,' she said dismissively and raised her cheek for Alyssa to kiss.

Adam guided Alyssa out the front door and she narrowed her eyes against the high summer sun as she tied the ribbons of her straw bonnet and descended the stairs towards the awaiting curricle. She was relieved the show was over and had been so successful. No doubt, back in the drawing room Lady Nesbit was putting her finishing touches to the story that would be delivered by the Mott sisters to all and sundry in Mowbray.

'That woman should have been a field marshal,' Adam said as he handed her up into the curricle and Alyssa laughed despite her nervousness.

'I know. I had no idea she was going to make such a production of it. Reports of the meeting will be delivered verbatim to everyone within an hour. Having Rowena there was a stroke of genius, but not quite fair to Rowena herself.'

He swung himself up beside her and took the reins from Lady Nesbit's under-groom.

'She did it for you,' he said offhandedly. 'They both did. They care for you.'

Alyssa shook her head.

'I am occasionally useful to them, that is all. I suppose Lady Nesbit considers this some kind of repayment of a debt, or an act of duty, I don't know.'

Adam glanced at her with a slight frown.

'You were the one intent on convincing me they weren't completely unfeeling. Why is it so hard to accept that possibility now?'

She shrugged.

'They are just caught up in the excitement of their own part in this farce. If there had been any genuine feeling for me, there were plenty of opportunities for them to have shown it when there was a real need for their help. Caring is giving when someone really needs you, not when it suits you to give.'

'It may be too little too late, but I think they do care—'

'Please stop,' Alyssa interrupted, putting up her hand abruptly. A wave of misery welled up so powerfully and without warning that she clutched her hands together, pressing them to her chest as though to hold something in by force. Her eyes were burning and she was grateful that her bonnet hid her face. She wished they would get back to the cottage before she broke. At the moment she could not cope with any more dispassionate discussions about their engagement and whether people cared for her or not.

Adam broke off, surprised by the sudden change in her manner. She had acted her part well, with a mixture of serenity and modesty that clearly found favour with Lady Nesbit. But now that he thought about it, he was not surprised she was upset. There was a wealth of pain and disappointment in her history with family members who should have stood by her and her siblings and had done nothing. Except, as she had said, when it had suited them. Before he could respond she spoke again, not looking up.

'I am sorry. I dare say I'm just tired. I did not sleep well.'

Adam breathed in. It was just a sign of how tenuous his self-control was that he would find her words in any way seductive. He was tempted to tell her he had not slept well either and that she was to blame. But she looked too fragile to deal with him on any level and he had no idea how to help her. Not that he had anything of value to offer. Or rather that whatever he had of value, at least what most society considered of value, held no interest for her.

'I'm sorry you have to go through this because

of me,' he said at last, aware of the inadequacy of his words.

'I wish it was all over,' she said urgently and her words sliced through him.

'Well, if whoever is plotting this finds me before I find him, you might have your wish.'

She finally turned to him, her eyes widening in shock.

'That is not what I meant! How could you think…?'

He shrugged and guided the horses over the bridge. He knew she hadn't meant that. He had no idea why he had lashed out at her. It was child-ish and unfair. Instead of easing her pain he was selfishly and unnecessarily adding to it.

'I don't think it,' he said more calmly. 'I'm sorry. I just don't know how to help you.'

Her expression relaxed almost into a smile.

'You don't have to. My family always brings out the worst in me. But I am all right, really I am.'

He shook his head at that obvious lie, angry that he was starting to succumb to precisely the kind of notions of responsibility he found so annoy-ing in her. His role was to make sure she came through this whole episode with minimal damage. It was not to try to help her come to terms with her parasitic and manipulative relatives and it was *not* to offer her comfort. Especially not when he knew very well he had powerful ulterior motives in wanting to comfort her. It was ludicrous that he had to remind himself so often she was not seduction material.

'No, you are not all right,' he said tersely, ignoring his better instincts. 'I would have to be a fool or blind not to see what it costs you to be in this situation. You don't have to confide in me, but don't bother lying.'

She turned away again to look at the passing trees, clasping her hands together more tightly.

'Fine. I won't. I'm too tired to fence with you anyway.'

They had reached the cottage and he drew up his team. He wanted very much to go inside with her, but he couldn't leave his horses outside unattended. He had purposely not brought Jem so he would be forced to resist the temptation of going inside with her. If he was going to have to behave, he would have to keep their encounters as much as possible to public venues. Now he regretted his good resolution. She looked brittle and cold and he hated leaving her in this state. She started rising, but he placed one hand over hers, stopping her.

'Are you cold?' he asked and the corners of her mouth lifted slightly and a glinting smile warmed her eyes.

'As *you* said once—I'm not a child.'

'No. You're not,' Adam said, but did not release her hand, holding back the need to take more than that. He would have thought that after a decade of having become acquainted with all forms of women and expressions of passion, a simple hand clasp wouldn't have this uncomfortable effect. But even with the barrier of gloves, or nothing more than her glinting, half-mischievous smile, somehow she set this feeling off, without effort or intent. And that was the worst of it. It would almost be easier if he could convince himself that this was simply a very clever trap, one that preyed on the almost forgotten need to receive and give comfort and to trust someone other than himself. He felt as tense as the reins holding a team of horses at a headlong gallop. He forced himself to let go.

'Do you think your father will answer her summons?' he asked and she laughed faintly.

'Of course he will. Cousin Harriet is the only one who truly scares Father. I wish I knew her secret.'

'Everyone is scared of something,' he said curtly. 'I will come by tomorrow to escort you to the Assembly. Meanwhile, if you must go somewhere, take Betsy with you, all right?'

She nodded and stepped down from the curricle, her smile fading as she moved towards the gate.

'I will see you tomorrow,' he said again and set his horses in motion again before he found an excuse to follow her inside.

Chapter Sixteen

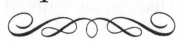

Once again Adam and Nicholas stood at the entrance to the Assembly Rooms, surveying the already crowded dance floor. But this evening, although only a week had passed since their last appearance, their reception was markedly different.

Most obviously, they were not alone. Alyssa stood on Adam's other side, her hand on his arm, looking very lovely and serene and unconcerned in her simple but elegant sea green evening gown held together in the front by silver clasps over a white muslin underdress. Another marked difference was that this time most of Mowbray nobility nodded politely and exchanged greetings with them as they made their way towards Lady Nesbit's usual corner of the hall, where she sat flanked once again by the Misses Mott and several other imposing dowagers.

'Oh, how the mighty have fallen,' Nicholas murmured under his breath.

'Quiet, Nick, or I will send you home.'

'Lissie won't let you. She likes me, don't you, Lissie?' Nicholas protested and Alyssa flicked open her fan to hide an undignified giggle.

'Her name is Miss Drake to you,' Adam said. 'Call her anything else and I will send you home with a broken nose.'

'How did the two of you survive ten years together without throttling each other?' Alyssa asked interestedly.

'Who says I didn't throttle him? Now quiet, both of you. The curtain is up.'

They stopped in front of Lady Nesbit, aware everyone was watching them, either overtly or covertly. Adam bowed to Lady Nesbit and introduced Nicholas, hoping his troublesome friend didn't indulge his worst nature too far. Lady Nesbit listened to Nicholas's practised charm for a moment with a small, appreciative smile before turning to Adam and Alyssa.

'Your father was kind enough to call on me today, Alyssa, and we had a most…fruitful discussion. I was very glad to hear that he has come to regard your alliance with Lord Delacort favourably. I believe you will find that Lord Delacort is most welcome at Drake Cottage from here on. I will convey you home in my carriage this evening and we can discuss some details of your nuptials on the way, child.'

Alyssa nodded modestly.

'Thank you, Cousin Harriet. You have been very kind—'

Lady Nesbit waved her fan dismissively, cutting her off.

'Nonsense. Now go and dance, you two. They are just striking up a waltz and I seem to recall you danced very prettily together last time,' she added archly. 'You, Mr Beauvoir, go and find some young lady to charm. With any luck someone from the area will snare you. Mowbray could use some new blood. All this excitement is doing us good. Well? Go on now!'

Adam bowed and withdrew, meeting his friend's alarmed look with a grin as he led Alyssa to the dance floor.

'I'm beginning to feel very much like a puppet on Cousin Harriet's stage,' Alyssa said once they had taken their places and Adam smiled down at her.

'Never mind. It is giving her a great deal of pleasure and it is certainly doing us a great deal of good, so we have no reason to complain. Though

I don't know what I feel about being told I dance "prettily".'

He watched appreciatively as her eyes lit up with laughter, accompanied by the appearance of her dimple. It was suddenly incomprehensible to him that he had been in this very place two weeks ago, dancing with her… So much had changed in such a short period of time. If someone had told him on that day that in short order he would be fearing for his life while becoming engaged to a very attractive young woman who was determined not to marry him, he would have thought them either mad or very creative.

'Is that what it means to dance "prettily"?' she asked as he pulled her nearer to him as they turned.

'Come a little closer and we'll show them what it means to dance beautifully, then,' he said, brushing his thumb over the palm of her hand with the rhythm of the music. Her lips parted slightly and the gold in her eyes shimmered and captured him, muting the music, the voices around them, everything but the tantalising revelation of watching the wild girl unfurl in his arms. Then her eyelids fluttered down and she smiled at him again, but he could see she had tucked that part of herself in once more.

He knew he should be grateful one of them at

least was being responsible, but contrarily he felt a flash of resentment and he forced himself to relax. It might be ridiculous that he was more on edge because of her than because someone out there wanted him dead, but that wasn't her fault. He changed the subject.

'Percy is looking rather worse for wear now that both Ginnie and your cousin have quit the field.'

Alyssa glanced over at Adam's cousin who was dancing with the rather plain young daughter of a local landowner. He was as flamboyantly dressed as ever, but he looked pale and his usually light-hearted smile looked rigid and forced.

'I still can't quite believe he is behind all this, but I have tried and tried to think of another plausible solution and I can't. Unless it is just some mad-man who hates all Delacorts?'

'From your tone you seem to find that possibility reasonable.'

She dimpled.

'Your predecessors did have a tendency to put up people's backs and, as you know, they were… deficient landlords.'

'That is putting it mildly, but mismanagement is rarely a cause for murder.'

'I know.' She sighed. 'If it were, you wouldn't be at risk.'

'Goodness, an actual compliment. But not quite merited. It was no secret I never planned on staying at the Hall once I put it in order.'

She nodded, her gaze falling, and he wished he had kept silent. He had no idea whether he was trying to convince her or himself that he was still the same man he had been when he had come back to Mowbray. He honestly had no idea if he was, but he could not deal with it now. The question took him too far out on to thin ice.

She shook her head after a moment, following a train of thought of her own.

'No, it doesn't make sense. There must be more to it. It is either Percy or we are missing something.'

He pulled her towards him, amused and exasperated by her tenacity.

'Since the music is winding down, the only thing we have missed so far is the chance to enjoy this dance. I'm beginning to think that my only redeeming quality is that there is someone trying to get rid of me.'

Her eyes rose to his, intent and serious.

'You know that's not true,' she said, but her tone was almost scolding, like the voice she might have used with her siblings, and he felt disappointed. There was always something she held back, some private place from where she stood and surveyed the world. He told himself it was idiotic to expect her to allow him in. She owed him nothing. And it was best like that.

The orchestra played the last chords of the dance and they stepped apart. Then Nicholas came forward to lead Alyssa in the next dance and Adam moved away. Across the room Lady Nesbit beckoned to him imperiously and he sighed and headed in her direction. No doubt she had found him his next dance partner. Being reformed had distinct disadvantages.

Chapter Seventeen

Alyssa hurried along the High Street towards Milsom's. Her heart was thudding and the letter she had just paid for and collected from the postmaster felt hot and harsh even through her gloves, but she had a superstitious fear of letting it out of her grasp. She resisted the urge to stop in the middle of the street and break open the seal. She needed someplace private and Milsom's would do just fine if it wasn't crowded. Mr Milsom was used to letting her sit at the back of the store and read his books ever since she was a little child and she knew he would not bother her.

She pushed open the door to the bookstore and glanced in. Mr Milsom was behind the counter, talking with a customer, and after a brief greeting both men returned to their gossip. She hurried to a window seat that overlooked the backyard of the store and opened the letter.

Her eyes flew over the sentences, then again, her ears filling with a peculiar rushing sound. She put the paper down on her lap, then picked it up again. Her body felt cold inside, hot outside, and she thought she might be sick. She wanted to crush the letter to her, squeal with joy and show it to everyone. She read it again, trying to see if she was wrong. Or perhaps reading too much into those simple words. To be sure it wasn't utterly conclusive. And yet it was so much better than she had expected. Should she tell? No. Not until she was certain. She would have to go to London. Soon.

Very little could have distracted Alyssa from the contents of this particular letter, but the sight of Percy entering the store and heading towards her purposefully succeeded. She put the letter into her reticule, took a deep breath, stood up and waited.

Percy stopped in front of her, a bit too close for polite conversation, and she could smell brandy on his breath. She glanced over at Mr Milsom, but after greeting Percy he had once again returned to his conversation. Still, she felt comforted by his presence. Surely she was not in danger with Mr Milsom there.

'Miss Drake. Good thing I found you. I want a word with you. I went by the cottage. Your girl said you would be in town. Thought you might be here.'

'Did you, Mr Somerton? How can I help you?' she asked and Percy rushed into speech, as if her cool request had been an invitation to indulge in full confidence.

'Listen, I know you don't like me. I mean I know you wanted Mary for Charlie, not that I think she'll have him. He's just a boy. But other than that… And it's not that I particularly wanted to be married, but I'm not saying I wouldn't have tried to make a go of it. I'm tired of Mowbray anyway, nothing ever seems to go right for me here. First Adam cuts me off, and then that whole thing with Mrs Eckley and Mary leaving… I don't know why I've stayed so long except it's been comfortable, you know, when I was at the Hall, and I suppose I've been too lazy to do anything else, but it's no fun any more.'

He paused, his eyes moving from her face to the books behind her as if he had lost his train of thought and might find it on their leather spines.

'The point is, now that you're engaged to Adam, you could get him to do something for me. I'm not greedy, whatever he may think, but he has more money than he'll ever know what to do with. He won't want me here now he's setting up to stay anyway. We never did get along. I mean he didn't pick on me like Timothy and Ivor, except that one time he near broke my nose over Charlie, but I suppose that was my fault, in a way, but he always looked down on me. So will you talk to him? You've always been decent...'

Alyssa listened to this rambling monologue with growing confusion. She did not know what she had expected, but it wasn't this. There seemed nothing to connect this slightly inebriated and petulant appeal with the cunning she had expected from someone who had patiently and violently schemed over several years to inch his way into the Delacort title.

'What exactly would you like me to ask him?' she questioned, trying to gain time to think.

'What? Ask him if he'll give me something to set me up away from here. Make a new start. I'd have to take Libbet with me, of course. He's been with us for ever and frankly I don't know what I'd do without him. Maybe the Americas. Boston. No, too strait-laced. Maybe South America. Or India. A fellow could do well there. Look at Adam. But I need some capital over and above my income to get myself started, you know.'

She was just about to answer when the door opened with more violence than was usual in Milsom's establishment and Adam entered, barely acknowledging the startled greetings directed at him. His gaze scanned the store, settled on her and moved forward with a single-minded force that penetrated even Percy's spirit-laden fog. He blinked and inched to the side, putting her between them nervously.

She raised her hand slightly, holding Adam's gaze with hers, and he slowed perceptibly.

'Hello, Adam,' she said calmly. 'I am glad you are here. Percy and I have just been talking and—'

'I am aware of that,' he interrupted. 'I have just been by the cottage and Betsy informed me Percy came to look for you. And that she told him you were in town—'

'Lovely,' she intervened again, ignoring the nervous twitch of Percy's hands, 'since this involves you directly. Percy has expressed an interest in your advancing him some funds so he could go abroad somewhere and make a fresh start. He asked for my help in approaching you, since he knows you two did not get off on the right foot since your return to Mowbray.'

Adam's expression did not change, but the look in his eyes was eloquent. She raised her brows slightly.

'I rather think this is a good idea,' she concluded simply.

Percy nodded, obviously encouraged by her calm support.

'It doesn't have to be a lot. A few ponies should do it. Enough to get a go somewhere else. You know, I could even go out to my mother's family in Barbados. Lots of English there. Good people. Could cut a dash there on very little, I should think. Dare say my income would go further there than here.'

The rising enthusiasm in his voice had obviously finally caught Adam's attention and Alyssa could almost see his thoughts and doubts mirror her own.

'Barbados,' Adam repeated slowly and Percy nodded, his light blue eyes filling with sudden hope.

'My mother was from there. I remember her telling me about it when I was small. I might even like it.'

Adam stood considering him for a moment. Then he glanced around the store.

'I see. I think it would be a good idea if we discussed this somewhere else. Perhaps you should come by the Hall this afternoon...'

Before Percy could reply, the door opened once more and Libbet stepped in. He nodded to Milsom and the man at the counter, then bowed towards

Adam and Alyssa, greeting them with his usual calm deference before turning to Percy.

'I have completed my errands, Mr Somerton. Will you be returning to Turl Street?'

Percy hesitated and turned to Adam.

'I'll come by this afternoon, then? Say around four?'

Adam nodded, watching Percy's valet as the man stood near the door, his gaze neutral.

'Four o'clock. Mr Beauvoir is away, so we can sit down and discuss your suggestion in private, but I think going to Barbados sounds like a very good idea.'

Once again Percy's angelic face lit up with an engaging grin. He nodded and hurried out, as if afraid Adam might change his mind. Alyssa watched Libbet as he bowed once more before turning to follow Percy. For a moment his pale blue gaze met hers and she wondered what this dapper man would think about Percy's plans. It seemed unfair he had no say in a matter that affected him so closely. But surely he could always resign his post if he did not wish to go with Percy. She was sure Adam would say she was being ridiculous worrying about him. Still…

'Come. I want to talk to you,' Adam said, taking her arm and leading her towards the door.

'Good. So do I,' she replied, nodding to the two men at the counter. 'Good day, Mr Milsom, Mr Grantley.'

They stepped outside on to the High Street where Thunder stood patiently by the pavement, gazing off into the middle distance and ignoring a small boy who stood staring up at him in awe.

'Hello, Johnny,' Alyssa said and the boy turned to her.

'Miss Drake! He's so big! Roddy says he eats rocks!'

She laughed, realising suddenly how tense she'd been. Too much had happened in that short time at Milsom's.

'Roddy is very creative, but I think Thunder prefers apples. Right, Adam?'

'He does, and carrots, but especially turnips.'

'Turnips!' The boy wrinkled his nose in disgust, eyeing Thunder suspiciously. He turned back to Adam. 'You're the scary lord.'

'Am I?' Adam asked politely.

'Roddy said you slayed a giant and stole his gold, but you don't look very scary.'

'I'm glad to hear I don't look very scary and I think Miss Drake was right when she said Roddy is very creative. And now we have to go, so make your bow, Thunder.'

The boy watched, delighted, as Thunder serenely bent one knee, moving back on his hind legs slightly to sink into an impressive bow.

'I've got to tell Roddy!' Johnny announced, dashing off down the street.

'Who on earth is Roddy?' Adam asked as he took Thunder's reins and they began walking down the High Street.

'Johnny's very mischievous older brother. They are Mr Curtis's sons. He's the greengrocer and postmaster.'

'Do you know everyone in Mowbray?' Adam said curiously and she smiled.

'Pretty much, I suppose. I've lived here all my life.'

'So have Percy and Rowena and I sincerely doubt they know either of those boys.'

They turned off the High Street on to the narrower road leading in the direction of Drake Cottage and she shrugged.

'They have other interests. Speaking of which, I admit I don't know what to think about Percy. I know he was a little the worse for wear, but he really didn't sound like a man who had either killed anyone or who was plotting to do so. He just sounded like a spoiled little boy who was tired and discouraged and wanted to get away.'

'Alyssa, so help me…if you start telling me you feel sorry for him, I don't know what I will do.'

'I don't feel sorry for him precisely. Well, a little. I feel worse for Libbet actually. It can't be easy to have your future decided for you without having any say in the matter.'

'I see you are already proceeding on the assumption that Percy is not involved in the attacks. And before you put Libbet on your ever expanding compassion list, remember he is so well respected a valet he could easily get employment elsewhere if he wished. No one is forcing him to stay with Percy.'

She frowned. 'I suppose. But I think he will. He has been with the Somertons since he was a boy, I think, and you could see that he is obviously very attached to Percy, goodness knows why. But the main point is that either Percy is a supreme actor, much better even than your delectable Mrs Eckley, or what we saw was sincere. In which case he isn't involved. Frankly I've never managed to convince myself he was behind all these years of murderous plotting. What on earth do we do now? This is almost as bad as it would be if Percy *was* guilty.'

'May I remind you that Ginnie is not *my* Mrs Eckley, but very happily married to a good friend of mine? And as for Percy…' He trailed off, looking ahead and obviously lost in thought.

She looked up at the strong lines of his profile and realised suddenly, no longer with surprise but with familiar warmth, how natural she felt with him. More secure on the ground. As if she had been walking on a rope—like the fair people who came through every spring and set up in the field outside Faringdon—and he had come and helped her down to level earth.

She remembered the letter folded in her reticule. Whatever happened, she would not get back up on that rope. He turned to look at her and she smiled, full of gratitude and joy and even an acceptance of the hurt that was yet to come. She knew without a doubt that she would not have forgone knowing him and loving him simply to be spared pain even if she had had the choice.

He stopped walking all of a sudden, looking down at her. He seemed distant and almost stricken, as if a painful memory had occurred to him. She wished it was her right to reach out to him. To step forward and put her arms around him, give him comfort and feel the heat and strength of his body against hers.

'As for Percy…?' she prompted after a moment and he frowned and the intent expression faded.

'Percy. Yes. It occurred to me… You might be right. Do you remember Percy's father? You would have been quite young when he died.'

'I do remember him. I think I was eight or nine. He was rather like old Lord Delacort, but much worse. Very dark and brutish. They lived in the old dower house, but Percy went to stay up at the Hall nursery with Timothy and Ivor to share a tutor with them when his mother died. I don't think his father was very fond of him. People used to say it was because Percy looked so much like his mother. Apparently she was very lovely and angelic, but frail. I can't imagine why she married someone like Somerton, but then she must have been very young and had very little say in the matter. I just think he was an extremely nasty individual and couldn't be bothered with a young boy around the house. Why? What are you thinking?'

He shook his head again and turned away to stroke Thunder's neck.

'Nothing. Nothing that makes sense. None of this makes sense.'

'What are you going to do? About Percy?'

'As you suggested, send him, and Libbet, to Barbados. I will tell him today when he comes.'

She sighed.

'I'm glad.'

He looked back at her with a wry smile.

'You are incorrigible.'

'So I am. However, this doesn't solve our problem, does it? Now we have no idea who is behind the attacks and we have no apparent motive for them. We might as well be back with my theory of a Delacort-hating madman.'

'Perhaps. But it is not *our* problem, but mine. Is there anywhere you could go and stay for a couple weeks outside of Mowbray? Perhaps with your sister or brother?'

'What?' she gasped, too surprised to hide it. 'Why?'

'Because Percy is a known quantity. If we take him out of the equation, we have to introduce an unknown quantity. And so far none of our other enquiries has borne fruit. Which makes me think we are dealing with someone a great deal cleverer than I had originally thought. I would be much easier if you were out of the line of fire for the moment.'

'I am sorry I am so much in the way, Lord Delacort,' she said coldly, moving ahead. They had reached the cottage gate and she opened it, but he reached out, stopping her.

'You are not… Well, yes, you are, but don't make it sound as if I am being ungrateful. I am very grateful for everything you have done for me, but I need to be focused on this problem completely and I can't be if I have to worry about your welfare.'

'No one asked you to worry about me.'

'Don't be facetious,' he replied. 'Of course I worry about you being hurt because of me. It would only be for a week or so. Please.'

'Asking prettily does not make it any more acceptable, Lord Delacort!'

'Just think about it for the moment. I will come to you after I speak with Percy and we will see what is to be done, all right?'

She looked up at him, her green eyes full of suspicion, and he wished she would smile at him again. That open, accepting, enfolding smile she had flashed up at him before he had ruined it. It had caught him off guard, like a soft warm hand reaching through a thicket of brambles. He had been unarmed and unprepared for the burst of emotion it had evoked. He could still feel its aftermath, like a sharp, bitter thorn lodged at his centre, unwilling to be ignored.

He wanted to say something else to her, but she promptly stepped through the gate, closing it behind her with a snap, and strode off towards the cottage without another word.

Adam watched her disappear and then swung on to Thunder's back, turning him towards the Hall. He rubbed his chest as if that could dispel the stabbing ache, resisting the urge to go back to her and…and what?

He had no idea what had just happened, just that her smile had prised open a Pandora's Box and there was no going back. He had no idea how this need had come to dominate everything else. It was ludicrous and irrational. And undeniable. And irrelevant. Because if he was not safe, there was no point in even considering any of this. If he could not lift this cloud that hung over him, there was no way he could drag her under it even if she was willing. And he had no real idea if she was. The wild girl might enjoy his seduction and the little crusader enjoy championing him, but he knew there was much more to her than those two extremes of her nature.

He wanted the warm, generous woman who had just smiled up at him on the lane with a powerful need he could hardly believe was something that existed inside him. He leaned forward, stroking Thunder's neck, as if that could calm the rush of heat and desire that struck him, leaving him mute and confused under its control.

He wanted to go back and force himself, and her,

to deal with what was happening, but he knew he couldn't, not yet. Right now he just had to make certain she was protected from what he was about to set in motion. She was obviously hurt and angry at him, but he could not let that weigh with him at the moment. Once she calmed down, she would see he was right.

In any case, if his suspicion was correct, which was doubtful, he might know within the week. And until then he had to have her safe, away from Mowbray. Because every time he let his fear for her dominate him, he made mistakes. Like that night in the woods. Even this afternoon when he had come to call on her and Betsy had innocently revealed Percy had come looking for her as well. He had made that short ride into town in record time and, until he had seen her safe and sound at Milsom's, he had been possessed by sharp clawing fear he'd never experienced before. No matter what he told himself, that it made no sense that she should be in any danger, he could not stamp out the fear that something would happen to her, because of him. And that was not acceptable.

It had never been so imperative to resolve this issue. Permanently. Because for the first time he admitted he had no intention of leaving Mowbray. Even with all the madness and the absurdity of his situation, he felt comfortable here, a completely unfamiliar sensation. At home in a way he could not remember ever feeling, not even as a child. Because of her. He had to fix this. And then, once it was over, he had to find out how she felt.

He knew that aside from often being exasperated with him, she did like him, was even attracted to him, but perhaps she knew him too well to feel anything more profound. Sometimes he thought she regarded him as no more than the object of her latest quest, a useful distraction from reality. He would have to make certain he was more than that. Because he now knew he wanted everything from her. Whatever it took.

He must have tightened his hands on the reins for Thunder whinnied in protest. Adam leaned forward and patted his neck apologetically.

'Sorry, old boy. You wouldn't mind if we stayed here, would you? It would be a relief not to be moved about all the time. I'd find you a nice mare and we'd see if you can sire anything half as fast as you.'

Thunder ignored the suggestion but allowed Adam to urge him into a canter.

Chapter Eighteen

Adam glanced up from the papers on his desk at the knock on his door.

'Come in,' he called and Stebbins opened the door.

'Mr Somerton, Lord Delacort,' he said with a slight bow. Standing, he stood back to let Percy in.

Adam stood and motioned Percy towards two armchairs placed by the large fireplace. He appeared to have sobered up and looked as neat as always, but there was a still a slight flush on his face, making him look younger and less urbane than usual. Adam noted he was also wearing a much more subdued waistcoat than normal. He sat down and Percy rushed to speak.

'Listen, I wanted to apologise for this morning. I was a bit under the hatches, you know, Dutch courage and all that. I hope I didn't offend Miss Drake. Never meant to do that.'

Adam did not particularly want to discuss Alyssa with Percy. He sat down on the other armchair.

'I don't think she was offended, Percy. Shall we get down to business?'

Percy laughed uncomfortably and rubbed his palms over his pale yellow pantaloons.

'You always were direct. Very well. It's up to you anyway. I told you I don't need much, just enough to get me started. Will you do it?'

'I will. I will provide you with enough blunt to get you and Libbet to Barbados and set up there. In addition, I own a property in Jamaica which is currently under the management of a local agent and yields an income of around eight hundred pounds a year. I will sign this income over to you on condition that neither you nor Libbet ever return to England without my express permission. If you do, the deal is off. Understood?'

Percy stared at him.

'That's more than I expected,' he said with unusual honesty.

'Do you want it or not?'

'Yes. Of course I do.'

'And you accept my condition? About you and Libbet?'

'Of course!' he repeated with growing enthusiasm. Adam scanned the good-looking, eager face across from him.

'It must have been a sore disappointment when you realised I had come into the title and estate,' he stated abruptly and Percy's eagerness dimmed under the weight of a bemused frown.

'A disappointment? But I always knew you would inherit. You were next in line, so it stands to reason. In fact, I always thought you were the most likely of the lot of us to settle down and have a brood of brats, whatever everyone thought. You always were the serious, bookish one. And I was right, too, in the end, wasn't I?'

'So you didn't want the title yourself?'

'Me? Not to say I wouldn't have liked the money, if it didn't mean doing all the work. But the place was a shambles and costing more than it gave out, so it would only have meant a lot of headaches and having to deal with things I know nothing about. Timothy and Ivor always complained everyone was always after them to take care of this or that… crop rotations and livestock and tenants hounding them with grievances. I like not having to think about things like that. Not in my line at all. I just wanted things back the way they were…'

Adam considered this ingenious attitude. He was not surprised at Percy's combination of modesty and venality. It suited his understanding of his cousin much more than the image he had tried to construct of a clever, patient plotter. He changed the subject.

'Will Libbet want to go with you?'

Percy looked surprised.

'I should think so. Been with us for ever.'

'He was your father's valet, as well?'

Percy grimaced.

'He was. Took over from his own father when old Libbet passed. Don't think my father was very fond of him, or vice versa. He abused Libbet roundly, but he knew his worth, especially since we couldn't afford many servants. Well, he abused everyone. Mama most of all. Don't know if you remember her.'

'I do, vaguely. We came to the Hall one Christmas long before we moved to Mowbray. I remember thinking she looked like an angel.'

'She did, didn't she? Never should have married my father, but she was barely seventeen when they handed her over to him. He had these moods. She knew when they were coming and she'd take me up to Libbet's room and tell him to keep me safe until it was over. I suppose it became a habit with him, looking after me. Or maybe because Mama was always kind to him. Never treated him like he was beneath her. She was a good woman.'

He rubbed one finger moodily along the silver stem of his quizzing glass.

'I remember her telling me about Barbados. How much she missed it. Said she would take me there one day.'

'And now you're going.' Adam said quietly and Percy's expression lifted.

'So I am. Strange world. So what do I do now?'

'Now I will have Thorpe draw up and deliver a draft on my bank in Oxford. He will also accompany you and Libbet to Bristol and will book you on a ship to the West Indies. Be ready to go by the end of the week.'

'So soon?' Percy gaped at him and Adam nodded.

'So soon. Any objection?'

'No…no.' He grinned suddenly. 'Dash it all, I'm looking forward to this! I've never been further than London. What an adventure! I think I'll like it much better than being married!'

Adam almost smiled at Percy's ingenious take on his offer. He stood up and extended his hand.

'You had better go and tell Libbet, then, and start packing.'

'I will.' He shook Adam's hand and wandered

out, looking slightly stunned. Adam closed the door behind him. He had a great deal to take care of in a short amount of time. Perhaps he should have waited until the following day, but he could not count on his antagonist waiting on his pleasure.

He hoped Nicholas would return soon; he would need him at his back now. He headed out towards the stables. He needed to see Jem. And then he needed to convince Alyssa to leave as soon as possible. It would be too late for her to set out today, but tomorrow morning would have to do. He would send her in the Delacort carriage. There would be nothing unusual about that, since they were engaged. That way he could have Jem go with her and keep an eye on her until she was safely away. Just in case.

Chapter Nineteen

Half an hour later he hitched Thunder up in his favourite corner in the orchard and headed towards the cottage. Alyssa answered his knock.

'Have you seen Percy already?' she asked immediately.

'May I come in or shall we do this on the doorstep?' he enquired politely.

She stood back, her dimple flashing. Apparently she had recovered from her annoyance, or at least it was subordinate to her curiosity for the moment.

'Do, pray come in, sir,' she said graciously and led the way into her back parlour. 'Well? Did you?'

She sat down and clasped her hands, looking up at him as expectantly as a little girl awaiting a gift. He looked down at her, wishing he could just forget everything and sit down next to her, take her hands and convince her she needed to be with him. He intended to do whatever it took to make it clear to her this engagement was no longer a sham. But right now the most important thing was to keep her safe.

'I did,' he replied.

'And?'

'And he has agreed to go to Barbados. With Libbet.'

'For a price.'

'Of course.'

'I see. And you are quite convinced it isn't him?'

'Yes.'

Her shoulders sagged slightly.

'So...what now?'

He took a deep breath. There was no way around this.

'Now you go somewhere for a few days until I can figure out what is to be done next.'

Her reaction was as he'd expected. Her eyes darkened to forest green and her mouth flattened ominously.

'No. I told you, you can't just pack me off somewhere. I am not your property.'

'I am not packing you off. I am asking you, as a favour, to please go and stay with your brother or sister, just for a few days. Please.'

Her glare didn't lighten, but when she did not answer he pressed forward, keeping his voice calm.

'This has nothing to do with not wanting you here, or not wanting you to interfere. Whether you accept it or not, the fact that you are at risk because of me is a distraction. And when I am distracted I might make mistakes. I don't want to make a mistake that might put you at further risk—'

He broke off at the sound of the squealing gate and footsteps hurrying up the path to the house.

'For heaven's sake, can't we have *one* conversation without someone interrupting?' he said, exasperated.

Alyssa didn't answer but stood up and went to the door just as Betsy knocked and opened it. She glanced in and seeing Adam she flushed and bobbed a curtsy, handing Alyssa a sealed letter.

'Mr Curtis said you hurried out so quickly this morning he did not get a chance to give you this letter, miss. It's been franked! By a lord!' She giggled and backed out rapidly.

Alyssa, who had taken it from her with a puzzled frown, smiled suddenly.

'It's from Charlie! It was franked by… I can't quite make out the name… Lord Barsford? Oh, could you wait just one moment? I must see if everything is all right.'

She didn't wait for his approval and Adam smiled ruefully. Clearly he would not get any attention from her until she found out if her little brother was well. Perhaps the interruption was well timed. It would give a chance for her temper to cool and for her to absorb what he'd said.

She broke the seal and frowned at the scrawled lines. He watched her face—the soft parting of her lips as she smiled at something in the letter, the way her thick lashes met and then finally swept upwards, revealing her amazing eyes, liquid and inviting in a way she was completely unconscious of.

'He's writing in response to my letter about Mary,' she explained, her eyes twinkling with amusement. 'He says he hopes Mary will have a fine time up at the Lake District and that he hopes she meets "a fellow worthy of her" and then he proceeds to tell me what a marvellous time he is having with the Barsfords who live near Ely. He thinks that I would like them and particularly Miss Barsford, who knows Greek and Aramaic and is a "devilish good horsewoman, too". Which explains all, I suppose. Must I admit you were right about my foolishness in trying to endow poor Charlie with my silly notions of love?'

She folded the letter and sighed, but the dimple was still there. Again he stopped himself from reaching out to touch her. Under the amusement she looked more vulnerable than ever, as if in dis-

arding his first love so easily, Charlie had somehow betrayed *her* rather than Mary. He moved
towards her.

'Simply because he is enjoying a series of infat-
uations doesn't mean he is suddenly the authority
on whether you ought to believe in love or not.'

She fingered the folded letter and laughed
slightly.

'That, coming from you? But you are right again,
I suppose. And it is too late for me anyway...'

She spoke lightly, but there was something in
her voice which sharpened his senses, as if the
danger was present right there in the room with
them. When he spoke, his voice was harsher than
he intended.

'What do you mean?'

She looked up, surprised.

'Nothing.'

'Not nothing. What did you mean? Are you in
love with someone?'

She blinked and looked down, but he had seen
the sudden glaze of tears.

'It was years ago,' she said simply, but her voice
was husky and everything changed. He felt very
far away, as if the room had suddenly expanded
and he could see everything at a distance. He saw
her, whom he had ridiculed for wanting to love,

who did love… And there was an echoing, child-ish denial that spoke in him.

You can't be in love with someone else. You have to love me.

Everything from the moment she had come to his study weeks ago came back to him, like beads finally strung together. He should have seen this. How could he have not realised? He must have realised, somewhere along the way. Because he wasn't surprised. Just in agony. He should have left long ago. He should have guessed there was more behind the fact she had never married. Beneath the vulnerability and the pain he had preyed on for his own purposes.

'What happened?' he forced himself to ask.

She shrugged, not looking up.

'Nothing. He didn't want me.'

The pain hit again and he waited for it to peak and subside. He wanted to tell her she would get over it and forget it, as he had with Rowena, but he said nothing. Because it was obvious that she had not forgotten it. The pain was still there and the loss. Emotions that had nothing to do with his blind, childish fixation on Rowena. He could feel them and for the first time he really knew what they meant and he didn't know if he could bear it. He reached out to the anchor of violent fury he felt against this man she wanted. He wanted to hurt him. Annihilate him. He would erase him. He strode forward and took her hands, drawing her to her feet.

'He's a fool.'

Her lips parted, but he didn't give her a chance to respond. He raised her face and kissed her with a desperation he could do nothing to mask, pulling her against him, wishing he could strip her bare, strip the universe bare of anything that separated her from him. She didn't pull away and her body shuddered against his with a tremor that shot through him like a galvanic force, tightening his body unbearably. He wanted to clear her mind of everything but him and what he was doing to her. He wanted her naked, crying out his name as she climaxed. He wanted to be buried in her so deeply he would never come out.

He bent to find that spot just below her ear that had made her cry out before. She did not disappoint him, whimpering as his mouth abraded the soft skin, her hands fisting on his coat, and he was swamped by a surge of both triumph and torture. He could make her desire him. But he wanted more. Infinitely more. He couldn't stand the thought she might be thinking of someone else.

He kissed her, carefully, softly, the atavistic urge

held back by a strange fear. Her hands released his coat, moved gently against his chest, mirroring the soft brush of his lips over hers, and he gave in, sliding his hands into her hair, deepening the kiss, and she moaned against his mouth, sinking against him once more, her hands pulling him to her. He felt her body shaking against him and the strange tentative fear was swamped by heat and triumph and resolve—he would show her what pleasure was; he would erase any thoughts she had of anyone but him.

'Say my name,' he demanded hoarsely.

Her eyes drifted open, already dreamy and lost. Her mouth opened, but no sound came out and he traced his fingers over the damp, flushed curve of her lower lip before bending to brush his mouth over it, coaxing, teasing.

'Say my name.'

'Adam…' It was barely audible, a slide of air on air, but it burned through him and he moved away slightly. She reached up, her hands around his neck, pulling his head back to hers.

'Adam.' This time his name was lost against his mouth as he kissed her fervently again and her lips parted without protest, slanting under his to give him full access. He bit gently into her lower lip, running his tongue lightly across it, and she moaned.

He slid his hands over her back, her hips, pressing her back until they both came up against the desk. He raised her so she was seated on the wooden surface and he moved between her legs and he felt himself hot and hard against the juncture of her thighs. Her body jerked slightly as if in surprise and then melted, her hands pulling herself against him so that her breasts were pressed to his chest. Adam's knees buckled for a moment under the intensity of his body's response to that sign of her need.

'Alyssa...'

Her eyes opened again, but there was nothing dreamy in them now; they were hot with emerald fire that fed the stretching, demanding urgency that ran like a vortex through his body.

'My wild girl,' he whispered, his hands threading through her hair, loosening it from ribbons and pins until it spilled over them, a warm, honeyed waterfall that gleamed even in the dim light. He drew one silky lock down over the soft skin above the bodice of her plain muslin dress, over the beautiful breasts he was aching to uncover. Her legs clamped against him, as if trying to draw him closer or reject him, but he ignored her and slid the dress from one shoulder, following its descent with his mouth.

'Adam…' she whispered, her head arching back in unconscious surrender and he obliged, sliding the fabric slowly over her breast. She shivered as he bared her, her hands tightening almost painfully on his arms as he touched his mouth to the soft swell. He kissed her breast slowly, just skimming the heated, tightening flesh. He could feel her breaths, short and hard, beneath his lips and her hands moved against him almost jerkily, grasping his shirt, dragging it up until her fingers found his skin as if she needed to attach herself to him directly. Her touch spread over his sides to his back, and as she moved, his blood rushed to follow the torturing path of her hands until it was unbearable.

He pulled up her skirts enough to slide his hand over her thigh, under her backside, raising her against him, a cry of protest and desperation gathering deep in his throat at the unbearable silkiness of her skin and the undeniable heat that met his erection even through their clothing. He hadn't realised how hard he was until he felt himself against her. He was prepared for her to pull away, but she just tightened her legs against him, as if to anchor him there.

'Adam, please,' she gasped, her eyes locking on

his, translucent and demanding. Her mouth was open and moist and her brows contracted as if in pain. But the maddening, burning, wonderful movement of her hips against him spoke of another suffering.

'Adam, please,' she repeated hoarsely, her hands skimming down his chest to his waist, burning him. He knew what he had to do, what he wanted to see... He bent his head to kiss her neck as he moved his hand between them. His body bucked as his fingers slid down to the moist fire below and he almost exploded there just from touching her. Her body shuddered at his touch, but the shudder turned into an almost animal cry as his fingers brushed that small, essential inch of skin. He stroked her there again and again while his other hand traced a line from her throat to her shoulder, pulling down more of the bodice of her dress to reveal both breasts, trailing his fingers lightly over the warm, pliant skin. Her flesh tightened under his touch and a moan deep in her throat sent thunder through his veins. He bent to brush his lips across her breast again, coaxing her with his fingers, his senses filling with her. He could feel her whimpers echoing through her body wherever he touched her. He drew back slightly and saw disbelief, wonder and an incredible need in her un-veiled eyes.

He had never seen anything even close to that look on her face and he wanted it. He *needed* it. Her eyes closed again as he increased the pressure of his fingers, then relieved it to brush her just lightly. He was shaking with the effort to hold back, but he wouldn't stop now. He wanted more from her.

'Look at me,' he bit out, his voice a tight growl. He withdrew his hand slightly and her eyes flew open at the sudden loss of contact.

'Look at me,' he commanded as he returned his hand, stroking her once, lightly. He wanted her looking at him as she climaxed, he wanted to see the need, the pleasure in her incredible eyes. He wanted his face burned in her mind when she came.

Her eyes locked with his, the blood rushing to her cheeks as she half-realised how far she had gone, but his hand was there again, the other moving to the breast his mouth had abandoned. She gave in fully, her eyes on him, squirming against his hand, trying to increase the pressure. His rhythm controlled her breathing now and she followed, shaking with each touch, her eyes drowning in his blackened gaze.

'My name,' he rasped. 'Say my name.'

'Adam…' she complied and her head arched back, her eyes closing, her hands tightening on him as she came.

Adam didn't move, torturing himself with the last of her shudders. At that last moment before she had closed her eyes he had seen the wonder there, the sudden incredible joy. And he cursed himself for wanting to see that. His whole body was so tense he didn't think he could move away if someone shoved a pistol into his back now. He wanted to take her. His body told him there was no stopping now. She wanted this. He could take her, make her unequivocally his. There would be no going back from it. He would take away her choice to refuse their marriage.

The implacable brutality of that final thought cut through the blaze of desire. He wanted this more than he could remember wanting anything, but he knew he could not force her hand. She already thought him thoroughly ruthless and manipulative. To take advantage of her like this would only confirm it. And she would be right. He could not do that, no matter how desperate he was to keep her. He wanted more from her and that meant he had to demand more from himself.

But he had marked her. He had seen her as no

one had ever seen her. And in his present state he thought he might kill before he let anyone else witness that. The primitive possessiveness of this thought shocked him back into some sanity and for the first time he felt the cold air against his skin. He forced himself to draw down her skirts. Her eyes flickered open, meeting his with a languid, faraway look that seared through him. He was about to throw caution to the wind when her expression changed to consternation. In one lithe movement she slipped off the desk, turning her back to him as she arranged her dress.

He watched her back, his body tense and singing with the need to turn her around, take her back to that peak of pleasure and join her there. He had no idea what to say. Should he apologise? Words would hardly answer here. Yet he did not know what else to do.

'I'm sorry,' he said and saw her stiffen. 'I should never have taken advantage—' He stopped abruptly. There was nothing he could say that would explain or justify it. 'I have to go now. Pack and we will discuss tomorrow if and where you should go. Please stay indoors.'

He didn't wait for her to respond. He needed to leave before what was left of his resolve melted completely.

Chapter Twenty

Alyssa pulled the blanket more closely about her, wondering if she had the strength to set a taper to the wood stacked in the fireplace. She was not sure if the weather had really turned, or whether this was just the numb cold of confusion. Since it was punctuated by burning heat when the memories of that afternoon intruded, as they often did, she thought it must be just a symptom of her internal chaos and not a sign the unseasonably warm summer weather was abating.

She could hardly believe she had acted as she had, with such total abandon. She had practically begged to be touched. She'd had no idea it could feel like that, that her body was capable of such pleasure. It seemed incredible that such capacity for joy had been dormant in her all this time, waiting for release. She felt larger, more present in the world. And she knew that no matter what happened with Adam going forward she would not be able to put the genie back in the bottle. It was only terrible that after such a cataclysmic upheaval in her little world, he had dared to apologise. She felt again the blaze of fury she had experienced at his words, a blaze that had contrarily held her silent, too shocked and ashamed even to speak. She wished she had…

It occurred to her suddenly that though Adam had apologised, perhaps he had known precisely what he was doing. He had played her skilfully. She might be innocent, but she was not a fool. He had taken it into his mind that the only way to proceed was as he had initially suggested. To turn this sham engagement into a marriage of convenience. And he had taken her as far down that path as his honour had permitted him.

And it was her fault. She had put the final card into his hand with her foolish admission about having been in love and rejected, adding the potent ingredient of pity into his considerations of duty, responsibility, propriety and convenience. And lust. She had no doubt he wanted to bed her. She had seen the blazing desire in his eyes as he had turned to leave and it had been a kind of mercy, but if she was brutally honest with herself she would have to face that she was not unique in this sense.

Just so, he had probably wanted to bed his string of mistresses and Venetian countesses. As much as she might want to, she would not delude herself that the passion he'd bestowed on her was as extraordinary for him as for her. But until he had pitied her he had never crossed the line of true seduction as he had that afternoon. And even then he had drawn back, though she would never have stopped him. Her whole body flushed with shame and remembered pleasure. She'd had no idea it could feel so good, so right...

She knew it might take more strength than she had to oppose his will if he really wanted to go ahead with this marriage. Or perhaps she was already there. She tightened her hold on the blanket. At the moment the thought of sharing his life with his other...interests seemed more than bearable. And perhaps, if she really set her mind to it, could she make him care for her?

After all, she was smart and she understood him. She was not blinded by the rakish charm. What drew her to him was what lay beyond it, the struggle between his strength and vulnerability, the irreverent humour and the need to be taken at face value. She straightened slightly. Whatever he might think, she was better equipped to give him what he needed than anyone she could think of, selfish countesses included. And she already knew he could give her what she needed, if only he was really willing...

She started in alarm as the door out to the garden swung open. For a moment she thought it was just the wind. It was already getting dark and all she could see was the shaded lines of hedge and trees. She moved towards the door, reaching out to secure it.

'Please don't call out, Miss Drake. It would force my hand and I would prefer not to shoot you.'

Alyssa froze, staring at the thin figure that had moved into the doorway, and the pistol that was aimed at her unwaveringly.

'Consider,' Libbet continued in the same low, calm voice as he stepped into the study, forcing her to move back. 'If you were to cry out, that little maid of yours might come running and I shall be forced to hurt her, which is not at all what I would like. Your father, on the other hand, would probably not come, would he? Or if he did, I would hardly suffer the same qualms. A very unsatisfactory parent, by all accounts. Not at all what a father should be.'

Alyssa listened, her mind racing as she tried to rearrange her thoughts.

'What do you want, Libbet?' she asked as calmly as possible.

'Your company, Miss Drake. Unfortunately you hold the only other piece in this puzzle and so I am afraid you must come with me. I am willing to pay you the courtesy of a chance to say your goodbyes to Lord Delacort. This is because you are a kind person and you have simply been caught in a situation not of your making. I am asking you, please come with me and don't make a fuss.'

Out of everything he said, she reacted to the only thing that mattered.

'Where is Lord Delacort? What have you done with him?'

He considered her.

'He is safe, for the moment,' he replied slowly. 'Do you want to see him or not?'

'Where is he?'

'Come with me and I will show you.'

'Is he hurt? Have you hurt him?'

'Not yet. Will you come or must I end this here?'

Alyssa could feel her nails digging into her palms. She had never felt such fury, but she knew she could not afford to indulge it. This madman had Adam and therefore he had her.

'Let us go.'

He nodded and indicated the door to the garden.

'Your usual mode of egress, if you don't mind.'

She stepped out into the garden, her mind slowly sliding the pieces into place, rearranging everything that had happened since Adam's return in light of this one shocking fact. She knew now that this quiet man had been spying on them all these weeks, watching Adam and her. Knowing everything about them, plotting...

She looked back at him over her shoulder. She had to keep him talking. Perhaps she could discover something, some leverage.

'You are Percy's father,' she said wildly and the blue eyes softened for a moment.

'I could tell you realised...the way you looked at me this morning at Milsom's.'

'You're wrong. I didn't...not until... I was just thinking how terrible it must be for you to have to be uprooted like that, without any say in the matter. That Percy never considered asking you if you even wanted to go with him. That's all. It never occurred to me that...'

Libbet cocked his head to one side, considering her.

'Of course I would go with him. He is my son.'

'Does he know?'

'Of course not. When she was dying Edith made me promise never to tell him. She knew if Somer-on ever found out, he'd make the boy's life a living hell. My Edith was a beautiful angel, she never could stand up to that old brute. I never had a thought above my station until she walked into the house that first day, the loveliest thing I had ever seen. And the most miserable. I never meant for it to happen, but I could not help myself, nor could she. I swore to her I would take care of our son and make him a fine man for all to admire. And I have. I will see him in his rightful place.'

The simplicity of that statement clicked the last pieces of the puzzle into place.

'Timothy. And Ivor.'

He nodded, directing her down a path she knew led only to the old dower house which now stood empty. Now that they were so close, her fear began to overcome her need to understand. She just wanted to find Adam and find him alive. And she wanted this quiet, gentle man dead with a certainty she couldn't even begin to comprehend but which muted her fear.

'This way,' he said calmly, directing her off the lane and into the forest.

'No. Where is Adam?' she demanded.

'This way. In the old icehouse by the dower house. I doubt many remember it. It was already disused when I was a child, when old Delacort built the new icehouse up near the Hall. The old one is completely overgrown and a bit of a shambles, but it has been useful as a base for my activities these past weeks. I replaced the padlock and there is no way for anyone to hear you out here in the forest. Ah, here it is. Come along.'

Alyssa stared at the tangle of bushes that topped a small hillock at the end of the narrow trail they had followed off the main lane to the dower house. She knew icehouses were often built well outside the grounds of houses, to take advantage of the coolness of the forest or their proximity to a body of water so that ice could be carted there during the winter frosts, but she had forgotten this old structure. She could see nothing more than a furrow in the ground leading to a wooden door in the hillock, half-lost in a hairy mass of bushes and vines. There was an old mining lantern hanging there and he pulled back the black shade and a faint light illuminated several steps which led to a padlocked door. The thought that Adam was in there, in God knew what state, was unbearable.

Libbet unlocked the padlock and pulled the door open, keeping his pistol on her, and then stepped back.

'You first, Miss Drake.'

It was pitch-black inside. A very short corridor

opened suddenly on to a room and for a moment in the dim light which entered from the open door she saw a pile of wooden crates in a jumble against the far end of the small room. The space was a peculiar shape, almost like the inside of an egg. She stepped forward, scanning the space, searching for Adam, her mind prepared for the worst, but then suddenly the door shut behind her, plunging the room into darkness. She surged against the door, groping desperately for a handle. Libbet's voice, calm but muffled, carried through the wood.

'I will be back with him soon enough, Miss Drake. Please try to remain calm.'

And then she heard nothing. She slammed her hands against the surface, crying out his name in fury and frustration, but there was nothing. The thought that he had duped her, that she had walked into this trap like a fool, burned red-hot. She filled her lungs and screamed, furious and terrified. But when the last echoes of her voice were absorbed into the brick walls, she closed her eyes and leaned her forehead against the door and forced herself to think. She had been a fool, but she would not let this man win. Adam was smart; he had been in danger before and survived. Somehow, they would win. And she had to think.

Think! Think of where you are. What you saw.

There must be some way to get out or at least to prepare for the madman's return.

An icehouse. During the winters as a child she and her siblings had often come to watch as they had skimmed the small lake at Delacort for ice and hauled chunks into large crates, then dropped them through the broad hatchway at the top of the large Delacort icehouse behind the stables. Her mind froze on the memory and she looked up, even though she could see nothing in the dark. She thought of the narrow corridor and the long chunks of ice and the crates. There was no reason this icehouse would be substantially different, even if it was smaller.

The mound had been overgrown, but Libbet had said he'd had to provide a new padlock for the door, which might mean the hatchway, too, was unsecured, long forgotten. Even if it was overgrown she might be able to get through, if she could get up there. If she could somehow stack together those crates she had seen. And she had to, because she had to stop Libbet before he hurt Adam. Just as he had used her fear for Adam to lure her here, he would use Adam's sense of responsibility to do the same to him. She had given Libbet the means and now she would have to find a way to prevent him from using them to hurt Adam.

She closed her eyes as she always did when she needed to imagine something, summoning the image she had seen for that brief moment before he closed the door. Then she inched forward, hands outstretched. Her foot encountered it first and she leaned down cautiously and found a crate. It was damp and she shivered involuntarily, drawing back as if from some slimy creature. She forced herself to reach out again, closing her hands on the lip of the crate, dragging it towards her and turning it over.

The crates were roughly made but sturdy and her arms were aching by the time she had managed to stack them in what she hoped was a kind of pyramid. At one point as she was tugging one of the crates towards her something fell to the earth with a loud clang and her eyes flew open. She realised, feeling quite ridiculous, that she had kept her eyes closed the whole time, as if it made the pitch-black less frightening. She groped along the floor for the source of the noise and found what felt like a rusted crowbar with a long curved end. She remembered from those winters the long metal hooks used to crack and snare pieces of ice from the lake and for the first time she felt a surge of hope pierce through her mindless focus.

She inched over to the makeshift stack of crates

and began to crawl up the step-like structure. It groaned but held her weight until she reached the top crate. Balanced on one knee, she raised her hand cautiously and jerked back as she scraped her knuckles on a rough surface. She could have cried out in relief. She felt around and found the rim of the hatchway almost directly above her. It creaked as she gave it a sharp shove and a shower of dirt descended on her, but it did not rise. She steadied herself and raised the thin end of the rusty metal bar, sliding it between the hatchway and the ceiling. It entered a few inches and stuck and she paused. She had no idea if her little mountain of crates would hold if she made too sharp a movement. It could hardly be more than six or so feet to the ground, she told herself reassuringly. If she fell, she would just have to build it again.

She braced herself, then leaned all her weight against the crowbar, using it as a lever against the hatchway. Her pyramid groaned and wavered, but held as there was a ripping sound above her and a torrent of dirt and leaves came down upon her. The pitch-black separated into shades of darkness and she knew she had broken through. Her heart thudding, she reached up through the gap and into a tangle of roots and leaves and earth.

She braced herself once more on the crate and

hauled herself through the narrow gap and up into the bushes. It was almost too narrow and as she pushed up on the hatchway with her back she felt her pyramid waver and the crates fall away under her as if she had been standing on water. But she was already halfway out, her hands clinging to the roots and branches of the bushes, and she managed to get one knee out, then brace herself and push through. She stayed there for a moment, kneeling on the mossy earth, caught in the piercing tangle of bushes, fighting back tears. Then she levered herself to her feet and stumbled through the bushes. She had to find Adam before Libbet hurt him.

Chapter Twenty-One

Adam looked up as the library door opened. He stood up slowly.

'You showed yourself in, I see, Libbet,' he said calmly as the valet closed the library door behind him.

'I did, My Lord. I am still probably more familiar with the ins and outs of the Hall than you are. I see you have made a great many improvements here.'

'Which you hope to appreciate, I gather?'

'It is not a consideration with me, My Lord. Please step back from your desk. I know you probably keep a pistol in the drawer you opened and I really do not want to have to shoot you here. Nor do you want to shoot me here, I promise you.'

'I don't know about that. It might ruin the carpet, but that can be replaced.'

'But Miss Drake cannot,' Libbet said simply and Adam froze.

'Leave her out of it. She has nothing to do with this.'

'Too late for that, I am afraid. Oh, she is not dead. Yet. But I really had no choice. This morning when she looked at me with compassion I thought she might have guessed I was Percy's father and from here it would be short work to realise I was the one responsible for everything that had happened. Well, that was my mistake, but it cannot be helped now.'

He did not have time to react before Adam had him against the wall, his hand on Libbet's throat and his other hand pinning the valet's hand with the pistol to the wall. Libbet's pale blue eyes widened in shock, but he did not try to resist.

'It won't do you any good,' he whispered past the chokehold Adam had on him. 'You kill me and she will die before you find her. And I might get what I want anyway if they hang you for my murder. Even you might find it hard to explain my throttled body in your library. It will be difficult to convince anyone that I am connected to any of the Delacort murders or recent attacks. And then my Percy will be Lord Delacort anyway. Your choice.'

Adam held him for a moment longer, fighting against the murderous, desperate rage, knowing he could not afford to feel anything yet. When Jacob had returned with the news that although Percy was in Turl Street, Libbet was nowhere to be found, he had prepared for something to happen that evening. But not this. He hoped Jem and Nicholas would continue to follow his cue.

'You have the upper hand now,' he said distinctly. 'For the moment. But after this. When she is safe. I will kill you.'

He pushed away and Libbet remained leaning against the wall for a moment, breathing deeply. Then he adjusted his coat.

'Where is she?' Adam demanded.

'Someplace secure. I don't know how much air she has in there, so if you want to see her still before both of you die, I suggest we go now.'

'When she is safe. I will kill you,' Adam said again, crushing the need to carry through on his threat right there, but Libbet merely indicated the long doors leading out on to the veranda and Adam opened them and strode through into the night. Libbet followed, indicating the path leading down towards the lake and the dower house. Once they were clear of the hall, he spoke again, his cool, even voice carrying in the still evening.

'I am prepared for that possibility. But as I pointed out, murdering me might serve my purpose as well, though I would obviously prefer to live to see my Percy claim the title. I have tried to avoid a direct confrontation, but it was you who forced my hand from the very beginning. You made no secret of the fact you never meant to stay here beyond a few weeks, which meant I had to act fast. I could not afford to bide my time as I had with Ivor...'

Adam only half-listened. He walked swiftly following the path towards the empty old dower house. This was one project he had not yet managed to get around to and he knew very little about the dilapidated old structure. He tried to remember anything about that house which could give him a clue as to where Libbet might be keeping Alyssa. From what he had seen of the cellars there they were in such a ramshackle state they would hardly be an effective prison, and certainly not someplace where the supply of air could be limited. Or had that just been a threat to make him obey?

He wished he could take the cur by the throat and choke the truth out of him, but he knew Libbet had spoken the truth when he'd said he held all the cards. Or the only card that mattered. Whatever this madman had planned, Adam would do whatever it took to get Alyssa to safety. If that meant putting himself in Libbet's hands for now, then so be it. For the moment he needed the man occupied and distracted.

'You have brewed your potion with a great deal

of patience, Libbet. When did you start planning all this?'

'But I didn't plan it. Not at the beginning at least. It was just providence, you might say. It started with Master Timothy. That winter when everyone was ill. My Percy was, too, and all I wanted to do was to care for him. My darling Edith, his mother, had placed him in my care when she died trying to birth Somerton's sickly brat. But Master Timothy's own man was ill. I had to wait on the master and got nothing but abuse. For years I had had to watch Master Timothy and Master Ivor make game, or worse, of my Percy. Always threatening to put him out of the Hall. And that night when I feared for Percy's life, Master Timothy kept me by him and wouldn't let me go back to my boy. It wasn't that hard, in the end, he was as weak as a kitten. I put the pillow over his face and held it there until he was quiet. And then I went and looked after my Percy.'

'And Ivor?'

'Master Ivor? He was as like old Somerton as peas in a pod. Horse mad but cow handed and always ready to strike out at those weaker than themselves. I was on my way back from Mowbray when I saw him fall and went to help. He lay there bellowing at me to help him back on his horse when t was obvious his leg was badly broken. I went to find a branch for a splint, but he kept cursing and then he said something about my Percy. I don't recall what. I hit him with the branch and knocked him out. And then I knew I had no choice. That if I didn't act he would have me sent away or worse and that it was nothing more than another moment of resolution that stood between my Percy and Delacort. So I finished it and left him and went away and waited.

'The madness is that for a moment I had completely forgotten about you. That you stood between my Percy and Ivor in the succession. Everyone had become so accustomed to expecting to hear of your death I had almost come to believe you would never survive. I realised soon enough after I had done the deed that I had rejoiced precipitously, but I still hoped you would not make it back to Delacort. But once you did, I knew there was nothing for it but to go forward, especially when you cut my Percy off, forcing him to go and try his luck making up to that silly little chit, then that *demi-monde* widow. I knew Edith would never have approved of her.

'The problem was that you made no secret of the fact you weren't going to stay here long. I could not afford to wait for a provident situation. I had to create it. The rope was a good idea. If only you had fallen harder or if Miss Drake hadn't come along and I could have finished the deed as I had with Master Ivor and then taken the rope away. The scaffolding was a sad failure. I was still close with all the servants at the Hall even though we had been forced to move out, and I knew you were going to inspect the work on the east wing that morning. I didn't like the idea others might be hurt, but I was, I admit, becoming desperate. The closer we came to your departure the more I realised I could no longer indulge in the idea of an accident. And I did not want to attack you directly, not if I could do it by other means. I was well aware I would be no match for you directly.

'So I watched you whenever I could. I know this land as well as anyone. Every moment my Percy did not require my services I was here, learning. I knew of your solitary walks and I was lucky enough to witness your argument with Moresby. I came that night with a knife and thought to have done with it, but I am no fool. And the idea came to me, complete and ready. I made sure Percy would be at the Duck and Dragon and then came to see that you had gone out walking as usual and would not be able to account for yourself. Then I ran to Moresby Hall to see what I could contrive. I thought my luck was truly with me when I saw Moresby coming out of the stables alone just as I approached. But striking the blow myself was harder than I had thought it would be and when he cried out I am ashamed to admit I ran. Still, I thought I had finished him and went quickly to clean up and write that note for Sir James. It is just a little bit further. This way.'

'You must have been quite upset the next day at the White Hart,' Adam commented.

'I was. I could hardly credit it when she lied, but there was nothing I could do. It is a great pity, since I have always liked Miss Drake. It is a great sorrow for me to involve her in this, but I have no choice.'

'Of course you do. You made your choice,' Adam responded brutally, wishing he could kill the man now and have done with it. They had gone past the turn to the dower house and the path dwindled to a trail leading into the forest. Adam tensed, wondering where they could be going.

'And she did serve me well, in a way,' Libbet continued, as if there had been no interruption. 'That night when I came to shoot you. I should have suspected you had realised that it was not mere chance at play, but I did not suspect that you were out to trap me. It is a pity I cannot repay her the favour, but there is too much at stake... Ah, here we are.'

Adam stared at the hillock, the horrible image of her being buried there beating in his brain. Libbet waved him down an overgrown trail and he went, alert but terrified of what he might find.

'Jerome...' A faint, breathy whisper flowed out from the darkness of the forest and both men froze. Libbet kept the pistol extended in Adam's direction, but his other hand had gone to his throat.

'My Jerome...' The sound was even fainter now, just a quiver of wind, but Libbet gave a strange keening cry.

'Edith?'

The voice came again, muffled. 'I let her out... She's not in the icehouse... Come...'

The pistol wavered and lowered slightly and Adam did not wait. He forced Libbet down on the ground, shoving his pistol hand under his knee, keeping his own hand on the man's throat even as he scanned the shadows.

'Alyssa!' he called out, praying she was all right.

Libbet's eyes grew wide with shock and confusion and they did not waver from the sight of a pale figure moving swiftly through the shadows towards them. As the figure, in a torn and ragged dress, her hair down about her shoulders, resolved itself from the dark, the valet gave an odd despairing cry and closed his eyes. Alyssa stopped as two other figures moved out from behind the trees on the other side of the path. Nicholas and Jem rushed forward, both holding cocked pistols.

Adam wrenched the pistol from Libbet's limp grasp and flew to his feet.

'Hold him,' he said to Jem and strode over to where Alyssa stood, staring at them all. She was holding a long metal bar in both hands, like a croquet mallet, and he took it from her gently and dropped it on the ground.

'Are you all right? Are you hurt?' he said urgently, taking hold of her shoulders. He wanted to crush her to him, but he needed to be certain she wasn't hurt. There were scratches along her arms and leaves in her hair and her simple muslin dress looked more brown than white. And he had never seen anything more beautiful. She shook her head mutely, her eyes on his.

'Blast you! I locked you in! Who let you out?' Libbet cried out with sudden fury and Alyssa looked at him, the anger kindling in her own eyes.

'You did, Libbet. Icehouses have hatchways in the ceiling. I climbed out. Did you really think I would just sit there and let you use me as bait?'

Her voice rose as she spoke and, hearing the

shakiness underneath the anger, Adam drew her against him.

'It's all right, sweetheart, it's over,' he murmured against her hair, and despite his own fury at Libbet he realised he was smiling in wonder and a kind of resigned pride. Of course she would not just sit anywhere and wait. When had she ever?

Nicholas laughed outright.

'Unbelievable. All those years climbing trees paid off, I see. And who the devil is Jerome? You scared the wits out of me there for a moment.'

'Jerome is Libbet's given name,' Alyssa replied, still leaning against Adam. 'I thought that was what Percy's mother would have probably called him if they had been lovers. I had to try something to distract him and to stop him from taking you down there, but I didn't want to scare him into shooting you, Adam.'

Adam raised her chin and gently brushed away some moss that clung to her cheek.

'I don't think there is one person in a hundred in Mowbray who would know his given name, you brilliant girl.'

She shivered against him and he tightened his hold on her. After a moment he stood back and shrugged off his coat and put it around her shoulders before turning back to the others.

'Let's get out of here. Jem, I need you to go fetch Sir James. And let's keep this between us for the moment.'

Jem nodded stolidly and stood back a step. 'On your feet now, Libbet.'

Libbet dragged himself to his feet, his head hanging, and began moving towards the path. He looked so broken none of them were prepared for the move. He had not gone two steps before he suddenly reached down, grabbed the discarded crowbar and with a roar of rage raised it, surging towards Adam. Adam pulled Alyssa behind him, raised Libbet's pistol and fired, just as Nicholas did the same.

The two shots rang out in the forest and Libbet jerked back as if tugged by an invisible string before toppling to the ground, his knees bent under him awkwardly, and the crowbar hit the ground with a muted clang.

He lay staring at the trees, a look of almost child-like surprise on his face until Jem stepped forward and lowered his eyelids gently.

Chapter Twenty-Two

Alyssa stared at the clock and the clock stared back. Three o'clock in the afternoon. Why hadn't he come yet? She felt like she had been awake and waiting for years.

She had understandably not slept well after the madness of the previous night. It was bad enough that Adam and Nicholas had taken her back immediately to the cottage and left her there with nothing more than the equivalent of a pat on the head, heading off to fetch Sir James and Dr Hedgeway. It was arguably worse to receive around noon a short note from Adam informing her he was busy with Percy and would come by later to discuss 'their plans going forward'. And still worse to be still waiting, as patient and obedient as the mythical Griselda, and just about as foolish, when it was increasingly obvious he was delaying this meeting because he knew what had to happen now and he didn't want to hurt her.

She knew she had to face the inevitable. Whatever he had said about the option of marriage being open, now that the danger was over, she knew he would want nothing more than to leave Mowbray and get on with his life far away from painful memories and demanding burdens. And she would have to decide whether to be selfish and compel him to marry her—even if it was to be a soulless union—or to grant him his freedom, and she did not know if she was strong enough to make that decision. She felt as if she was being torn apart.

Suddenly it seemed unbearable to be sitting there, waiting for him to come and inflict misery on her. She went over to her desk and took out two letters from the top left-hand drawer, spreading them out side by side. The first was from her mother's friend, extending a warm welcome to Alyssa to come stay with her in London whenever she wished. The second was an equally inviting missive from Mr Burnley, of Burnley, Smith and Elder Publishers.

She stared at them. A few weeks ago the plans she was forming in her mind would have been the culmination of all she might hope for, all she had strived towards. Now she just felt empty, aching.

Even with all the fear, over the past few days and weeks she had felt alive, more alive than she could remember feeling. She hated that he had that power over her. It should not be like this. It could not be that once again she was letting her happiness ride on the decision of a man who fundamentally did not need her, who regarded her as an obligation. It was unbearable.

She folded the letters and went to find Betsy. If she packed quickly, she could still make the London mail coach.

Adam hitched Thunder's reins to the gatepost and looked up at the cottage. Its windows winked happily in the late-afternoon sun and everything looked sharper, more defined today, as if after a long stretch of grey weather a burst of rain had cleared the clouds, leaving only scrubbed blue skies and summer flowers at the bright pinnacles of their bloom—perfect yellows and oranges and reds.

There was something brutal about the fact that it had taken a man's death to make room for this sensation of clarity, but life *was* brutal. His only regret about the way the threat had been removed was that Alyssa had been exposed to any of it. He would make it up to her somehow. He'd had no chance to talk to her privately after the dramatic events of the previous night; there had been too much to take care of.

Now that it was over he was finally beginning to realise what a hellishly long night and day it had been. Once he had taken her back to Drake Cottage, he had gone with Nicholas to find Sir James and Dr Hedgeway. But confronting their shock and their questions and the arrangements about the body had been minor compared to dealing with Percy. Nicholas had had to leave that morning to fulfil a family commitment in Berkshire, but thankfully Sir James had insisted on coming with Adam to break the news to Percy.

Adam had been unsure whether to tell Percy the whole truth, but he had given in to Sir James's insistence on a full revelation. When Percy had collapsed and they'd had to send for Dr Hedgeway, he had wished they had held their peace. He wanted nothing more than to leave the lot of them and go to Alyssa. But he had stayed until Percy had recovered and finally calmed down, and Adam had convinced him to go ahead with his plans to sail to Barbados as soon as he felt able. Percy had surprised him by wanting to act immediately, though Adam supposed he shouldn't have been surprised. It was clear Percy couldn't stand to stay in Mowbray. And so he had sent for Thorpe and together they had made what arrangements they could to allow Percy to leave immediately.

And now Adam was finally free to deal with his own affairs.

He strode down the gravel path, and though it might make no sense he felt almost as tense now as he had been the previous night when he had thought Libbet had Alyssa in his power. With the threat of danger removed, he was free to do as he wished. The problem was that the only thing he wished to do was to marry Alyssa and he wasn't at all certain she was willing, even after the amazing interlude at the cottage the previous afternoon. He couldn't forget the pain in her eyes as she had revealed she had been—might even still be—in love…

He knocked firmly on the door. Come hell or high water she was going to marry him as soon as he got his hands on a special licence. He wanted her safe. With him. He wanted her in a way he had not known was possible to want anything.

Betsy opened the door and blinked up at him.

'Is Miss Drake in?' he asked.

'Oh, no, My Lord.'

Adam felt a surge of disappointment and annoyance. Had Lady Nesbit come to her with more demands?

'Where is she? When will she return?'

'I don't rightly know, My Lord. She didn't tell me. I mean, she went on the afternoon mail to London, but she didn't exactly say when she was to return. She packed enough for a week or so, so perhaps—'

She broke off at his expression and took a small step backwards.

It took Adam a moment to find the words.

'London. She went on the mail to London.'

'Y-yes, My Lord,' Betsy stammered.

'This afternoon.'

Her head bobbed up and down nervously. 'Yes, My Lord. An hour ago, My Lord.'

He turned without a word and headed blindly back towards where Thunder was hitched to the gatepost and automatically swung himself on to the horse's back. His mind felt empty except for the memory of the moment she had told him about the man she had loved. Surely she must have gone to London to see him. She'd told him she was planning to go to London when the danger was over, but he had never imagined...

After what had happened between them at the cottage she should have known... He shouldn't have stopped. He should have claimed her. He had to stop her. By whatever means. Even if he had to kidnap her, he...

He tightened his hands on the reins and Thunder shook his mane in annoyance, dragging him back from the depth of his thoughts.

This was Alyssa, he told himself, fighting down the clean sharp pain that cut through him at the realisation he had no right to force anything or demand anything of her. She deserved whatever she wanted in life, whatever gave her joy. He had no right, none, to make another selfish demand on her. To become another person who needed and used her for their own purposes. His agony was a poor trade for her happiness. He had made a thorough mess of his life and deserved to pay his stupidity. She deserved infinitely more.

He hardly even noticed he had arrived at the Hall until Thunder stopped at the foot of the front stairs and a footman ran down to take the reins. Adam walked blindly up the stairs and past Stebbins, who stood waiting.

'Is there anything you need, My Lord?' Stebbins asked hesitantly and Adam felt a wave of protesting fury and despair. There was only one thing he needed, one thing he wanted in this whole useless world. He stopped and spoke without turning.

'Stebbins. As of now I will not be receiving any visitors. Any problems you encounter—deal with them yourself or bring them to Thorpe. And when the door to my study is closed I am not to be disturbed for any reason unless the whole house is on fire. Understood?'

Stebbins blinked but bowed in assent and Adam strode into his study, shut the door behind him and moved towards the long windows overlooking the lake. It was a lovely view. The setting sun had turned the lake into a rich, gleaming gold and the sky into a cacophony of orange and pink and purple.

He pulled the heavy curtains over it.

Chapter Twenty-Three

Alyssa stepped down from the mail coach in the White Hart's large inner yard. She was the only passenger disembarking in Mowbray, but the cobbled yard was busy with traffic and she remembered it was market day. She had been gone only a week, but already she had lost the rhythm of Mowbray.

She had hoped going to London would give her the strength to face what must come, but she felt as bruised now as she had the day she left. No, worse, because she missed Adam with an unrelenting ache that only seemed to increase with time, like thirst. Every day she woke up wondering what he was doing and every night she went to sleep wondering the same. Even the success of her trip to London felt hollow. All she wanted, all she had wanted all week, was to see him again. The only thing that had prevented her from getting on the first coach back to Mowbray had been the conviction that she would be coming back to a choice she was not sure she could live with. She had tried to prepare herself, but the truth was she did not know how she was going to hide her need and pain from Adam when she saw him again.

She glanced down at the portmanteau the coachman had laid on the cobbles by her side. She knew she had to move, do something, but she felt rooted to the spot. Mr Curtis, the postmaster, nodded to her as he took the delivered mailbag, but did not address her. The uncharacteristic diffidence of the usually talkative postmaster dragged her momentarily out of her abstraction and she realised she was receiving quite a few unusually conscious and cautious glances from the employees and patrons of the White Hart. She flushed slightly. She should have known the events of the past few weeks would lead to a certain degree of notoriety and it was best to act as oblivious as possible.

'Is the scary lord dying?' asked a young voice behind her and she turned abruptly to face Johnny, Mr Curtis's boy.

'What?' she asked in shock.

'The scary lord with the big black horse. Your friend. Roddy said maybe he's dead already be-

cause no one has seen him, or his horse, for a week
ever since Mr Libbet died. Is he dead, too?'

'Johnny!' Mr Curtis advanced on them rapidly
his face beetroot red. 'Enough of your prattle, run
along now!'

'Mr Curtis! Has something happened to Lord
Delacort?' Alyssa demanded, throwing caution
and propriety to the wind.

The postmaster's complexion deepened to an
alarming shade of puce and he scowled at the re-
ceding back of his youngest born.

'No, no, not that I am aware of. You know
Johnny, Miss Drake. It's just—' He broke off awkwardly and looked helplessly towards the entrance
to the inn as if salvation lay there.

'Just what?' Alyssa demanded, her heart beating
furiously. 'For heaven's sake, tell me!'

Mr Curtis's love of gossip overcame his embarrassment. 'It's true he has not been seen this week
since Mr Libbet...died and Mr Somer...Mr Percy
left for Barbados. And you went to London. He
won't talk with none but Mr Thorpe. Naturally
there's talk with all what has happened. People
say he won't stay long now. The Delacort people
are right worried.'

At that moment Will entered the courtyard from
the taproom, alerted by some publican's sixth

sense, his face reflecting the same avid but embarrassed interest as Mr Curtis's.

'Miss Drake! Welcome back—'

'Thank you, Will,' she interrupted. 'Do you have
a gig I could borrow by chance?'

'A gig? Well, of course, Miss Drake. Here, Jack,
go bring round the gig, will you? Right away.'

Alyssa thanked him as calmly as possible and
waited with agonising impatience as Jack pulled
out the gig and handed her into it. Finally they
were ready and she could feel Will and Mr Curtis
and practically everyone in the courtyard watching as they drove off in the direction of the Hall.
The ride was not long, but the road seemed end-
less and her nerves tightened with each mile. She
had no idea what was happening or if she would
be welcome, but none of that mattered at the moment. Johnny's words had set off an almost superstitious fear in her and she had to see Adam, make
sure he was all right, no matter what he thought or
what he was planning to do.

When they finally reached the broad drive leading up to the Hall the afternoon sun was glinting
off the window panes and warming the Oxfordshire stone walls, turning them a burnished gold.
It looked bright and happy and inviting and contrarily she felt so nervous her palms were damp

and she was sure she was as flushed as she would be if she had run the whole way from Mowbray.

Jack pulled up the gig and she jumped down and hurried up the wide stone steps. Their passage up the drive must have been noticed by someone because before she had even made it halfway up the stairs the door opened.

'Good afternoon, Stebbins,' she said as she ascended the wide steps.

Stebbins stared at her with a peculiar look on his face and her nerves tightened further.

'Miss Drake!' he said at last, but he did not move and her fear grew.

'Hello, Stebbins,' she repeated. 'Is Lord Delacort in?'

Stebbins nodded, flustered, and waved her inside.

'Yes. Yes. In the study. Come in. Come in. He does not wish to be disturbed, but I think...' He stopped, aware he was falling out of his role, and straightened.

'This way, please, Miss Drake.'

She followed him, so nervous now her hands felt stuffed with hot, rough sand. The hallway was empty and clean, but somehow darker than she had remembered. Then she noticed that a trunk and a portmanteau stood at the foot of the steps and her heart contracted.

'Is His Lordship leaving?' she asked in a rush and Stebbins stopped.

'I don't know, miss,' he replied simply and continued towards the study.

Alyssa shook her head, trying to assimilate everything through a mist of fear. Stebbins stopped again at the study door and glanced over his shoulder at her. He stepped back and motioned towards the door.

'You go in now, miss,' he said quietly, turning and heading towards the back of the hallway.

She stared after him in surprise and then took a step forward and opened the door, her heart working hard and loudly.

She did not know what she had expected, but there seemed to be nothing in there to merit Stebbins's peculiar conduct or to give credence to the gossip. Quite the opposite. The room was rather dark, since the long velvet curtains blocked out most of the afternoon light, but it looked neat, quite different from her memory of her first visit to the Hall on Adam's return. And it was empty. She frowned, untying her bonnet, and stepped inside.

'What part of "don't disturb" is unclear? Get out.' Adam's voice, harsh and angry, bit out from the back of the room and she took another step in.

He was seated with his back to her, in an armchair facing the empty fireplace, dressed in buckskins and top boots and a plain white shirt. He was leaning over an elaborate book of maps open on the low table in front of him and he did not turn around upon her entry. Even just the sight of his back filled her with an almost overwhelming feeling of relief and joy. She had no idea if she was welcome, but right now she could not think further than the fact that he was here, close enough to reach in a few short steps, and that she loved him.

'I said—' He turned and broke off as he saw her and she stopped. The silence stretched out and she tried to read his expression, but the gloom defeated her.

'So. You're back,' he said at last. There was no anger in his voice now—it was flat, uninterested.

She nodded and cleared her throat, but he spoke first.

'What do you want?'

She struggled to even begin to answer that loaded question.

'I came… I thought… People said you aren't talking to anyone. I was worried…'

He stood up abruptly and moved towards her. In the dark he looked even taller and once again she had the sensation of facing a stranger, but this time rather than a cynically detached stranger, he looked dangerous and she had to forcibly stop herself from taking a step back. When he spoke his voice was tight with a red-hot fury she had never heard before.

'I am not a damn cause! Don't you dare come here dripping pity!'

'Pity? Are you m-mad?' she stammered.

'That's one way of putting it,' he said scathingly and stopped short of her, his hands fisted, and she stared up at him, her shock and confusion overcoming even her pain.

'I don't understand. Has something happened? Are you angry at me for going to London without speaking with you first? I told you I meant to go, and that day... I couldn't wait any longer. I had to go,' she finished lamely.

'Angry!' The word seemed to break something in him and he turned and went to sit down again, placing his hand on the map, blotting out most of the Continent.

'Are you going away?' she asked fearfully as she finally began to accept the meaning of the trunks and maps. She should not have left. She should have stayed and locked him to her. The thought of him leaving, of not seeing him again, was unacceptable.

'Perhaps,' he answered in the same flat voice as before.

She moved towards him, trying to think of how to stop him. She could not let him go.

'Where?'

'Does it matter?'

'It does to me.'

He surged to his feet again.

'Don't play games. You've made your choice! What did you come back for? To tell me the good news in person?'

'Yes, but...'

'I don't want to hear it.' He held up a hand, his gaze furious and full of hatred, and she shook her head, trying to find some stable ground. He moved towards her again and she just stared at him. She felt as though she had been caught in the jaws of some giant relentless beast and was being shaken and torn to shreds. She spread her hands as if to ward him off and he seemed to realise what he was doing. His expression changed, softened.

'Alyssa. Don't do this,' he said, his hands closing on her shoulders. 'Don't do it. He doesn't deserve you. I know that is unfair, I don't know a thing about him, but I know you. I am asking you not to do anything yet. You've seen me at my worst, but I can do better, I swear. Stay here for a while.

He can't love you more than I do. I don't believe it. Give me a chance. All I am asking is that you don't make any decisions yet.'

Alyssa stared up at him. His words were so strange and confusing and unrelated to anything that she almost missed what he was saying.

'A decision about what?' she asked dumbly. 'It's just a novel.'

There was a moment's silence as he stared down at her, clearly as bemused as she was.

'A novel?'

'Yes. I sent it to them some weeks ago and they want to publish it. I went to meet the publisher, Mr Burnley. What on earth are you talking about?'

'A novel?' he asked again. 'You wrote a novel? You went to meet a publisher?'

'Yes, I—'

His frown returned and he interrupted her brusquely, his hands tightening on her shoulders. 'What about the man...the one you were in love with? I thought you went to see him.'

The shifting ground beneath her settled and she surveyed the remains of the storm. She had been so caught up in her own longing and fear it had never occurred to her she had the power to hurt him. The enormity of what he was telling her was finally reaching her, filling her from within with joy and hope. She reached up to touch his cheek, but he brushed her hand away, the anger resurfacing.

'I told you I don't want your pity any more than you wanted mine!'

She looked up at him, past the anger and suspicion, to the man she knew and loved and who needed her. It was so clear to her now, she wondered at her own blindness in not seeing it before. She had been too caught up in her own emotions, but there was no room for caution now.

'Adam, the very last thing I feel for you is pity. I never guessed you might care for me. Not the way I did. There never was anyone else. When I said what I did, that day, I was talking about *you*. It's only ever been you.'

He grasped her face in his hands, his fingers pressing against her cheekbones, suspicion and need at war in his dark grey eyes. The tension did not leave his mouth and he shook his head after a moment.

'No…you were just a child.'

'To you perhaps. I might not have seemed it next to Rowena, but I was just about to turn eighteen. When you came back I told myself I had just been a silly girl with romantic fantasies which had nothing to do with reality, that I had been no better than Mary. But I knew it wasn't true. I may have been young, but I saw what you were even then, Adam. I never felt more alive, and myself, as I did with you. That hasn't changed. I know it's very selfish, but I can't help it. I just can see it more clearly now. I love you.'

He shook his head again, his eyes darkening, but she knew it wasn't a negation. She reached up to touch his face again, her amazement only growing now that she was beginning to believe him. He pulled her against him, closing his arms around her as if he could absorb her. His voice was muffled by her hair, but she could feel every word.

'Alyssa. You don't know... I kept telling myself that if you found what you wanted I should be happy for you. But I wanted to kill him. And kidnap you. And keep you. I just wanted you back here, with me. I kept waiting for the axe to fall and I couldn't stand it. Tell me again.'

There was a raw, almost fearful need in his voice and she drew back, looking up at him.

'I love you, Adam. I've never wanted anything in my life as much as I want to be with you. I need you not to give up on me. Ever.'

He dragged her back into his embrace and she wrapped her arms around him as well, her cheek pressed to his chest, listening to the sharp striking of his heartbeat. She felt his breath shudder against her.

'Oh, God, Alyssa, I love you. I could just as well imagine giving up breathing. I can't stand it. Don't ever leave again!'

She shook her head, filled with a joy she had never experienced before. That she had not known could exist.

'I won't. I love you, Adam...'

He tilted her face up, his eyes locking on to hers, filled with a fierce, uncompromising demand that did not need to be voiced. His arms pulled her to him as he bent to kiss her, gently and slowly, as if she might still be frightened away, his lips sliding over hers, leaving heat and tingling wherever they touched. It was melting her, burning her from within, and she wanted more, she wanted him to take her back to that unbearable peak of pleasure he had shown her once before.

'Adam, please...' She pushed up against him on tiptoe as if she could shed all the layers between them by sheer force and tear down every barrier between them. 'Please...'

He groaned, tightening his hold on her, digging his hand into her hair as he gave in and kissed her the way she wanted, the way she needed him to. There was something wonderful and terrifying in he feeling of being erased and released all at once. She kissed him back, dragging up his shirt so she could feel the hot, hard muscles of his back.

'Alyssa, I want you...' he breathed against her mouth, his hands searing her skin even through her dress. She wanted it off her; she wanted her skin on his, her breasts against him; she wanted him to touch her as he had in her study. She scraped her fingers down along his back, urging him towards her, but he pushed back slightly, his breathing harsh and his eyes fixed on hers.

'I'm not letting you go this time,' he said and it was clearly a warning. 'Last time I did the right thing and stopped, but I'm damned if I am going to play by the rules again. If you want me to stop, you're going to have to leave now. Do you understand?'

Alyssa shook her head impatiently. She had no more intention of playing by the rules at this point than he. She shrugged off his hands and strode towards the door and had almost made it when he grabbed her arm, turning her. She looked up, surprised at the expression in his eyes.

'No. You can't go yet. I didn't mean to scare you, Alyssa. Stay, I won't do anything. I promise...'

She stared up at him, amazed he had so little faith in her. She had thought she had made it abundantly clear she was extremely willing and had no more wish to wait upon propriety than he.

'That's a pity. Then there's no point in locking the door?' she asked.

'Locking the door?'

'I know you have scared everyone into leaving you alone, but since we always seem to get interrupted just when…matters are getting interesting I thought it would be a good idea to lock the door. I really, really don't want anyone bothering us for a while. So, should I?'

Adam breathed in, his body visibly relaxing, before he shook his head slowly and reached past her to turn the key in the lock.

'An excellent idea. Come here, wild girl. We have some unfinished business, you and I. And you're marrying me as soon as I procure a special licence, are we clear?'

He grasped her hand and drew her towards a broad, Empire-style sofa. She followed happily but felt the urge to protest on one count.

'Oh, no, that's ridiculously extravagant. An ordinary licence should do just fine…'

Adam pulled her down next to him and tipped up her chin, his finger stroking her mischievous dimple, his own eyes filled with reluctant laughter and beneath it the banked heat that made her aware of every inch of her body and made her dress feel harsh and heavy on her sensitised skin.

'No, it won't,' he replied, his voice as soft and warm as his fingers as he slid her sleeve from her shoulder. 'It has to be very special and with a great deal of licence. By this time next week I want you living here with me.'

She arched forward as his fingers moved lower. She grasped his other hand and pressed it to her breast, too impatient to be embarrassed. He laughed and bent to kiss her flushed skin.

'Is that a yes?' he whispered against her and a shudder ran through her that she hardly realised as he slid off her dress, baring her, his hands moving hot and urgently, pulling her on to his lap so she could feel his need. She tilted back her head as he kissed her neck, her breast, his hand moving against her thigh, finding her again, melting her. She no longer knew what he was asking, just what she wanted of him, what she wanted to do to him.

'Yes, Adam. My Adam…'

* * * * *

*If you enjoyed this story,
you won't want to miss Lara Temple's debut
LORD CRAYLE'S SECRET WORLD*

MILLS & BOON®
Large Print – January 2017

ROMANCE

To Blackmail a Di Sione	Rachael Thomas
A Ring for Vincenzo's Heir	Jennie Lucas
Demetriou Demands His Child	Kate Hewitt
Trapped by Vialli's Vows	Chantelle Shaw
The Sheikh's Baby Scandal	Carol Marinelli
Defying the Billionaire's Command	Michelle Conder
The Secret Beneath the Veil	Dani Collins
Stepping into the Prince's World	Marion Lennox
Unveiling the Bridesmaid	Jessica Gilmore
The CEO's Surprise Family	Teresa Carpenter
The Billionaire from Her Past	Leah Ashton

HISTORICAL

Stolen Encounters with the Duchess	Julia Justiss
The Cinderella Governess	Georgie Lee
The Reluctant Viscount	Lara Temple
Taming the Tempestuous Tudor	Juliet Landon
Silk, Swords and Surrender	Jeannie Lin

MEDICAL

Taming Hollywood's Ultimate Playboy	Amalie Berlin
Winning Back His Doctor Bride	Tina Beckett
White Wedding for a Southern Belle	Susan Carlisle
Wedding Date with the Army Doc	Lynne Marshall
Capturing the Single Dad's Heart	Kate Hardy
Doctor, Mummy... Wife?	Dianne Drake

MILLS & BOON®
Hardback – February 2017

ROMANCE

The Last Di Sione Claims His Prize	Maisey Yates
Bought to Wear the Billionaire's Ring	Cathy Williams
The Desert King's Blackmailed Bride	Lynne Graham
Bride by Royal Decree	Caitlin Crews
The Consequence of His Vengeance	Jennie Lucas
The Sheikh's Secret Son	Maggie Cox
Acquired by Her Greek Boss	Chantelle Shaw
Vows They Can't Escape	Heidi Rice
The Sheikh's Convenient Princess	Liz Fielding
The Unforgettable Spanish Tycoon	Christy McKellen
The Billionaire of Coral Bay	Nikki Logan
Her First-Date Honeymoon	Katrina Cudmore
Their Meant-to-Be Baby	Caroline Anderson
A Mummy for His Baby	Molly Evans
Rafael's One Night Bombshell	Tina Beckett
A Forever Family for the Army Doc	Meredith Webber
The Nurse and the Single Dad	Dianne Drake
The Heir's Unexpected Baby	Jules Bennett
From Enemies to Expecting	Kat Cantrell

0117 GEN STD HB

MILLS & BOON®
Large Print – February 2017

ROMANCE

The Return of the Di Sione Wife	Caitlin Crews
Baby of His Revenge	Jennie Lucas
The Spaniard's Pregnant Bride	Maisey Yates
A Cinderella for the Greek	Julia James
Married for the Tycoon's Empire	Abby Green
Indebted to Moreno	Kate Walker
A Deal with Alejandro	Maya Blake
A Mistletoe Kiss with the Boss	Susan Meier
A Countess for Christmas	Christy McKellen
Her Festive Baby Bombshell	Jennifer Faye
The Unexpected Holiday Gift	Sophie Pembroke

HISTORICAL

Awakening the Shy Miss	Bronwyn Scott
Governess to the Sheikh	Laura Martin
An Uncommon Duke	Laurie Benson
Mistaken for a Lady	Carol Townend
Kidnapped by the Highland Rogue	Terri Brisbin

MEDICAL

Seduced by the Sheikh Surgeon	Carol Marinelli
Challenging the Doctor Sheikh	Amalie Berlin
The Doctor She Always Dreamed Of	Wendy S. Marcus
The Nurse's Newborn Gift	Wendy S. Marcus
Tempting Nashville's Celebrity Doc	Amy Ruttan
Dr White's Baby Wish	Sue MacKay

MILLS & BOON®

Why shop at millsandboon.co.uk?

Each year, thousands of romance readers find their perfect read at millsandboon.co.uk. That's because we're passionate about bringing you the very best romantic fiction. Here are some of the advantages of shopping at www.millsandboon.co.uk:

* **Get new books first**—you'll be able to buy your favourite books one month before they hit the shops

* **Get exclusive discounts**—you'll also be able to buy our specially created monthly collections, with up to 50% off the RRP

* **Find your favourite authors**—latest news, interviews and new releases for all your favourite authors and series on our website, plus ideas for what to try next

* **Join in**—once you've bought your favourite books, don't forget to register with us to rate, review and join in the discussions

Visit **www.millsandboon.co.uk**
for all this and more today!